"Don't you realize how helpless I am?"

Rachel asked. "Do you have any idea how desperate and hopeless I feel, knowing that no one, not the police, not even the FBI, has been able to find my child?"

She moved until she stood directly in front of Jake, staring up at his veiled expression. "Sh-she's lost, and no one can find her... except...maybe you...."

Jake tried to distance himself from the pleading voice, the expression of stark pain on Rachel's pale face, but it was impossible. One look into her eyes and he recognized the agony she was going through, but he had no words of comfort to offer her. He was frozen inside.

A voice within spoke to Rachel, demanding that she continue to try to persuade this man to help her. He was her—and her child's—last hope.

Dear Reader,

Spring is on its way in at last, but we've got some hot books to keep you warm during the last few chilly days. There's our American Hero title, for example: Ann Williams's *Cold, Cold Heart.* Here's a man who has buried all his feelings, all his hopes and dreams, a man whose job it is to rescue missing children—and who can't get over the tragedy of failure. Into his life comes a woman he can't resist, a woman whose child has been stolen from her, and suddenly he's putting it all on the line all over again. He's back to saving children—and back to dreaming of love. Will his cold heart melt? You take a guess!

Mary Anne Wilson completes her "Sister, Sister" duet with *Two Against the World.* For all of you who loved *Two for the Road,* here's the sequel you've been waiting for. And if you missed the first book, don't worry. You can still order a copy—just don't let Ali's story slip through your hands in the meantime!

The rest of the month is filled with both familiar names—like Maura Seger and Amanda Stevens—and new ones—like Diana Whitney, who makes her Intimate Moments debut, and Dani Criss, who's publishing her very first book. I think you'll enjoy everything we have to offer, as well as everything that will be heading your way in months to come. And speaking of the future, look for some real excitement next month, when Intimate Moments celebrates its tenth anniversary with a can't-miss lineup of books, including Patricia Gardner Evans's long-awaited American Hero title, *Quinn Eisley's War.* Come May, Intimate Moments is definitely *the* place to be.

Yours,
Leslie J. Wainger
Senior Editor and Editorial Coordinator

AMERICAN HERO

COLD, COLD HEART

Ann Williams

Published by Silhouette Books New York
America's Publisher of Contemporary Romance

SILHOUETTE BOOKS
300 East 42nd St., New York, N.Y. 10017

COLD, COLD HEART

Copyright © 1993 by Peggy A. Meyers

All rights reserved. Except for use in any review, the reproduction or utilization of this work in whole or in part in any form by any electronic, mechanical or other means, now known or hereafter invented, including xerography, photocopying and recording, or in any information storage or retrieval system, is forbidden without the permission of the publisher, Silhouette Books, 300 E. 42nd St., New York, N.Y. 10017

ISBN: 0-373-07487-5

First Silhouette Books printing April 1993

All the characters in this book have no existence outside the imagination of the author and have no relation whatsoever to anyone bearing the same name or names. They are not even distantly inspired by any individual known or unknown to the author, and all incidents are pure invention.

®: Trademark used under license and registered in the United States Patent and Trademark Office and in other countries.

Printed in the U.S.A.

Books by Ann Williams

Silhouette Intimate Moments

Devil in Disguise #302
Loving Lies #335
Haunted by the Past #358
What Lindsey Knew #384
Angel on My Shoulder #408
Without Warning #436
Shades of Wyoming #468
Cold, Cold Heart #487

ANN WILLIAMS

gave up her career as a nurse, then as the owner and proprietor of a bookstore, in order to pursue her writing full-time. She was born and married in Indiana, and after a number of years in Texas, she now lives in Arizona with her husband of twenty-three years and their children.

Reading, writing, crocheting, classical music and a good romantic movie are among her diverse loves. Her dream is to one day move to a cabin in the Carolina mountains with her husband and "write to my heart's content."

To Leslie Wainger
for all your encouragement,
your kindness
and your help

Prologue

It was eleven o'clock on a quiet Sunday morning in mid-June. The sweet perfume of wildflowers, mixed with pine and newly turned earth, filled the balmy air. The sky overhead was a deep Wedgwood blue.

In the distance a dog barked, letting the cry trail off into a long mournful howl. The engine of an automobile purred down the country road, trailing a thin streamer of yellow dust in its wake. The dust billowed, wafted to and fro by the breeze, thinned and settled lightly on whatever stood in its path.

A bright summer sun rose steadily, spilling Texas sunlight onto an ancient, spreading-oak tree. It filtered slowly through the branches, casting leaf-dappled shadows on the bowed heads of the somber group of people gathered below around two open graves.

As the minister took his place at the head of the graves, a shiny black crow swooped through the air and landed on a top branch of the tree. It hopped from one limb to another until it stopped, perched low, directly over the party beneath.

Bending its sleek, glossy neck, turning its head this way and that, it settled a small, inquiring black eye on the silent group. The hum of the minister's soft voice as he began to speak mixed with the drone of insects and floated away on the breeze.

A solitary figure, dressed all in black from the top of his dark head to the shine of his boots, stood back from the other mourners. With bowed head and hands clenched in the pockets of his jacket, he focused hazel eyes unblinkingly on the white wood grain of the nearer coffin.

After a while, the man's head lifted and he directed his glance toward the solemn faces of the people assembled around the two graves. One at a time, he peered intently at each face, probing the damp eyes, noting the stiffly held lips. And each time his eyes shifted to the next face, he asked himself the same question.

Did this one know? This one? Or this one? Did any of them know that *he was the one*—the one responsible for the death of this woman and her child?

If only he could have another chance... if only he could go back... go back and change the past....

Chapter 1

Jake rose from his kneeling position, hunching his shoulders against the cold wind. It ripped through his clothing, ruffled the too-long hair lying against his collar, and tumbled a brown curl into deep hazel eyes.

He'd been working since eight o'clock that morning to reset the two gravestones at the head of the two graves. They'd been knocked awry by violent storms and flash flooding during the last three days.

Straightening, he arched his back to try to remove a kink caused by the strain of shifting the three-hundred-pound marble stones without help. He placed a hand on a spot in his lower spine where the pain was the worst and rubbed hard. From his spine, his fingers worked their way around to his right hip where he massaged the pain in muscle and bone.

The storms weren't over yet; the leaden sky overhead attested to that fact. But he'd have known in any case, because the ache down the length of his right side was as good as a barometer, gauging the changes in the weather.

Jake frowned, adding to the series of lines marking his face. Gray hair had recently added a new maturity to the mass of thick brown waves covering his head, but he didn't notice. He never took notice of his appearance anymore.

Returning to his kneeling position, he began to gather the debris he'd removed from the immediate area into one large mass. A trash bag, weighted down with a rock, lay waiting for it.

As he stretched, reaching for a beer bottle someone had no doubt thrown from a passing car or truck, his knees slipped in the mud and his hand came down hard on the bottle's broken edge. Sharp pain bit into the palm of his hand and laced up his arm.

"Damn!" Fighting to regain his balance, he pulled back his hand and stared down at its palm. Blood welled from between the ragged edges of a deep wound and spilled over the sides of his hand.

In frustration, muttering curses, he felt around in the side pocket of his dark green jacket and found a handkerchief. It wasn't very clean, and it was damp from the rain, but it would have to do for now. Later, he'd take care of the hand at home.

Just for a moment, as he stared down at the wound, thoughts of Janet came to mind and what her reaction to such a wound would have been.

Janet? When had he stopped thinking of her as Mother?

Had the change come about the week after she'd died— when he'd found the newspaper clippings? Or had the change come about more recently, when he'd awakened in the hospital, his body racked with pain and his mind filled with memories he'd kept safely locked behind an impenetrable door for most of his life?

Shaking the bleak thoughts from his mind, he secured the handkerchief and went back to work. It really didn't matter. Nothing mattered anymore, except trying to make up a little for what he'd cost Mary and Lacy Tolbridge.

He'd spent the last five months trying to make up for what he'd cost them. He'd paid for their burial plots in this cemetery and all the funeral expenses, but he knew that wouldn't make up for the loss of their lives.

The only good thing that had come from their deaths was this time he'd spent by himself. He liked living in the Texas hill country alone. It gave him plenty of time to think. And he'd done a whole lot of thinking since the day he'd stood for the first time in this cemetery five months ago, watching mother and child being laid to rest.

As a result, he'd evaluated his past and reached some true, if painful, conclusions about himself and what had brought him to this juncture in his life. He'd been arrogant and cocky and he'd thought himself... infallible.

Never before now had Jake ever consciously examined his motives for what he'd done with his life. But somewhere inside he must have at one time thought he was doing what he did for the right reasons.

Now he knew the truth. He was a fraud. His whole life had been built on deception.

For the last ten years he'd fooled himself into believing he was a humanitarian. And that he restored missing children to their parents out of a sense of duty. In all those years, he never once returned a child without making a thorough investigation into the child's home life, and if there was ever a question of child abuse in any form, he involved the appropriate local authorities.

He'd always thought he was being so careful, because he wanted to be certain that the children he returned were being placed in the proper environment for their safety and well-being. But that was a lie—whitewash for his true motives.

He wasn't doing all that checking for the children. At least, he wasn't doing it for the children as much as he was doing it for himself—*to punish the parents*—to get back at all those who were like his own....

A sudden crash of thunder jerked Jake's attention to his present surroundings. His glance darted upward. Black clouds raced across the sky, with terrible, twisted forks of lightning dancing across their paths. Wind slashed at the mighty oak above him, bending and lashing its sturdy branches as though they were no more than twigs.

Something—some inbred instinct—caused Jake to whirl abruptly and stare through the gathering darkness. His breath lodged in his throat. He wanted to run, but his feet were glued to the spot. He wanted to blink, positive that what he was seeing would disappear once he closed his eyes, but the muscles of his face remained rigidly frozen in place.

A pale figure with flowing white robes floated slowly toward him. The violence around him faded abruptly into oblivion as Jake's eyes widened and his mouth grew slack.

Into his mind rose the image of his long-dead mother. *She'd come for him!* Just as she used to come for him when he was a child....

"Hello! I'm lost—at least, I think I am."

Jake shook his head to clear it, felt his muscles relax at the sound of her voice, and took a bold step in her direction.

"Who are you?" he asked harshly. "What do you want?"

The woman moved closer, fighting to stay on her feet as a sudden, powerful gust of wind shook her small frame. Clutching at the skirt of a white raincoat as it flapped wildly around her knees, she raised her voice to make it heard above the wind and asked, "Do you know a man..." the wind caught her slight figure and threw it off course "...by the name of Jake Frost?" She managed to regain her footing.

Jake's defenses moved instantly into place. "Why?"

She was standing only a few feet from him now. "I'm looking for him." Her eyes probed his face and something in his expression made her ask, "Are you Jake Frost?"

"Why?"

She moved closer. "I've been searching for you."

Again, giving nothing away, he asked, "Why?"

"Because I need your help—*desperately*." One frozen-looking white hand snaked out of the cover of her raincoat and fastened like a vise onto his arm. "Please, you must help me. It's my daughter...she's been kidnapped."

Jake felt himself freeze up inside, "I'm sorry, you've got the wrong man."

"You aren't Jake Frost?"

"1 told you—" the words were buffeted about by the wind, but she had no trouble hearing them "—you've got the wrong man."

"Wait!" He was walking away. "Please!"

A bolt of lightning slashed through the air, striking a large branch of the tree beneath which he stood. A puff of gray smoke shot upward, the sound of popping and cracking wood came sharply to ear as cold rain began to beat an insistent tattoo against the ground.

"Look out!"

Jake heard the crash, smelled the scorched wood and glanced up, realizing immediately the danger he was in. A slight, soft body hit his, and they both tumbled to the ground. But the danger wasn't over yet—now they were both in danger's path.

Jake wound his arms instinctively around the delicate body lying atop his and threw their combined weight in the opposite direction of the falling limb. They rolled several times, Jake ending on bottom as their momentum gradually slowed to a stop.

For a moment he lay there, panting, feeling the surge of adrenaline course through his veins like liquid power. And then, grasping the woman by the shoulders, feeling the rain wash his face, he pulled her head from his chest and asked in a breathless whisper, "Are you all right?"

"Yes."

Shaking the mass of wet brown hair from her eyes, she nodded slightly, tasting the rain, and answered again, "Yes...I'm fine...you?"

Their glances tangled and locked. Jake regarded her impassively, very much aware for the first time in a long time, what it was like to lie with a woman stretched along the top of him. She was so close he could see the dark rings of blue surrounding the gray irises, feel her uneven breath blowing against his wet skin.

As he watched, something flared behind the gray eyes and Jake felt his insides quicken. The hands gripping her shoulders tightened. This new pressure propelled her toward him, until her lips were a mere breath from his.

"Who *are* you?" Jake whispered, the question burning its way to his brain.

Pale lids descended suddenly, shielding the expression in her eyes from his probing stare. She couldn't speak over the sudden pounding of her heart. Who was this man, that he could provoke such a reaction with a mere question and a glance from those young-old eyes?

Jake moved her abruptly from him. The rain was coming down in a steady sheet as he climbed quickly to his feet. After a momentary hesitation, he offered the woman a hand up.

She grasped the hand without looking, heard his sharp intake of breath and glanced down at the red-soaked handkerchief tied loosely around its palm.

"You're hurt. What have you done?"

Jake pulled his hand from her grasp and shoved it into one of the many pockets in his jacket. "It's nothing." Turning away, he strode purposefully toward the debris now floating in a growing puddle of water.

Grabbing the trash bag from beneath the rock, he fumbled with it for a moment before finding the opening, then dropped to his knees and using one hand as a scoop, began pushing the pile of trash inside it. *Why didn't she go away?*

The woman stood over him, watching. "Did you hear what I said? My daughter has been kidnapped and I have to find her.... Where are you going?"

Jake was on his feet, moving toward the rusty iron gate set in the wall surrounding the cemetery. The trash bag was slung over his shoulder, and he paused momentarily to deposit it in a receptacle just outside the gate.

"Where are you going?" she asked again, trotting along at his side.

"Home—where you ought to be in this storm."

"Please, you have to listen to me! You're my last hope! I've got to find my daughter...."

"Then go to the police."

"I have—they can't find her." She tugged on the sleeve of his jacket, bringing him to a sudden halt. "Don't you understand? My little girl's life may be in danger."

Jake felt his chest squeeze tight. "I can't help you."

"Oh...please...they said you were the best." Tears choked her voice, welled up in her eyes, mixed with rain and ran down both cheeks. "She's only a baby. She needs me. She needs her mother...and I..." She choked and shook her head, unable to continue. Dropping her hand from his sleeve, she put both hands over her face and fought for control.

"I'm sorry." Jake stared somewhere over her shaking shoulders toward the graveyard, spotted a small white headstone and hardened his heart. "I'm not the man you want." The gate was open, and he was about to pass through it, when her voice lashed out at him.

"I saved your life just now! Doesn't that count for anything? Isn't that worth a few minutes of your precious time?"

Jake turned back to look at her with dead eyes. After a long frozen moment, he shook his head, just once, and answered, "No."

"No! What do you mean, no? Are you telling me life means nothing to you?"

"My life," he explained softly, "my life means nothing to me. Now, if you'll excuse me, I'm going home."

"How can you just walk away? What about my daughter? My b-baby is in danger of losing her life and you just walk away? What kind of man are you?"

"The kind who knows when he's beat."

"What does that mean?" she asked angrily. "I didn't come to listen to conundrums. Just answer me one question—are you Jake Frost?"

What difference did it make if she knew? "Yes."

"Then you're the man I'm looking for. Why are you being so difficult?"

"I am *not* the man you are looking for," he refuted with emphasis. "Go to the cops," he added, turning away.

"I told you, I did. They couldn't find her and neither could the FBI. That's why I'm here. Please, just hear me out. Listen to what I have to say. Then..." these words, apparently came with great difficulty "...if you still refuse to help me...I'll leave without a fight. I promise."

For a long moment she thought she was lost. He gave no sign of having heard her final plea. On the other side of the gate, he hesitated and muttered, "Who sent you?"

"I'm sorry..." she tried to step closer, fighting her own battle with the wind "...what did you say?"

"I said..." he whipped his eyes to her face "...who sent you?"

"A man named Davison."

"Gus Davison!" The words were a curse.

"Yes." She nodded. "That's him."

Jake strode through the gate angrily and stood holding it open. "Well?"

She realized he was waiting for her to join him.

Closing it after her, Jake jammed both fists into his pockets and started down the road at a brisk trot. After a few yards, he stopped and turned back to look at her.

"Well, are you just going to stand there, getting soaked? It's cold and I'm beat."

A moment later, she was at his side. "I'm Rachel Dryden."

"And your daughter?" He didn't want to know, but the words seemed torn from him against his will.

She hesitated before answering. "Amy...her name is Amy. Do you know what it means?" Rachel glanced up at the man's stern profile. "It means, beloved."

Jake's jaw tightened and his steps quickened, but he made no comment.

The house was a good two-mile walk from the cemetery in the bone-chilling rain, but Rachel kept up with his quick pace and made no objection when he didn't defer to her shorter stride. She was just thankful to have him agree to hear her out, a thing she'd thought was beyond hope when she'd first looked into those hollow dark eyes.

Gazing into them had been like getting a glimpse inside hell and after the initial shock had worn off, though she didn't know the source of his own private hell, her sympathy had gone out to him. If she hadn't been living in a hell of her own, she'd have turned right around and left the man to find whatever comfort he could from the thing that was slowly destroying him.

Gus Davison hadn't explained what had changed this man into the shell of a man she now saw. He'd only warned her that after a recent tragedy he'd become a recluse. He'd also said if anyone could find Amy, it was this man, marching grimly at her side.

Thanks to the pace set by Jake, they reached his house in what must have been record time. The house lay down a short gravel walk surrounded by tall cottonwood trees and a four-foot stacked-rock fence. It was very old, built during the period when Europeans were settling central Texas, and constructed from the rocks cleared from the area. A sloping porch with a metal roof ran the length of the house and at one end a fireplace chimney climbed up past the red-painted roof.

Rachel slowly followed Jake inside, noting he hadn't paused to unlock the door. He took his jacket off in the small entrance hall, hung it on a coat tree, and removed his muddy boots.

He didn't look at her as he held his hand out for her rain-coat. Neither did he bother waiting for her when she stopped to slip off her damp shoes and socks before following him into the short entrance hall. There were two doors, one on either side of the hall, but she had no idea how the rooms beyond were used, because both doors were shut. At the end of the hall was a short flight of stairs leading to the second floor.

Jake reached for the doorknob on the right and moved into a small, sparsely furnished room. Striding to the fire-place, set at the end of the room, he removed a long match from the container sitting on a corner of the stone mantel. He knelt to set flame to the wood already laid.

Holding cold hands out to the flames, he noticed the soiled handkerchief and was once more aware of the steady throb from the wound in his hand. He supposed he ought to go upstairs and take a look at it, but first he wanted to hear this woman's story and get her out of his hair.

"I'm listening," he prompted with his back turned toward her.

"I was taught that good manners required that you face the person speaking to you," she rebuked him softly, thinking the lack of comfort and warmth in the room's furnishings accurately reflected the man's nature.

Jake's jaw tightened. He stood and turned toward her slight figure, hovering near the door. "Are you here to give me a lesson in manners or tell me about your daughter?"

Rachel bit her lip, but there was a slight air of defiance in the glance she allowed to rest briefly on his face. Then her glance slipped downward. "Your hand!" she gasped.

Jake looked at the hand he clutched unconsciously by the wrist. The handkerchief binding it had become saturated with blood. The cloth dripped slowly onto the floor, leaving dark red splotches against the wood.

Cupping his other hand beneath it with a disgusted air, he moved toward her, passing close by her as she stepped swiftly out of his way. "This will only take a minute," he threw back over his shoulder as he slid around the corner and out of sight.

Upstairs, Jake unwrapped the hand over the sink. The deep gash appeared to go almost to the bone and it was going to need stitches. The medicine closet standing beside the sink held everything he'd need. It would be awkward, using his left hand, but...

"Let me help."

Jake glanced into the mirror and saw Rachel's image float into view. "I can manage," he said shortly, then dropped a plastic bottle of antiseptic he was attempting to open onto the floor.

"I didn't say you couldn't," she responded, bending to recover the brown bottle.

Jake opened a plastic tray resting on the side of the sink and reached for a small square package. Lifting it, he placed it between strong, white teeth. But before he could rip it open, Rachel reached for the package, her eyes on the dimple in his chin. She tugged lightly, and when he didn't release it, her eyes moved upward. The message in his eyes was clear. Playing nursemaid to him wouldn't win her any brownie points.

After a moment, his jaw relaxed and Rachel removed the package from his teeth. He followed her movements with narrowed eyes as she ripped it open. Removing the needle and suture, she laid it on the small utility table at her side and reached for his hand.

"Uh-uh." Jake clenched his fingers and pulled them out of reach.

"What?"

His uninjured hand snaked out past her shoulder and retrieved a sealed package off the shelf behind. Handing it to her he said, "Germs."

Rachel's lips compressed, but she opened the package and pulled on the tight-fitting rubber gloves. Firmly taking hold of his wrist, she raised cool gray eyes to his face and said, "Be brave now, it will only hurt for a little while."

He let that pass to ask skeptically, "Do you know what you're doing?"

"Of course," she replied without batting an eyelid.

"You've done this before?"

"What do you think?"

Jake opened his hand slowly. Rachel swallowed, took a deep breath and cupped his injured hand in her smaller one, drawing it close. As casually as she could manage, she asked, "How did you do this?"

"Glass. I slipped in the mud."

"I think we'd better wash it out, just in case there are any broken pieces of glass . . . or anything foreign inside."

Jake allowed her to peel back the edges of the wound, exposing the bluish-white membrane covering the bone. He heard her quickly smothered gasp and felt a glimmer of satisfaction.

"This is going to sting," she murmured insipidly, pouring the antiseptic directly into the cut. Jake clenched his jaw tight, but except for a slight tremor in the hand resting in hers, he evidenced no other sign of discomfort from the sharp sting of the medicine.

Rachel licked dry lips, pushed an errant strand of hair back from her damp forehead with the back of one hand, and tilted his hand slightly over the sink. The second stream of medication washed over the open wound from top to bottom.

"There," she said, breathing a little unevenly following the flow of pink liquid into the basin with her eyes, "how's that?"

"It hurts like hell," Jake answered succinctly.

"I'm sorry," she murmured.

There wasn't a glimmer of apology in the gray eyes resting on his face. *Touché*.

"Get on with it," he said impatiently, tearing his glance from the sight of her full bottom lip. The wound was ready for suturing.

"Don't you have something . . . some kind of medication to deaden the area—"

"No! Just sew it. If you're afraid to, then give it to me and let's be done with it."

"Y-yes, all right."

During the next fifteen minutes it was hard to say who suffered more. Rachel concentrated completely on the job at hand, feeling every stab of the needle as it passed through Jake's tough hide.

Jake withstood her efforts in grim, tight-lipped silence. If he was in pain, no one would know it. When the last knot had been tied and cut, Rachel stood staring at the not-so-neat row of black knots and shook her head remorsefully.

"Maybe you *would* have done a better job of it."

Jake closed his fingers, hiding a wince, and made a fist. "It's done, that's what counts."

Rachel insisted, despite his protestations, upon wrapping a strip of white gauze around his palm to protect the stitches. But when she started to clean up the mess, he pointed toward the door and told her to get out.

"It will only take a moment—"

"I'll do it myself!" he barked shortly.

Rachel was halfway down the stairs when the slamming door echoed loudly throughout the house. She'd accomplished more than she'd hoped with her first aid. Now he knew she wasn't someone who gave in at the first sign of an obstacle.

When he joined her a few minutes later, she was sitting with folded hands staring into the fireplace. He pulled a straight-backed chair, twin to the one on which she sat, before the fire, and sat facing her. "Okay, let's hear your story."

Rachel stared down at her hands clutched tightly on the lap of her black wool slacks. She knew without his having to say it that he'd already made up his mind. The instant he'd entered the room, she'd known that what had taken place upstairs had lost her the advantage. She just couldn't figure out how.

"I don't know where to begin. Maybe I'd better tell you a little bit about Gary—"

"Gary?"

Rachel nodded. "Yes—Gary, my ex-husband. He...we...met in college. I was a student and he taught literature—"

"He's a teacher?"

"College professor—yes. He's a few years older than me. After we got married, he wanted to have a child right away, but I insisted we wait. I didn't know...."

She twisted her fingers into impossible shapes, trying to think how to tell him all that had happened in as few sentences as possible. The cool, controlled woman who'd matched him tit for tat upstairs was gone. In her place was a distraught mother, frightened for her child's safety.

"How was I to know?" She met his glance with troubled eyes. "How was I to know he was...sick?"

"Sick?"

"I...yes...this isn't making any sense to you, is it?"

Jake just looked at her.

Taking a deep, calming breath she said, "Let me start again. Gary and I met in college and fell in love—oh, not right away, but soon after we started dating.

"We got married a year after I graduated. I was teaching school—I'm a kindergarten teacher. Anyway, we got married and were happy. Gary wanted to start a family right away, but I talked him into waiting for a while. I liked there being only the two of us...." She hesitated. "Do you know what I mean?" she asked, meeting Jake's unflinching dark eyes.

"Go on."

"I became pregnant a year later and we had...Amy." She smiled, lost in the memories of those first few days home from the hospital. Everything had been perfect. Gary had been kind and loving and so solicitous of her welfare. He'd even gotten up at night to take care of the baby so she could sleep....

"I should have known something was wrong when he insisted I go back to work immediately after my six-week checkup. We'd talked about it—about when I'd return to work—and decided I'd stay home with the baby for the first year.

"But he finally convinced me having a woman in to care for Amy would be all right. And besides, I had worked four years to get my teaching certificate, I agreed with him that I should use it. I love teaching and though I love Amy more, I let him convince me he knew what was best.

"I would never have known what was happening if the head of the English department hadn't called me and asked if there was something seriously wrong with Amy. It seemed Gary had been leaving his classes, turning them over to graduate students, and going home during the day quite frequently in the months since Amy's birth.

"I felt like such a fool!" She twisted at the gold band on her left hand. "I didn't know what he was talking about, all I could do was stumble through an apology and half pretend I knew what Gary was doing. That evening, when I went home, I got Maida—the woman we'd hired to look after Amy—aside, and asked her what was going on.

"You see," she admitted slowly, "I thought Gary was...having an affair.

"But Maida told me she, too, had been puzzled when Gary began coming home in the middle of the day and sending her home. She said she'd thought she wasn't doing a good job. But when she approached Gary with her fears, he'd told her she was doing an excellent job, and assured her he had some free time and just wanted to enjoy being a daddy. Then he'd told her they should just keep this between themselves and he'd given her a raise.

"That's when I began to think back and realized how he'd gradually been pushing me out of my own daughter's life."

She stopped, swallowing back tears and cleared her throat. "And the awful thing about it is that I let him get away with it! I was so caught up in my work, I didn't see what was happening."

She took a moment to compose herself and then continued. "When I confronted him with what I'd been told by both Maida and the head of the English department, he flew into a rage. I was stunned. I'd never seen him angry. He was always in complete control of his emotions."

Jake slanted a sharp glance. Always in control? Surely there were times, when they were alone, that his control had slipped.

"Gary said he knew what was best for Amy and we wouldn't discuss it again." Her voice thinned. "That's when he moved out of our bedroom and into the spare room on the other side of the nursery. Things worsened after that. He fired Maida without consulting me and left every morning with Amy, before I went to work.

"I didn't know what to do. I tried talking to him and he became violent. So, I called a close friend and explained what was happening. She suggested getting Gary professional help. I was afraid to even mention the idea to Gary. When I did . . . he hit me."

Rachel compressed trembling lips, unable to continue for a moment. After taking a steadying breath, she murmured, "I filed for divorce the next day—the day after he hit me.

"I had to leave the house with Amy under police guard, because he threatened my life. He began to call me at home, and sometimes at work, and say vile things over the phone, so I got a restraining order against him.

"The first day of the divorce hearing Gary showed up in a rage, he cursed the judge in his chambers and made threats against Amy and me. When the child custody hearing came up, I won sole custody of our daughter.

"I never saw him again, not until about three months after the divorce was final. He caught me in the parking lot of a grocery store after dark. Amy was with me. He forced us into his car and drove us into the country. There, he jerked open my door and shoved me out onto the ground. He said..."

"Yes?" Jake prompted when it looked like she wasn't going to continue.

"He said...if I came after Amy...he'd kill her—and then he'd kill himself."

Jake felt the words like a blow to his gut.

Chapter 2

No! This was too much like the last time! He couldn't do it—not again!

"Please, will you help me find my baby...before he hurts her?"

On the point of refusing out of hand, Jake pushed himself abruptly to his feet, caught a brief glance from her desperate eyes, and turned quickly away. Staring into the flames, he considered what helping this woman might mean to him and decided he couldn't take the chance.

"No."

"W-what did you say?"

"No—I can't help you."

She couldn't believe her ears. After all that she'd told him, he was refusing her.

"Three weeks—he's had her three weeks. God only knows what he may have done to her, and you say no...no, you can't help m-me?"

Rachel began to shake all over, and she didn't know if it was caused by despair or rage. Her teeth chattered together loudly and nausea rose in her throat. She wanted to be strong—she had to be strong—for Amy, but this constant fear about Gary's threat was slowly destroying her.

She wanted her baby! Why couldn't anyone understand that all she wanted in the whole world was her baby? Maybe, if she could make him understand...

"D-do you know—do you have any idea of w-what I'm feeling?" The deepest, darkest anguish she'd ever known mixed with fury churned inside her. "Have you any idea of the helpless—hopeless—feeling inside me?"

Raising herself slowly from the chair, she looked into his face, even though he refused to meet her eyes. "Every day, when I awaken, the first thought in my mind is of Amy. I think of seeing my child, holding her warm, wiggling little body close." Rachel crossed empty arms over her chest. "And feeling her chubby arms wind their way around my neck." She touched the side of her neck in memory. "And hear her soft childish voice whispering in my ear, 'I love you, Mommy.'" Her voice broke, and her jaws clenched tightly to try to still their spasmodic quivering as she struggled to get control of her breathing, so she could continue.

"And then I remember... I remember she's gone... and I can't find her." The tension grew tight within her, making her words come out in jerky spurts. "I don't know where to look for her." She gestured wildly with her hands. "Outside this room is the whole world. There's so much of it. And she could be anywhere—*anywhere!*

"Do you know how helpless that makes me feel? Do you have any idea how desperate, how *desperate and hopeless* I feel, knowing that no one, not the police, not even the FBI, has been able to find my child?"

She moved until she stood directly in Jake's path, staring up at his veiled expression. "S-she's lost and n-no one can f-find her... except... maybe you...."

Jake tried to distance himself from the pleading voice, the expression of stark pain on her pale face, but it was impossible. Because he'd felt that same hopeless despair himself. One look into her face and he recognized the agony of spirit she was going through, but he had no words of comfort to offer her. He was frozen inside. And so he did the only thing he could do at that moment. He left the room in silence.

Rachel stood where he'd left her, a feeling of defeat now added to those of anguish and despair. She should just go. He'd made his decision.

But can you accept it? Can you give in so easily? This is your child's life!

A voice inside spoke to her, demanding that she continue to try to persuade this man, Frost, to help her. It was the same voice that had driven her to fly to Washington, D.C., and seek out Gus Davison; to beseech him to do something more to find her child, because weeks had passed and no one in the field had come up with a lead. Jake Frost was her last hope. Somehow, she simply had to get him to agree to help her.

She was ready for him when he reappeared, but he surprised her by returning with a cup of steaming liquid in one hand. He further surprised her by crossing to her chair, reaching for her hand, and wrapping it around the cup.

"Don't touch me!" She jerked away from him.

Jake grew still, a muscle working in his jaw, but he didn't speak, only stood, holding the cup out to her. After a long, tense moment, she accepted it with a shaking hand. The hot liquid immediately sloshed over the cup's rim and onto the floor at Jake's feet.

Now Jake had no patience with her. Cupping the back of her head, he wrapped a firm hand around hers and guided the cup unerringly to her mouth. Rachel hesitated, slanting him a look of suppressed fury, but declined to struggle against his hold.

The rim of the cup bumped against the edge of her lower lip, splashing it with liquid. Slowly she unclenched her lips and reluctantly tasted his offering with the tip of her tongue.

Jake watched grimly, explaining in terse tones, "It isn't laced with arsenic. My...mother believed strongly in the curative aspects of hot, honey-sweetened, tea."

Rachel noted the slight hesitation before the word mother and filed it away for future contemplation. The thought uppermost in her mind was his refusal to help her.

Taking a deep breath, hands steadier now—strangely enough, the tea seemed to be helping—she took a large, bracing gulp before whispering, "Please, won't you reconsider? Won't you change your mind...and help me?"

No! Again, the answer fought its way to the tip of his tongue, but this time his lips refused to shape it.

"Why me?"

Rachel looked confused. "What do you mean?"

"Why did you come to *me?*" he repeated. "If you talked to Gus Davison, then he must have told you that I no longer work for the agency. I don't do that kind of work anymore."

"But you're the best—"

"Don't you understand?" he asked angrily, her single-mindedness beginning to get to him. "Must I repeat myself yet again? I no longer work for the agency—I quit! Find yourself a good private detective, someone who specializes in missing—"

"I did," she interrupted impatiently. "I found you!"

"But I'm not available."

"You're the best!"

"*I'm not!*" he yelled, whirling on her angrily. "I'm not the best. Can't you get that through your head? *And... I ... will ... not ... take ... this ... case!*" he thundered.

"You must," she said quietly, refusing to get into a shouting match with him. "He said you were the best there ever was and ever will be," she argued doggedly.

"Gus Davison said I was the best?" he asked quickly. She nodded. "I don't believe you." Gus had been there the night he was shot. Gus knew all about Lacy and Mary Tolbridge. He couldn't believe that Gus could recommend him.

"Did Davison tell you where I was?" he asked abruptly.

"Yes."

"Damn him!" Jake swung toward the fireplace and slammed a fist against its unyielding surface, feeling the impact all the way down his spine.

Rachel jumped, her eyes drawn to the spreading red stain on the white bandage wrapped around his fist. He'd probably torn the stitches loose.

"Look..." She climbed to her feet, still holding the cup, and moved toward him, setting the cup on the mantel. "I don't know why you left your job, or what you have against Mr. Davison. And I don't care," she added quickly. "I only know, my child—my little Amy—needs me. She's in trouble...." Her voice broke and she hesitated, swallowing tightly, fighting to keep things in balance and retain control of her emotions. "She's in trouble." She was losing the battle. Her voice quivered, "She needs me...she needs her mother."

Grabbing hold of his shirt with both hands, she tried to force him to look at her. "Do you understand? *My baby needs me!*"

Jake's glance touched the trembling lips and quivering chin before moving up to her smoldering eyes and then darting quickly away. What would it take to get her off his back?

"Your help," she whispered desperately, as if in answer to his silent question. "Help me and I swear you'll never see or hear from me again. As soon as I have Amy in my arms, I'll forget your name. I promise, no one will know it was you who helped me—if that's what you want."

Her hands bunched and tugged tighter on his shirt with each word. "Will you help me?"

Lifting unfathomable dark eyes, Jake made himself look into hers. He searched the gray eyes, reached past her thoughts and delved into her soul. What he saw there disturbed him. It also made it impossible for him to refuse her. "Yes." The word was dragged from him against his will.

"Oh, God..." Rachel collapsed, sagging against him in sudden relief. "Oh, thank you! Thank you!"

Jake carefully extricated himself from her touch, telling himself he didn't want her gratitude, all he wanted was her silence and her quick removal from his life. But the feel of her soft cheek, pressed to his shoulder, lingered long after they moved apart.

"Don't thank me yet," he answered darkly, striding toward the door. "You may wake one morning and find yourself bitterly regretting the day you ever set eyes on me, or asked for my help."

Rachel watched his quick exit with puzzled eyes, but followed quickly in his wake, eager to get the search started, now that he'd agreed to it. Three whole weeks. It had been three whole weeks since Gary had snatched their frightened child from her helpless arms and disappeared with her.

"What do we do first?" she asked, only a step behind as he marched down the dark, narrow hall.

Without answering, Jake flipped a switch set in the wall just inside the kitchen door and flooded the room with bright, yellow light. When he did answer, it wasn't what she wanted to hear. "*We* do nothing. I'll need to know everything you can tell me about your husband's background and your life together before your divorce."

"That's all?" Rachel asked bleakly. "You just want to talk?" She wanted action! She'd spent the last twenty-one days answering questions and waiting for someone to *do* something besides write things down and ask more questions.

"For now," he answered coolly.

Placing an old-fashioned teakettle beneath the faucet, Jake filled it with water. He turned to find Rachel standing directly behind him as he moved away from the sink. She glanced up into his flat, expressionless eyes and stepped quickly out of his path, swallowing the argumentative words she'd been about to bombard him with.

"All right," she conceded with faint grace, watching him place the teakettle on the stove and light the burner beneath it. "I've got most of what you'll no doubt want in the car." She couldn't help adding in fed-up tones, "I've spent a lot of time these past three weeks answering questions."

Jake glared at her momentarily before his head disappeared into a cabinet in search of clean cups. Gus must have been awfully sure of him if he'd entrusted official documents, intended for him, to this woman.

"You get the paperwork, and when the tea is ready, we'll get started."

"It's all in the car. And my car's parked at the cemetery," she added ruefully. In the ensuing silence, pistol-shot rain slammed against the roof of the house as though to remind them of the inclement weather raging outside its warm cocoon. Jake straightened from the refrigerator with a pitcher of milk in one hand and shrugged in resignation.

"Give me your keys." He set the milk on the round wooden table and held out a reluctant hand.

Rachel looked from the blood-stained bandage to his face. "I can go after it. It isn't that far."

"The keys," he repeated.

She fished in the pocket of her slacks and held them out to him. Jake took them, shoved them into his jeans, and turned toward the door.

"When the water's hot," he threw the instructions over his shoulder as he moved down the short hallway, "pour it into the teapot and let it steep, the tea is already inside. It should be about ready to drink by the time I return."

Grabbing his coat from the coat tree, he shoved his arms into the sleeves and bent to retrieve a boot.

"You'll get soaked," Rachel protested quickly, as he pulled on the mud-caked boots, noticing the circles of dried mud on the knees of his jeans for the first time.

Jake shrugged, opened the door and closed it between them without another word. Outside, he breathed a quick sigh of relief. It was the first easy breath he'd drawn since he'd turned and spotted the ghostly pale figure coming toward him in the cemetery.

He really didn't mind the brisk walk in the pouring rain. It soothed the unsettled feelings the woman stirred inside him with her presence in his house. She reminded him of things he wished he could forget and aroused emotions better left alone.

Jake found her car, a dark blue Volvo, sitting beneath the trees near the back entrance to the cemetery. Climbing quickly inside, unmindful of the damage his soiled clothing might cause, he drove the two miles to his house without using the heater.

On the passenger seat, he spotted a neat stack of folders and gathered them into his arms before leaving the car. Inside the house, he quickly divested himself of jacket and boots and strode down the hall toward the kitchen. He was looking forward to that cup of hot tea. The only thing that would make it better would be to find the woman and all trace of her presence gone from his house.

As he passed the stairs, Rachel suddenly appeared at the top. Jake glanced up at the same instant she saw him and paused with her hand on the newel post. She must have towel-dried her hair, because it lay in soft fluffy waves about her head and floated gently to her shoulders.

Her face was flushed pink with her efforts and there was a faint glow in the gray eyes. The top two buttons of the white blouse she wore had been unfastened and the sleeves rolled up past her elbows. Jake's eyes took in the rosy hue of her cheeks, set against the pale creaminess of her skin, and noted the hint of a shadowed hollow where the gaping blouse partially exposed her breasts, as he strode by without pausing.

"I hope you don't mind," Rachel called to his rigid back, "I took the opportunity to wash up."

In the kitchen, Jake slapped the folders down on the table, poured milk and tea into one of the blue ceramic mugs, and took a large gulp. A slight step behind warned him she'd followed.

Rachel stepped up to his side and eyed the manila folders. "So, you found them. Good. Now we can get started"

Jake raised a dark brow, and mindful of his burning tongue, took a small sip of the hot tea before asking, "We?"

"Yes, I'm going to work with you on this." She saw refusal in the hazel eyes and added quickly, "Please—I *need* to do this."

Jake took another sip from his cup, picked up the folders and headed toward the door.

"Where are you going?"

"To read these."

"What about me? What should I do?"

"Keep still, unless I ask you a question."

"That's all?"

"For now."

"But time is slipping past. What about going after him? When do we go after him? He could be anywhere—anywhere in the country! We can't just let him slip—"

"And where do you suggest we look?" Jake asked curtly, twisting to face her.

"I…" Rachel shook her head. "I don't know—that's up to you."

"Exactly." He left the room without a backward glance.

Rachel poured herself a cup of tea, spooned in a generous amount of sugar from a mushroom-shaped bowl sitting in the center of the table, and hurried after him. Whether he liked it or not, she was going to take part in the search for her daughter. It wasn't going to be the way it had been with the San Antonio police.

All she'd gotten from them was advice about keeping the home fires burning and letting them do their jobs. She'd done that, and what had it got her? Amy was still missing, and they were no closer to finding her.

And as far as the FBI was concerned, the agents she'd dealt with so far had been closemouthed and formally distant. All, that is, except Gus Davison. He'd been kind and concerned.

Entering the living room, she found Jake sitting stiffly in the same chair he'd sat in earlier. The only concession he'd made toward comfort was in crossing his feet at the ankles and turning the damp bottoms of his stocking feet toward the heat of the fire. His cup of tea rested on the floor beside him, and the first folder lay open on his lap.

Rachel took a seat and sipped her tea. For the next thirty minutes, except for an occasional snap from the fireplace and the rustling of paper as he turned one page after another, the room remained silent.

It wasn't easy, but Jake did his best to concentrate on what he read and ignore the woman perched on the edge of the chair directly across from him, her eyes glued to his face.

"Well?" Rachel prodded when he'd dropped the last page onto the folder lying on the floor beside his chair. "Have you any ideas?"

"Several," Jake responded laconically, lifting his mug of tea, "but none concerning the whereabouts of your husband."

"Ex-husband," she corrected swiftly.

"It's late." Jake swallowed the last sip of tepid tea and got to his feet. "I've had a long day . . . and so have you. Where are you staying?"

"Staying?" She looked at him blankly.

"Yes, where are you planning to stay while you're here?"

"I . . . don't know . . . I came here directly from the airport. I didn't even think about . . ." She let the words drift off.

Jake gave her a look that said he wasn't surprised to learn she didn't have a place to stay for the night. "Well, there aren't any guest houses or motels in the area, it's too remote for that. I thought maybe you had friends living somewhere nearby."

"No . . . I'm sorry," she apologized, knowing instinctively that he wouldn't want her staying overnight in his house.

"I have a spare room," Jake admitted reluctantly. "I suppose you could make do with it for the short time you'll be needing it," he added with a pointed glance at her face.

He was letting her know his tolerance of her would last no longer than a day or two at the most, just until he'd sorted through the facts in the case. When she'd answered all his questions, she'd be on her way back to San Antonio.

Rachel let the implication pass without challenge. She knew what she had to do, and no one, not even this man who had finally, unwillingly, agreed to help her, could deflect her from that purpose.

"Would you like a refill?" Jake asked on his way to the kitchen for more tea for himself.

Rachel shook her head and glanced down at the face of her watch. It was only a little past eight, but it was pitch-black outside and the dampness of the weather made her feel dull and drowsy.

The drive from the San Antonio airport had been long and tiresome. But looking for Jake Frost, and withstanding his implacable attitude once she'd found him, had used up what little remaining reserve of strength she'd been able to muster in the last three weeks. She needed time to rest and regroup for the battles she was certain lay ahead with this taciturn man.

"All I want is a shower—or a bath," she added quickly, in case a shower wasn't available, "and a bed."

"Dinner—"

"No food." Rachel made a face and shook her head. "I couldn't eat a bite."

"If that's what you want." He shrugged, secretly glad he'd be spared more time that night in her presence. "If you'll follow me."

Jake led the way up the narrow flight of stairs. There were three doors along this new hallway, all on the same side and three windows in the opposite wall.

The first door led to his bedroom which he didn't bother offering to show her. The next one was a small bathroom. Rachel was already well-acquainted with that room by now.

Stopping at the third door, Jake twisted the doorknob and pushed the door inward. He stood back to let her precede him into the room. When they were both standing in the middle of the small, square room, he said, "It isn't four-star, but it's warm and dry. And there—" he gestured "—is the bed."

Rachel eyed the large, old-fashioned, four-poster sitting against one wall, covered with a thick colorful quilt. "Thank you," she replied, anticipating the few hours of oblivion she'd find now in sleep.

Jake pointed to a door centered in the wall opposite the bed. "That leads to the bathroom. We share. There are clean towels and washcloths in the closet at the end of the hall."

"Thank you," Rachel murmured tiredly.

"There's a lock on the inside of the bathroom door." He crossed the room, threw open the door to the bathroom and indicated the sliding bolt on the door opposite them. "Use it."

Rachel roused herself long enough to whisper, "I know this must be a terrible inconvenience for you and I'm sorry. I want you to know, I do appreciate your hospitality."

Jake brushed her thanks aside and was halfway down the stairs when he heard her call, "My keys!" He hesitated before turning back.

"I need my car keys to get my bag from the car," she explained apologetically.

"I'll bring it along in a few minutes." Without waiting for a reply, Jake resumed his descent.

"Thank you," Rachel called softly to his unyielding back, wondering what she'd said this time to upset him.

A short while later, Jake returned with her bag. He stood in the hallway and pushed the expensive leather suitcase through the door with his left hand.

Rachel had grown tired of waiting for him to return with her bag and had taken her bath. A large bath towel was wrapped around her slight figure and tucked beneath one arm.

"Would you like me to take a look at that?" she asked, opening the door wider and indicating the hand he kept protectively near his waist.

After one brief glance at pale ivory shoulders, Jake dropped the hand to his side and shook his head curtly, keeping his eyes on the door beside the narrow opening.

"If you change your mind about something to eat, there's food in the refrigerator." Having said that, he stomped down the stairs.

In the kitchen, he slapped together a sandwich. Fifteen minutes later, he'd taken only a bite from it, but he'd drunk a whole pot of tea. At the back of his mind a small voice taunted him with the fact that his visitor had come prepared to stay.

A picture of pale, creamy shoulders and a long, delicate neck rising from the blue of his bath towel floated through his mind. Jake shoved himself away from the table and threw the rest of his sandwich into the garbage. Just two days, that's all he'd give her, and then she was out of his house.

A few minutes later, Jake made himself comfortable in front of the fireplace and sat down to work. Sleep was a commodity that had been in short supply for the past several months. He was learning to live without it. He couldn't abide tossing and turning and staring into the dark, so he sat up and read most nights, or went for long walks.

Tonight, his sleeplessness would give him plenty of time for work. And the sooner he solved the riddle of her husband's disappearance, the sooner he'd be free of Rachel Dryden's disturbing presence in his life. When she was gone, things would return to normal—or what had become normal in the last five months.

Jake read the documents she'd provided him a second time and began to form a picture of Gary Dryden. What he imagined was a quiet, intellectual man, one who seemed to have few interests outside teaching.

Jake could imagine him existing day-to-day, living in the pages of the dry, dusty books from which he taught. And then one day, he must have looked up and seen Rachel's lovely, eager face staring back at him. For the first time in almost forty years, he must have discovered what it was to be a man hopelessly in love with a real flesh-and-blood woman.

He wondered if Professor Dryden had ever considered the fact that Rachel might be only infatuated with the idea of gaining attention from an older man, one who perhaps brought to life for her the romantic ballads of bygone years. How surprised he must have been to realize the fresh-faced young coed thought herself enough in love with him to consider marriage. A certain sympathy for the man began to grow inside Jake as he began to picture the man as victim.

He'd heard Rachel's side of the story. But there was a lot she hadn't said. What had taken place during the marriage to cause its dissolution? Was the man, as she'd intimated, mentally unstable?

And if not, then what had occurred after the divorce to make Gary Dryden rip the little girl from her mother's arms in such a cruel fashion? Had that part of Rachel's story even been true?

He'd read the transcripts of the divorce and custody proceedings provided by the court. Professor Dryden had indeed made threats against Rachel, but no threat had been mentioned against the little girl's life.

In his experience, Jake had learned that there were always two sides to every issue. Neither was ever all white or all black.

Had Rachel been a good mother?

The room grew cold around him as the thought popped into his mind. If she hadn't been, if perhaps she'd been too harsh—cruel, even—in her treatment of the little girl, that could be the reason her husband had taken the child away. Hadn't he seen what he believed to be an expression of guilt behind the woman's eyes a little while ago?

Jake stared into the fire's dying embers and remembered his own past. . . .

"Is that a chocolate handprint on the bathroom wall?" a *shrill voice bounced off the ceiling and walls, wrenching him from sleep.*

Jake sat up and rubbed chubby fists into sleepy dark eyes.

"Did you hear me? Answer me when I talk to you!"

Rough hands grabbed him by the shoulders, extricating him from the bedclothes, and shook him ruthlessly. "Answer me! Haven't I told you, over and over again, not to put your filthy hands on the walls?"

Bewildered at first, but becoming frightened now, Jake began to shiver in the woman's hard, hurting grasp. The large diamond-and-ruby ring she wore on her left hand cut painfully into his shoulder as she shook him harder with each word.

"I—I'm s-sorry . . ." he sniffed. "I f-forgot—"

"Sorry!" Shake. "Forgot?" Shake. "Do you think . . ." slap against the side of the face *". . . that gets you off*

again?" Slap to the other side of the face. *"Well, think again, little Master Frost! This time..."* Slap, slap. *"...you get what's coming to you—something to make you remember the next time you think you can soil the house with your filth."* Hard shake.

"A sound whipping," she promised, a note threading its way through the shrill tones, *"that's what you deserve. And remember, this is for your own good, so you grow up to appreciate nice things."*

She was sitting on the bed now, turning him over on her knees. Jake could smell her expensive perfume. It was a light, airy fragrance and it never seemed to fit the violent, exacting nature of the woman wearing it, not even to a mere boy of four years.

Crying now, he glanced up and spotted a tall, dark silhouette in the doorway. *"D-daddy! P-please..."* He reached toward the figure, crying harder when he saw the man turn silently and disappear.

"This is one whipping," the woman promised with relish, as she uncoiled the object in her hand—an object he hadn't noticed until now, *"you won't soon forget."*

A sudden crash of thunder brought Jake back to the present with a startled jump. Rubbing a tired hand across his face, the sound of those last words echoing in his brain, Jake thought about how wrong she'd been. He *had* forgotten the beatings. He'd forgotten them for a very long time.

He forced his thoughts on the woman upstairs. Had she threatened, perhaps whipped, her own daughter for "her own good"?

Obviously there had been a problem in the marriage before it broke up. By Rachel's own admission, they'd stopped sharing a bed long before the divorce. Had that really been Gary's idea ... or hers?

Despite how things had looked to the court at the time of the divorce and child custody battle, it was possible Gary Dryden had been the wronged party. What if the man had only been trying to protect the child, resorting to kidnapping her, because it was the only way he could ensure her safety?

Not every parent who had the custody of a child or children deserved it. That's a lesson he'd learned a long time ago.

He didn't know what to make of Rachel Dryden. True, she'd come looking for him, come from Washington, D.C., if she was to be believed. And he believed that, because she wouldn't have known where to find him if Gus hadn't told her. No one else knew where he was.

But there was no denying the guilt he'd glimpsed in her eyes. He just wasn't certain yet what had caused it.

Chapter 3

Rachel sat on the side of the bed and stared wretchedly at the floor. Sleep was impossible. She hadn't had a full night's sleep since Amy's kidnapping and tonight was going to be no different.

The last expression she'd seen on her husband's face, the almost inhuman glitter in his cold green eyes, flashed into her mind and she began to tremble. He couldn't hurt their baby—oh, God, he couldn't hurt Amy! Could he?

Bunching her fists angrily, she asked herself why, before it had got to this stage, hadn't she realized how badly he'd needed help?

Before the divorce she'd asked him several times to see a doctor, but he always refused. She should have insisted! She should have done something—anything—to make him see what was happening to him. To them. And then maybe she wouldn't be in this cold, unfriendly house with this awful man and Amy would still be with her.

Unable to sit still any longer, she jumped to her feet and began to pace the parameter of the tiny room. No matter how many times she went over things in her mind, she still couldn't understand what had happened to change the quiet, gentle man she'd grown to know and love into the angry, possessive man Gary Dryden had later become.

When had he changed? He'd always been different from other men, that's what had attracted her to him in the first place. His courtly manner and soft voice had easily charmed the shy, twenty-year-old Rachel, who was away from home for the very first time.

To her, his gallantry had made him seem like one of the gentle knights they studied in his classes. As though riding to her rescue, he'd stepped into her life when she'd needed someone most and made everything better.

How could she have known what twisted emotions lay hidden below the surface? Right from the first he'd treated her with a kindness and consideration lacking in most men with whom she was acquainted. And when they'd married and she'd become pregnant, he'd treated her as though she was more precious to him than life itself. There had been nothing he wouldn't do for her.

In the beginning, their life had been filled with happy times, times like the night Amy had been born. She could clearly remember the look of joyous astonishment on Gary's face, the first time he'd seen his baby daughter.

What had gone wrong?

Had *she* done something to cause him to turn into the kind of monster that could tear a frightened, weeping child from its mother's arms? The kind of monster that could threaten his own child's life?

She hated him! God, how she hated him! If he were here, right now, sick or not, she'd . . . she'd scratch his eyes out.

Raising her face toward the ceiling, arms held stiffly at her sides, hands knotted into fists, she whispered, "Why? Why has he done this terrible thing? Why have you let him? Oh, God, please, let me find my baby—let me find her safe and sound.

"Anything—I'll promise you anything—if you'll only let her be alive and well."

Taking a deep breath, she added on a note of desperate anger, "I'll find you, Gary Dryden, I'll find you if it takes a lifetime. If it takes every last cent I have, if I have to beg, borrow or steal, cheat and lie, I'll find you. And when I do, heaven help you. *Heaven help you—because nobody else will be able to!*"

Rachel strode toward the window, pounding a closed fist against her forehead, and muttered, "Think! Dammit, think! Where could he have gone? Where would he have taken Amy? It has to be someplace I wouldn't normally think to look."

Drawing back the drab brown drapes, she stared into the darkness outside while her mind busily considered Gary's possible destination. An occasional flare of lightning in the distance threw her image back at her.

It was during one such display that she caught a glimpse of the expression in her eyes. She drew back from the new, raw look of desperation in her eyes and quickly covered her face with her hands.

That expression. It was the one she'd seen on Gary's face the instant he'd stomped on the brakes, almost throwing her through the windshield, reached across her and thrown the car door open to shove her outside. She'd landed painfully on the rough gravel road, stunned by his behavior. My God, the look in his eyes—that's when she'd finally admitted to herself that he truly hated her and she didn't even know why.

For months before the divorce, she'd been asking herself the same question. Why? Why was this happening? She'd been a good wife and mother, hadn't she?

Hadn't she?

Leaning her hot forehead against the cool glass, she closed burning eyes so she wouldn't have to see her own image and tried to recall when things had first begun to change. The night of Amy's second birthday party came to mind. That was the first time it had been made glaringly obvious to her that Gary was jealous of the warmth and affection between Rachel and their little daughter.

Nearly all of the English department and their families had shown up that night, and everyone had seemed to be in good spirits. Many of the other professors had been well beyond the child-rearing age, and some had grandchildren.

Gary had been the youngest professor with tenure, and despite running up against a little jealousy now and then, he'd been well-liked by his peers.

But the night had belonged to Amy. She'd reigned like a little princess over the whole proceeding, charming everyone in sight with her huge blue eyes and bright, toothy smile. Rachel could still see her in the white lace-ruffled dress with matching panties, holding out her arms for Rachel to pick her up.

It was time to cut the cake, and Amy was jumping up and down with excitement. All of a sudden, Gary had whisked the little girl into his arms and hurried toward the table where the cake sat waiting to be cut. Amy's little face had looked startled at first, then suddenly puckered with tears.

For a moment, the anger in his expression had shocked Rachel into immobility. She'd never, in all their time together, seen such an expression on his placid, good-natured face. Amy began to whimper, and her tears released Rachel from her paralysis.

Gary had locked eyes with Rachel, and a moment later, released the child so she could run to her mother. After that, he'd disappeared and didn't reappear until the guests were saying good-night.

That was the first time Rachel had tried talking to him about his odd behavior. He'd angrily denied there being any problem with him, then accused her bitterly of trying to monopolize their daughter's affections.

She'd been stunned by the unfair accusation but hadn't been able to think of any way to address it. Later, he'd seemed his old self and denied ever making the allegation.

Perhaps it was her fault that things had turned out the way they had. She should have taken more notice of Gary's strange mood swings, followed by absolute denial. If she had . . . if only she had . . .

Rachel's cheek stuck to the glass and she realized she was crying. Twisting away from the window, she wiped both cheeks with the heels of her hands.

She had to get hold of herself! It wouldn't do any good to rehash the past. What had happened had happened. It wasn't Gary who was important now. It was Amy.

All her guilt was for Amy! She had to get Amy away from Gary before he hurt her, or infected her with his own particular brand of madness!

Calm. She had to stay calm. Taking a deep breath, she forced back the tears, hiccuped lightly and took another deep breath. She couldn't afford to allow herself to be governed by emotion. She had to think clearly.

Her lip trembled and she bit it so hard she tasted blood. *How could she stay calm, when he had her baby? He could be capable of anything—even murder.* She had to find her! She had to find her quickly!

All at once she shivered, becoming aware that the room was bitterly cold. She shivered again in the thin cotton nightgown and rubbed at her bare arms.

Her glance fell on the small electric heater sitting in a corner of the room. It left a lot to be desired when it came to staving off the room's damp chill. Rachel hurried to the suitcase sitting open on a chair at the foot of the bed, and began to rifle through it, looking for something warmer to put on.

A persistent gnawing in the pit of her stomach reminded her she'd turned down her host's earlier offer of food. The only thing keeping her from going downstairs to search the refrigerator was the possibility of running into the man.

Jake Frost was a strange one. He disturbed her in many ways. There was something about him...she couldn't quite put her finger on it...but...*his eyes*...something happened inside her, every time she looked into his eyes.

Rachel shook herself and forced the man's image from her mind. The idea that he occupied even a small portion of her thoughts irritated her. She didn't want to think about anything but Amy, and certainly not another man after her recent experiences with Gary.

But her mind had found a focus other than the painful thoughts about her missing child and refused to let it go.

Something Jake Frost had said, when he'd finally agreed to help her, teased the edges of her memory. . . .

You may wake one morning and find yourself bitterly regretting the day you ever set eyes on me, or asked for my help.

What had he meant by that?

Jake was deeply immersed in work when a light sound from the stairs abruptly shattered his concentration. A moment later, Rachel peered around the door's frame.

"Oh! I didn't know you were . . . did I disturb you?" she asked uneasily. She hadn't expected to find him downstairs working at this time of night.

"No," Jake answered shortly, closing the notebook and putting aside his pen. Easing long, cramped legs back from the narrow opening beneath the desk, he stood and stretched tiredly.

"I'm ready for a break."

Rachel felt suddenly tongue-tied in his presence. She wanted to ask him straightaway what he'd meant by the comment about her being sorry she'd met him, but something held the words back.

Moving with him as he strode toward the kitchen, Rachel was careful, without really knowing why, to keep a safe distance between them as they passed down the dark, narrow hallway. As for Jake, he seemed totally oblivious to her presence.

Passing through the kitchen door, he flipped on a light switch and strode directly to the refrigerator. The silence that had followed them from the living room grew tight with tension as he began to remove items from inside the refrigerator and set them on the counter.

Rachel stood awkwardly watching, too shy to admit she was starving, and wishing she'd stayed in her room. If she'd known he was awake, nothing would have dragged her downstairs before morning.

"Are you ready for that sandwich?"

Rachel jumped at the sound of his voice and murmured tentatively, "A sandwich would be good—and a cup of the tea we had earlier . . . if it's no trouble."

"I was just about to make coffee." He turned to face her, surprising them both with his next words. "Is that okay?"

Rachel nodded wordlessly as he turned back without waiting for her answer and took a plastic container from the freezer. He moved toward the coffeemaker. Removing the lid, he dumped coffee beans into an electric grinder and pressed down on the handle.

The sound of grinding coffee filled the air, grating on Rachel's already raw nerves. She was glad when he let go of the handle and removed the cuplike lid to pour the dark rich coffee grounds into a snowy white filter.

In a few minutes, while he gathered the ingredients for sandwiches, an unusual aroma began to fill the air. Rachel sniffed and frowned. Jake caught her puzzled expression and almost allowed himself a smile.

"What do you think?" he asked, after he'd handed her a cup of the steaming liquid and watched her take the first sip.

"It's . . . different." She glanced up into his face, but avoided looking directly into the hazel eyes. "What is it?"

"Coffee," he answered solemnly. Rachel almost smiled when a moment later he added, "And brandy. I soak the coffee beans overnight in brandy. Sometimes I soak them in rum. It adds a little something to the flavor."

Rachel took another hearty sip. "It's good," she decided. "I like it."

That pleased him. As insignificant as it was, the fact that she liked his own special way of making coffee eased a fraction of the mounting tension between them.

Their glances met. Rachel saw reluctant approval in Jake's eyes and her own defenses began to waver.

Suddenly, Jake dragged his gaze from hers and turned quickly away, wary of this sudden bond of understanding that had sprung almost naturally between them with little more than a shared cup of coffee.

"Cold cuts are all I have for sandwiches—"

"That's fine," Rachel said quickly. "Is there something I can do to help?"

"No! I... prefer doing things myself."

Feeling as though he'd reached out and slapped her for no apparent reason, Rachel pulled out a chair in confusion and dropped onto it. She lifted her coffee cup in unsteady hands and took a large gulp.

So, that's the way it was going to be between them. Well, that was fine with her. She'd already concluded that he was a man to be kept at a safe distance. So long as he found her daughter, that's all that mattered.

Jake peeled back crisp leaves of lettuce and held them under the faucet. It was awkward, using his right hand and trying to keep it dry. It hurt like the devil, but he refused to give in to the pain and ask for help.

Earlier, in the upstairs bathroom, he'd repaired the two stitches he'd ripped out when he'd allowed his anger to get the best of him. It hadn't been easy, but he'd managed alone. He'd been managing alone for a good many years.

He knew he'd been abrupt to the point of brutal with the woman just now, but he needed to keep a certain distance between them. For her sake as well as his, he couldn't afford to see her as a person. She must remain nothing more than the mother of the child for whom he searched.

It was bad enough having her stay beneath his roof. Gritting his teeth, Jake picked up the cutting knife in his left hand and prepared awkwardly to slice a tomato. The first attempt nearly mangled the soft vegetable.

"Dammit," he muttered beneath his breath.

"You know," the words came from somewhere near his right shoulder, "I'm very good at slicing tomatoes."

Jake offered her the knife without further protest, and despite his care, their fingertips met on the handle. Everything inside him grew suddenly still. His breathing stopped, trapped somewhere inside his chest. Even the blood in his veins refused to flow, while his eyes rested on their joined fingers, wavered, then slowly lifted toward her face.

Rachel's soft lips were half-parted in a moue of surprise. She stared up at him blankly, a disturbed light in the gray eyes.

Jake came to his senses abruptly, jerking his fingers from the shock of her touch. Stepping carefully around her, he moved away from the sink.

"Everything you'll need is there on the counter, so eat," he grated roughly before leaving the room.

It was a while later when he returned. Rachel was sitting at the table, slowly munching on a sandwich. She'd placed another plate with a sandwich on it directly across from her. A mug of fresh coffee sat beside it.

Jake took his place without comment, lifted the cup and drank deeply before reaching for the thick, deli-style sandwich. He bit into it cautiously, chewed slowly, and swallowed. But he tasted nothing. It could have been made of cardboard for all he cared, yet he was determined to eat every bite of it, even if it choked him.

"This will probably cause us both to have nightmares."

Jake stopped chewing and glanced in her direction.

"The food," she explained. "Eating this late at night and then going to bed is supposed to cause nightmares."

Jake resumed chewing, and they ate without speaking after that. When their plates were empty and a second pot of coffee had been brewed, Rachel couldn't stand the silence a moment longer.

"We don't have to like each other, you know, just because we're working together."

"What makes you think we're working together?" he asked without expression.

"Aren't we?" she asked quickly. "I'm not going to—"

"Tell me about your husband."

"M-my husband?" The quick change of topic threw her for a moment. "What do you want to know?"

"What did he do, when he wasn't teaching, or being a husband and father?"

"Do? You mean . . . like a hobby?"

Jake shrugged. "If you like."

"Well . . ." she frowned " . . . he liked to read."

"What about sports?"

"You mean, did he like watching Monday night football?"

"No." Scraping his chair back from the table, he picked up his empty mug and headed for the coffee pot. "I mean something *he* liked to participate in—like hunting, or fishing."

"Oh. I...don't know." A thin line appeared between the fine brows as she concentrated harder. "I don't remember his ever mentioning either of those things."

"What about friends?"

"What about them?"

Jake almost snapped at her in irritation, but he swallowed the angry words and asked, carefully, "Was there someone—at work, perhaps—that he was particularly close to? Someone who might not have come to the house all the time—a friend, who wasn't your friend, too?"

"You mean a man?"

"I mean anyone, man, woman, or child."

"I..." she shook her head "...I don't know."

"What about old girlfriends?"

"What about them?"

"Did you ever talk about them?"

"No. We never discussed anyone he'd...dated, before we met."

"Weren't you curious?"

Rachel hesitated before shaking her head, realized his back was turned to her and answered in a soft voice, "No."

"What about your old boyfriends—did you discuss *them* with him?" Jake turned from refilling his mug and leaned back against the counter, impaling her with a sharp glance.

"We didn't discuss either of our former...dates," she answered stiffly.

"How long did you say the two of you were married?" He raised an eyebrow.

Rachel swallowed uncomfortably. "Almost six years."

He gave a nod she didn't quite like and asked, "What about his family?"

"He didn't have any."

"No? What about his mother and father?"

"He...didn't talk about his father—ever. And his mother is dead."

"When did she die?"

Rachel shrugged.

"Where did she die?"

"Somewhere," she answered slowly, "here, in Texas, I guess." Running a finger around the rim of her cup, she felt compelled to explain, "He didn't like to talk about the past—"

"How do you know? Did he say that?" Jake fired the questions at her.

Rachel's eyes shot to his face. "N-no—he just didn't seem to want to talk about his life before we met, and I didn't like to pressure him."

"Weren't you interested in his background? His family? Where he grew up, or what he'd done, before the two of you met?"

"Y-yes...but not because it really mattered. What mattered was the way we felt about each other—"

"Had he ever been married before?"

"M-married? No—why do you ask?"

Jake levered his tall frame away from the counter and crossed the room to stand somewhere behind her. "He was quite a few years older than you...that doesn't seem to be an unreasonable question to me, under the circumstances."

"Twelve years," she muttered and then said in a louder voice, "He was only twelve years older than me—that isn't *so* great a difference."

Rachel felt embarrassed talking about her ex-husband with this man. Somehow, she felt as though she had to explain everything about her marriage to him, and still it wouldn't matter, because she knew he blamed her for the loss of her child—just like she blamed herself.

"I lost my parents my second year in college. Gary offered me...comfort...stability—"

"Is that why you married him?" Jake asked abruptly.

"No!" she turned toward him angrily, dealing his face a glancing blow with wrathful eyes. "I married him because I loved him."

"Do you still love him?" Jake asked with his eyes on her face, gauging the quickly changing expressions taking place there. "Do you hate him?" he asked softly before she could answer.

"Really!" Rachel was on her feet in an instant. "I don't see what this has to do with anything—"

"Answer the question!"

"I won't!"

"Why not?"

"Which one?" Rachel's fists were clenched at her sides, her breathing uneven, as she faced him across the narrow space separating them.

Jake shrugged. "You pick."

"He's not the same man I married—I'm not the same woman. I don't love him."

"Do you hate him?"

The nails on both hands bit painfully into the tender flesh of her palms. "He's stolen my child—"

"The girl is his child, too," Jake reminded her bluntly.

"My husband is sick! Dangerous! He's unstable. He flies into fits of rage—"

"You're very angry yourself at the moment. Did you ever get this angry before your divorce?"

Rachel frowned. "What do you mean?"

"Did you ever scream and yell at your husband? At your little girl?" he asked in a softer voice.

"What are you saying? What are you accusing me of?"

Jake swung away from her. "I'm not accusing you of anything. I'm trying to build a picture of this man—your husband—"

"Ex-husband."

"—in my mind, that's all. Anything I learn about him and your relationship with him will help me determine where he might have gone." He faced her suddenly. "That is what you want, isn't it? For me to find your ex-husband and little girl?"

Rachel continued to stare at him with narrowed eyes. It was a reasonable question. "Yes."

She relaxed her angry bearing and slowly sat down in the chair, her vision turning inward. "I don't think I can explain Gary, or our relationship, to you. All I know is that in the beginning, he was so...different, from what I expected—what I was used to in a man.

"He never came to see me without bringing me something—a flower, a book of poetry, a small box of candy."

Rachel blinked and met Jake's steady gaze. "We didn't rush into anything. We took time to get to know each other."

"Did you?"

She let the skepticism in the question pass. "He was kind and gentle. Wasn't knowing that enough?"

The question irritated him. "You tell me. Was it?"

Rachel pressed her lips together firmly, wrenching her gaze from his face. "This has nothing at all to do with where he's taken my daughter."

There was a moment's pause and then Jake took a last drink of coffee and leaned toward her to place his mug on the table. She moved quickly in the opposite direction. He paused and gave a slight shrug.

"Perhaps you're right," he said, straightening and moving away from her. "In any case, it's late, and we've both about had it for the day. I think it's time we called it a night."

Upstairs, he tried to leave her outside her door with the murmured suggestion that things would appear different in the morning, but Rachel had her own ideas about that.

"I know you said we had to know where to look, but isn't there something—some clue you've come across by now that will give you an idea where to start? My daughter is only four years old," she added anxiously. "She's very impressionable."

"We'll find her," Jake said, "but not tomorrow. Now, go to bed and get some rest."

"You didn't see his face—his eyes—when he made those threats—"

"We can't go off half-cocked," Jake interrupted, seeing the hysteria gathering behind her wide eyes. "What good would that do? It's a big country. We can't cover every square inch of it on foot, so we have to narrow it down, concentrate on one specific area at a time."

"But—"

"Let me do my job! I'm good at it...." A muscle worked in his jaw. "At least that's what *you* told *me*."

"But I want to help."

"You can do that by getting some rest, so you can answer more questions in the morning."

His hand was on the knob of his own door when he glanced back and saw her still standing where he'd left her.

"Go on." He nodded toward the door in front of her. "Go to bed and get some rest. I promise you—" his voice deepened against his will "—we'll find your daughter."

In his own room, Jake shut the door, closed his eyes, and leaned his head back against it. She drained him. It was too hard to keep up the pretense when he was with her.

There were times he felt certain she must see through his flimsy mask of self-confidence to the frightened man beneath. Yet, he kept on with the masquerade, because, at the moment, it was all he had.

Rachel lay down on the bed, pulled up the blankets, and closed her eyes out of sheer exhaustion. She hadn't bothered changing into a nightgown. The dark sweatpants and matching shirt were warm, and she was freezing again. Only this time she knew the cold was coming from somewhere deep within her.

Slowly, relaxing the tight rein on her emotions, she let her mind drift toward sleep, telling herself Jake Frost was right, she needed a few hours of rest. On the edges of consciousness, a sound she recognized with dread echoed loudly inside her head.

"I'll kill her! You'll never take her away from me again! I'll kill her—and then I'll kill myself!

Rolling over onto her side, Rachel felt the hot tears slide from the corners of both eyes. Jake said they'd find Amy...but would it be too late to save her?

If anything happened to her daughter...she'd want to die, too....

Jake stared into the darkness until his eyes burned and finally drifted shut. A long time ago, almost in another lifetime it seemed now, he'd questioned another mother about her missing child. That woman hadn't been quite so young, nor so well-educated, but she'd been just as distraught as Rachel Dryden to find her little daughter.

The echo of her bewildered voice, whispering desperately, "How was I to know...he was so quiet...so kind...so gentle—how was I to know?" echoed inside his brain.

Jake clamped his hands over the sides of his head to try to shut out the sound of her voice, but it didn't work. He could still hear her despair, see the timeworn eyes begging him to tell her it wasn't true; the man she'd trusted with her child's life hadn't abducted her, and her little girl would be returned to her any minute, safe and sound.

Sleep was impossible. Pulling himself up on the side of the bed, Jake sat hunched over, doubting he'd ever know peace again in this lifetime.

He shouldn't have agreed to take this case. He'd been learning to live with his guilt. As long as he didn't put himself in the position of being responsible for another child's life...

Climbing wearily to his feet, he moved about the room, finding his shoes in the dark. The storm had passed. It would be damp and cold outside, but he had to walk.

He'd walk until the sun had begun to finger the eastern edge of the sky, until his lungs burned with pain, and his limbs shook with cold and fatigue. That's when he'd return home, fall into bed, and find a measure of peace through sheer exhaustion.

Some nights it was like that. Some nights the voices refused to be stilled.

Chapter 4

Early the next morning, Rachel awakened feeling a little bit better. Once she'd managed to block Gary's threat from her thoughts, she'd actually slept. It didn't occur to her that Jake Frost's assurance that he'd find Amy had anything to do with this newfound peace of mind.

After she'd had a quick wash, she dressed in jeans, sweater and boots, and hurried toward the stairs, anxious to see if her host had come up with any ideas while she slept. Her enthusiasm waned somewhat as she hesitated outside Jake's door, recalling the rough question-and-answer period he'd put her through the last time they'd spoken together.

As she moved toward the top of the stairs the aroma of fresh-brewed coffee teased her senses. She decided she could put up with a lot, even an early morning confrontation with her unwilling host, for a good cup of coffee. As it turned out, she needn't have worried because her host seemed to have disappeared. He wasn't in the living room, nor was he in the kitchen.

Shrugging, she poured a cup of the dark, rich coffee and took it with her into the living room. She paused before the

Catching her breath, she stared at a small blue spiral notebook with satisfaction and a slight twinge of conscience. With one fingertip, she lifted the edge of the cover and flipped it back. The page was blank. She frowned and flipped the next page and the next. Again she found nothing but blank pages.

In frustration, she picked up the notebook, turned toward the back, and began to flip slowly through the pages. Her name leapt off the page at her. She stopped and turned back to it.

A list of character traits had been printed below her name. Some had check marks beside them. Her eyes stopped on the word truthful and she was immediately incensed by the question mark beside it. She was not a liar!

Slamming the book shut, she threw it back where she'd found it. This was not what she'd been looking for—but then what *was* she looking for?

Angry now, she jerked open the fourth and final drawer. It was wide and shallow and ran the length of the top of the desk. She'd found it! Or had she?

A folder of newspaper clippings spilled its contents into the drawer as she lifted it out. Rachel picked up the first clipping and read, Child Kidnapped By Babysitter! There were several others along the same line. Young Man Sought In Disappearance Of Four-year-old Girl. Little Lacy Tolbridge Mourned.

"What are you doing?"

Rachel stiffened, felt her heart flutter to a stop, and turned slowly to face the man standing less than two feet behind her. "I...I..."

Jake's eyes dropped to the newspaper clippings still clutched in her right hand. *"You're going through my things?"* Hazel eyes, filled with contempt, slammed into hers.

Twin stains of scarlet, like banners of shame, flew in Rachel's pale cheeks. She wished a hole in the floor would suddenly open and swallow her. "I was just..." She shrugged helplessly without continuing.

Jake's eyes had blackened with fury, but all he did was hold out a hand and wait for her to drop the clippings into it. If the hand trembled slightly, neither seemed to notice.

"I'm sorry," Rachel managed in a shaken voice, placing the papers in his hand.

Jake elbowed her aside and stuffed the newspapers into the desk drawer, slamming it shut. Damn her! *Damn her!*

His back to her, he stood with bowed head, fighting to restrain the tide of dark anger sweeping through him. Control, that was the key. Control had been the mainstay of his existence for as long as he cared to remember.

When he could speak without shouting, he turned and asked tightly, "What gives you the right to go through my personal belongings?"

She'd expected him to rage hotly at her and demand an explanation for her snooping. The question coming in such a subdued voice astonished her, but it also gave her the courage to answer back.

"Newspaper clippings are not personal belongings." He didn't appear impressed by her statement, and since she was in the wrong, she added a shade contritely, "I was only trying to understand things—understand *you* . . . a little bit better!"

"It isn't necessary for you to understand me!" he cried passionately, hands working like pinchers that he was finding difficult to control, because they wanted to reach for her neck.

In a voice little more than a whisper, he charged, "You came to me for help. I agreed to help you, didn't I? *Didn't I?*" He demanded an answer.

Rachel jumped slightly and nodded.

"And I'll continue to do so—but only so long as you stay out of my private life! Is that understood?"

Rachel's eyes dropped to the fingers knotted tightly at her waist. She couldn't sustain the contempt in his glittering eyes. "I didn't mean to . . . I'm sorry."

Jake showed no sign of acknowledging her apology. He simply made a wide berth around her and strode from the room. He knew his reaction had frightened her. And he knew, too, that she had followed him and stood watching as he mounted the stairs. But he didn't dare pause, because, right now, he needed very badly to get away from her.

In his room, he lifted shaking hands and stared at them. Bunching them into fists, he slapped them against his thighs in frustration. He was disgusted with himself more than her.

Why had he gotten so angry? The events depicted in the newspapers were now a part of the record. She'd probably read about the kidnapping in her local newspaper. It had made national headlines. Sometimes that happened—a tragedy that otherwise wouldn't rate more than a small article on the back page of a big-name newspaper, is picked up by the wire service and makes national news.

But that was all in the past now, and his anger had been all out of proportion to the situation. He should have gotten rid of the clippings months ago. He didn't know why he hadn't.

No, that wasn't strictly true. Why was he trying to fool himself with that crock of bull? He knew exactly why he hadn't gotten rid of them. It was the same reason he stayed in this house, close to the graves....

An hour later, Jake descended the stairs. He'd taken a hot shower and then a cold one, shaved, and changed clothes. He could at least try to behave like a normal human being while this woman was beneath his roof—while he was forced to endure her presence.

His eyes burned from lack of sleep, but he'd spent two hours in unconscious oblivion very early that morning after walking himself to exhaustion, and knew it would have to suffice. Entering the kitchen, he sniffed the air appreciatively.

"Something smells good." The words escaped his lips before he knew it, surprising him with their pleasant ring of normality.

From her bent position in front of the oven, Rachel quickly scanned his face for signs of the anger that had darkened it when he'd left her a short while ago.

All she saw was a man with bloodshot eyes who looked as though he hadn't slept in weeks. The rich brown hair appeared to be damp and lay in tight curls all over his head. Her eyes strayed to the cleft in his chin and she found herself suddenly very much aware of his virile appeal.

"It's only biscuits and sausage gravy," she whispered in uneven tones.

The slight catch in her voice affected Jake strangely. Going to the cabinet he began removing plates. He laid their places in silence, while Rachel finished cooking the meal and carried it to the table.

They sat down to eat without speaking, without looking at each other, and to all intents and purposes it appeared a companionable meal. But, though it lacked the tension of their previous meetings, a new, perhaps more dangerous force was now at work between them.

When the meal had been eaten, they cleared the table and did the dishes, sharing the work. By silent agreement, they then adjourned to the living room to begin another question-and-answer session.

By late afternoon, Jake was convinced that a trip to the college in San Antonio, where Gary had taught English literature, was a must. While he made calls to confirm appointments with some of the faculty who had known Gary best, Rachel searched the kitchen for food for their dinner.

Without knowing quite how, she had taken over responsibility for cooking their meals. She didn't mind. It gave her something to do besides answer questions she'd already answered a hundred times—and worry.

Jake finished making his calls and went looking for Rachel. He found her in the kitchen. Stationing himself near the doorway, he noted the scene of domesticity with a slight twinge of irritation.

"I've scheduled appointments for the day after tomorrow in San Antonio. We'll be speaking with Dean Anderson at the college, Charles Rothwell, and Marian Benning."

The knife she was using slipped. Rachel stopped slicing fresh vegetables into a large pot on the stove and turned to face him. "Why are we going to San Antonio?" she asked tightly. "Gary isn't there." Then she added tensely, "You're wasting time, and every hour wasted is one more..."

She caught sight of Jake's rigid jaw and swallowed the rest of her protest. With shaking hands, she turned back to her work.

When she looked back a few minutes later, he was gone. Putting the vegetables on the back burner to simmer, she looked out the window over the sink and saw that the rain had abated, for the time being at least.

She listened and realized the house was quiet. Where was Jake Frost?

Removing the towel she'd tied around her waist as an apron, she left the room. In the hallway, she spotted Jake shrugging into his jacket.

"Are you going out?" she asked quickly. She didn't particularly want his company, but on the other hand, she didn't like the idea of sitting here all alone with her thoughts, either.

"Yes," he answered shortly, "I'm going for a walk."

"May I come, too?"

"If you like," he answered almost grudgingly after a slight hesitation.

Outside, Rachel took a deep breath of fresh air. It was twilight, and a golden haze filled the western sky. The air was chilly and damp, but it had an invigorating effect on her.

Jake set a brisk pace and left it to her to keep up with him. They walked toward the back of the house, through the trees, and down to the stream running along behind it.

Following the narrow stream that sliced his property almost in half, Jake jammed his hands in his pockets and tried hard to ignore the woman at his side. They moved along the stream past pecan, oak and cottonwood trees, their naked branches reaching toward the sky. Suddenly Jake changed course and strode toward the water.

Silence loomed between them, broken only by their quickened breathing as they picked their way across a series of flat stones bridging the stream, swollen twice its normal size by the rain. Jake wanted to continue to ignore her, but a sixth sense kept him alert to her progress. When her foot slipped off the last stone and she teetered precariously, he was there to catch her.

"Thank you." Rachel brushed a strand of hair back from her cheek and looked up into his face. And though she'd been spared the shock of a plunge into the icy water, nothing spared her the shock of breathless sensation caused by his sudden nearness.

Jake gazed into her face and felt his insides twitch with a curious kind of ache. He struggled to remove his glance from the spellbinding sight of clear gray eyes and trembling, pink lips, but it lingered despite his efforts, refusing to budge until his brain had recorded every feature in his memory. He knew, whether he liked it or not, he'd remember each facet of her lovely face long after she'd disappeared completely from his life.

Rachel felt her heart jolt beneath his steady gaze. He looked as though he was photographing her with his eyes. She tried to subdue the dizzying current racing though her veins at the thought. The fact that he might find her attractive didn't bother her nearly so much as the fact that her body was responding to his attraction on a purely visceral level.

"Are you all right?" he asked hoarsely.

"Y-yes."

He could see that she was and knew he should let her go. He released her slowly, as though breaking contact with her was the hardest thing he'd ever have to do.

They moved on in silence, walking side by side, as though nothing momentous had occurred. But now, neither could easily ignore the proximity of the other.

"Have you lived here a long time?" Rachel asked, trying to bring a measure of the ordinary into the atmosphere between them. She'd managed to partially convince herself that what she'd seen in his eyes a few moments ago had been nothing more than a trick of the light.

"No."

"Are you planning to fix up the house?"

"What's wrong with the house?" he asked sharply, throwing her a narrow glance. Maybe he could find some refuge from confusion in anger.

"I just meant...are you going to add central heating and air-conditioning?"

"I don't know." He shrugged, retreating into a sullen silence.

He seemed more comfortable with the silence, but Rachel wasn't. "Why did you quit working for the FBI?" There, now she'd done it, she'd asked the one question that had been in her mind since she'd spoken with Gus Davison in Washington.

"Didn't Gus tell you?"

"No."

Somehow they'd ended up at the back entrance to the graveyard where Rachel had first seen him. She followed him through the gate and across the grounds, picking her way between the gravestones, until she stood alongside him, where he'd stopped at the head of two graves.

"Do you know the people buried here?" Rachel asked tentatively, inching close to his side. There was an eerie feeling about this place, as though not all of the souls of the people buried here were at peace.

"I know them," he answered shortly.

"Are they family?" On the point of turning away without speaking, Jake hesitated and answered. "They're the reason I quit the agency."

"I don't understand."

"You don't have to." He turned and walked away. Rachel stared at his retreating back with a slight frown, then she bent to try to read the names on the headstones. It was difficult to make them out in the gathering darkness.

"Oh, no," she whispered a moment later and turned to hurry after Jake. She'd thought the newspaper clippings were intended for a scrapbook he hadn't yet put together about cases he'd worked on. But it looked now as though something more were involved.

Was this child the same child named in one of the newspaper clippings she'd found in the desk back at the house? What had happened? How had the child died?

Was Jake somehow involved in her death? The thought made Rachel shudder in horror. What about her own child? Gus Davison had told her this man was her only hope in finding her daughter. Had he lied? She had to find out.

"Wait! Wait for me—please!" Rachel ran to catch up with Jake's quick stride. "How do you know the child buried back there? I remember reading a headline with the child's name in it. What happened?"

"I don't want to talk about it."

"B-but..." She was running out of breath by trying to keep up with him. "I want to know," she said, panting, "what happened?"

"They died."

"They?"

"That's right." He stopped suddenly and faced her. "The people in those two graves died."

"Who were they?"

"Mother and daughter." He stared at her stonily.

"W-what happened?"

"Look it up in the newspaper files." Hands in his pockets, he turned abruptly away and marched stiffly down the road, leaving Rachel to stare after him.

Why hadn't he told her no when she'd asked to join him on his walk? Jake fumed. He should have walked in another direction, but his footsteps had automatically followed the route they normally took. Why had he agreed to take this damned case in the first place?

After asking the same question three times, Jake looked up and realized Rachel wasn't paying any attention to him. She was staring out the window, oblivious to what was taking place in the room.

He'd been pushing her hard, ever since they'd returned from the disastrous walk a couple of hours ago. Maybe it was time he let up. Glancing at the watch on his wrist and then toward the window, he realized it was getting late.

"What is that tantalizing aroma I smell coming from the kitchen?" he asked softly, going to stand behind her at the window.

Rachel felt her pulse quicken uncomfortably. "V-vegetable soup."

"I haven't had homemade vegetable soup since..." Rachel forgot her own nervousness as she turned and surprised a peculiar expression on his face.

"In a long time," he finished with a shrug, swinging away from the window. He was tired of the tension between them, tired of the questions, tired of his own guilty conscience... tired of everything....

"It should be about ready, if you're feeling hungry," Rachel said gently, moved despite herself by the expression of suffering she'd seen in his eyes just then.

They moved toward the door together, Jake stopping and letting her pass through first, then following more slowly. He'd been watching her at intervals since their return to the house, and whether he liked it or not, she was beginning to fascinate him.

As the evening had passed, she'd grown more guarded. At first, he'd thought it was caused by the suspicion he'd seen in her eyes whenever they rested on him, a result of his refusing to divulge his past for her personal edification. But he'd slowly begun to change his mind about that and to wonder if there was something in San Antonio she didn't want him to know.

Rachel ladled soup into bowls with a shaking hand beneath Jake's examining gaze. And something in his eyes made her feel very uneasy.

She hadn't again broached the subject of the dead child, but it was never far removed from her thoughts. She was even considering making a call to Gus Davison later that night, when Jake had gone to bed.

Suddenly the soup dipper knocked against the side of the pot and slipped through her fingers. Jake reached to grab it before the hot liquid could spill down the front of her and Rachel jerked away from his touch, splashing it on the back of his injured hand.

The white gauze saved him from a painful injury, but nothing saved him from the anxiety caused by the incident. The thought of burned flesh didn't bother him. It was the sensation of soft skin brushing against his, burning hotter than any soup ever could, that lingered, scorching his mind with images he couldn't afford to imagine.

When they sat down to eat, Rachel barely touched her soup. The only word she uttered was a murmured excuse, a short time later, when she left the kitchen. Jake hardly touched his own meal but stayed behind to clean up.

This uneasy state of affairs between them only made him more certain that his plan to leave her in San Antonio, with or without her agreement, was best for the both of them. He'd always worked better alone. It seemed that, at least, hadn't changed.

Chapter 5

Jake's head rolled back and forth across the pillow. The skeletal remains of a woman with glowing empty eye sockets chased him through a dark graveyard, brandishing a belt with a large shiny buckle in one hand, and a straight razor in the other.

Sweat poured from his body. His hands gripped the sheets tightly and a soft moan escaped his clenched lips. All at once he jerked upright, instantly awake, and stared into the darkness with wide, frightened eyes.

Something had awakened him. Vestiges of the familiar nightmare lingered round the edges of his memory, making him think his conscious mind had jerked him from a horror too deep for his subconscious to endure.

But an instant later he knew that wasn't it. Something, some sound that didn't quite fit, had pierced his nightmare-world and brought him back from the land of the dead to that of the living.

His glance drew level with the narrow strip of light seeping into the room from beneath the bathroom door. A fear so intense it rendered him incapable of movement surged through him like a giant tidal wave, receding only to leave him feeling drained. This time, when it came, Jake heard the sound distinctly. He bounded from the bed and leapt toward the door. Grasping the knob firmly, he threw it open and froze on the threshold.

Rachel looked up, confusion widening her eyes as they met his over the gleaming edge of the straight razor clutched in one hand.

Jake lunged at her. "You stupid—*stupid* woman! What are you doing?"

Shocked, Rachel jumped back, avoiding the hand reaching for hers. "Get out of here!" She was only wearing her nightgown.

Jake ignored her words and caught her wrist in a strong grasp.

"Let me go!" Rachel cried, jerking her arm to shake loose from his hold. What was the matter with him, coming into the bathroom when she was in there and acting like a lunatic? "You're hurting my wrist!"

"Give me the—*ow!*"

Jake's breath left his body all at once as Rachel punched him in the stomach with her empty fist. She had no idea what was wrong with him, but she wasn't going to stand for another man using strong-arm tactics on her again.

Jake sidestepped an intended blow from her foot, but got caught with the next one. She had to be hurting herself as much as she hurt him since she wasn't wearing any shoes, but that didn't seem to slow her down.

"Let go of my wrist!" Rachel twisted and turned, writhing against his hold, shoving at him with the other hand when he paid no attention to her demands for release. Finally, in an act of pure desperation, she bent and tried to bite the hand hurting hers.

"The razor—give it to me and—*ow! Son-of-a...!* Let go of the damned razor!"

"Why?"

"Because I said to—that's why!"

"I won't!" She didn't trust him. He'd come storming into the room without a by-your-leave, grabbing at her, and now he expected her to let him have the razor?

A thunderous scowl darkened Jake's glance. "I said, let go!"

"No." Rachel clenched her lips and met his glance unflinchingly. She'd be damned if she'd give him the razor. Who did he think he was? Besides, she didn't trust him with it. Something in his eyes frightened her.

The hand on her wrist tightened. She continued to glare at him, but now her teeth worried her bottom lip. The fragile bones in her wrist felt as though they might snap at any moment under the increasing pressure. Closing her eyes to block out the fire storm of madness she saw in his, she tried, but couldn't quite hold back a slight whimper of pain.

"Drop it," Jake demanded in rough tones. This was a game he understood, a game of wills, and he was good— very good—at it.

"No," she responded stubbornly. If she gave in to him now, he'd have the upper hand and she refused to subjugate herself to any man, ever again.

"Drop it!" Jake demanded in a louder voice, increasing the pressure on her wrist. He was hurting her and he knew it, but he couldn't seem to stop himself. All he could see in his mind's eye was another woman with a razor in her hand and blood . . . everywhere. . . .

"Drop it!" he muttered through clenched teeth, forcing a knee between both of hers, despite her attempts to prevent it, and pressing his lower body intimately against hers. "Drop it," he whispered unevenly, "or I'll break your wrist."

Rachel's eyes widened until too much white showed. He was too close. She couldn't breathe—and the expression on his face . . .

Suddenly she knew beyond a shadow of a doubt that he'd do it, he'd break her wrist if that's what it took to make her drop the razor. Panic seized her. He must be insane!

"N-o-o—!" All at once, she brought her knee up hard against his groin, letting the razor drop from her hand and shoving against him at the same time. While he was off balance, she gave him another, harder push.

Surprise suddenly flared in Jake's eyes as he, unable to breathe, let her go. He doubled over then. The white-hot pain spread from his groin up into his belly, nauseating him, and, his knees weak, he fell back against the open door.

He managed to save himself from a nasty fall against the corner of the sink, but had to lower himself to the floor, because his legs would no longer support his weight. Watching helplessly, he saw Rachel bend, grab the razor, and disappear into her bedroom.

He'd failed—again!

Rachel slammed the door, locked it quickly and looked around frantically for something to wedge against it for added protection. There wasn't much in the room she could manage to move—certainly not the bed, nor the heavy oak dresser.

She finally settled on the single chair in the room. It wasn't heavy, but it was all that was available. Once she'd dragged it across the floor and stationed it beneath the doorknob, her eyes darted quickly toward the door to the hall. Hurrying to it, falling against it, she checked to make certain it was locked.

My God, he was crazy! The man was crazy! Why hadn't Gus Davison warned her about him? What was she going to do?

She had to call somebody! She hadn't seen a telephone, but there must be one someplace, because he'd used it to make the calls to San Antonio. But where? And who was she going to call?

Her eyes darted toward the door with the chair wedged against it. What was he doing? She didn't fool herself into thinking she'd done him any permanent damage just now. He'd come after her and when he did . . .

If she could just get outside to her car. Her eyes alighted on the window. It was the only other way out of the room. Moving across the floor as soundlessly as possible, she peered through the glass to the darkness outside. She couldn't see a thing, but she knew it must be a good twelve-foot drop to the ground below. With her luck she'd probably break a leg and then she'd never get away.

Rachel's eyes shot toward the bathroom door. It was awfully quiet in the next room. What was he doing in there?

The only sound she could hear was that of her own erratic breathing. He was still there—she knew he was still there—waiting on the other side—*waiting for her!*

Lifting the forgotten razor, still clamped between the trembling fingers of one hand, she considered it uneasily. It was the only weapon she had against him.

Could she use it? Her mind screamed yes, but in her heart she doubted it. She could never, deliberately, injure another human being....

A sound at the door jerked her eyes toward it. The knob turned slightly. She tensed, unable to control the spasmodic trembling coursing through the length of body. The hand holding the razor gripped it tighter, becoming stationary at waist level.

She would! She'd use the razor to protect herself if it became necessary. She had to. If anything happened to her, who would save Amy from her ex-husband?

Jake closed his eyes and rested his forehead against the door. The door was locked and she had the razor. *Not again,* a voice inside him cried, *not again!*

If he let loose the emotions ripping through him, he'd tear down the door. His fingers itched to do it right now. But a calmer, saner part of his brain was urging him to play it cool. Thanks to him, she was already in an overwrought state of mind. If he came through the door like a raging bull, there was no telling what she might do.

"Mrs. Dryden—" he called abruptly, causing Rachel to back away from the muffled sound coming through the door. "Mrs. Dryden—Rachel—listen to me, please."

Letting go of the doorknob, doubling his fists, telling himself to remain calm, he whispered hoarsely, "I wasn't trying to hurt you."

He paused to let that sink in. When she made no response, he asked in a louder voice, "Did you hear what I said? I wasn't trying to hurt you."

Rachel's glance slid to the red, painful welts encircling her right wrist. Liar!

"I thought you were trying to... harm yourself," Jake explained hesitantly. Pressing an ear against the door, he listened for sound coming from the other side. "R-Rachel... are you listening?"

Panic raced through him when he heard nothing—not even a whimper. Pressing closer, he whispered tautly, "Rachel—listen to me. I was *not* trying to hurt you. I wouldn't! I was only trying to stop you from hurting yourself."

"Liar!" she screamed suddenly, tears starting to her eyes. "You t-threatened to b-break my w-wrist!" She gulped and continued, "I just want out of here." Laying a wet cheek against the cold, painted door, she whispered unsteadily, "P-please let m-me go."

"I will," Jake responded quickly. She was alive! And she was talking to him! "I'll let you go. I promise. Just open the door—"

"No!" Rachel jumped back, gripping and lifting the razor like a knife. "Stay away! Do you hear? If you try to come in here—"

"I won't!" Jake assured her quickly. "I promise I won't. Let me explain. Will you just do that one thing? Will you let me explain what I thought... when I saw you with the razor?"

Rachel wiped the tears from her face with the back of one hand and sniffed. "All right, I'll listen—but that's all," she added quickly. "I'm not coming out, and you're not coming in."

Silence expanded between both sides of the door, before the soft sound of Jake's voice whispered, "I thought..."

Rachel pressed closer, trying to hear the strained whisper more clearly. "I thought you were trying to... kill yourself."

"What?" She gave a slight jerk and frowned in confusion.

Jake heard her startled exclamation and defended his explanation in louder tones. "I had reason to think you were trying to commit suicide."

"Suicide! Reason!" she spluttered. "What reason?"

"Your daughter—"

"—would be in my husband's hands for good if I did something so foolish. She needs me. *Alive,* not dead!" she cried indignantly.

"Why were you holding my straight razor?" Jake asked abruptly.

Rachel stared at the gleaming blade in her hand. So that was it. Yes, she supposed it was possible to assume—no, to jump—to the conclusion that she wasn't planning to shave her legs at three o'clock in the morning.

"I went into the bathroom," she explained carefully, "to get a drink of water. I knocked the razor off the shelf and into the sink. I was only picking it up—to replace it—when you jerked the door open and ... Why did you immediately leap to *that* particular conclusion?" she asked curtly.

She thought he was never going to answer when she heard his muffled reply. "It's happened before."

All at once, Rachel shivered, suddenly aware of the frigid temperature in the room. She glanced toward the electric heater and realized she hadn't turned it on when she'd come up to bed.

"I...want to tell you about it." Jake's voice seeped through the cracks around the door. "Perhaps that will convince you I'm not the crazy man you think me."

Rachel compressed her lips and stared hard at the heater. Her mind didn't want to deal with the obvious torment in the man's voice. She had a terrible grief of her own to deal with right now, and there was no room left inside her for more pain.

"I..." She licked dry lips and shook her head. How could she silence him without telling him she didn't want to listen to him? He'd listened to her....

Jake didn't wait for a reply. If he hesitated too long, he'd never get the words out. "You know the file you found in the desk downstairs? The clippings are from my last case.

"I was looking for a . . . little girl . . . a four-year-old girl."
It was hard to think about her, let alone speak about her.

Rachel closed her eyes. Lacy Tolbridge. The name swam
before her closed eyelids. She didn't want to hear this. The
hand holding the razor lowered slowly to her side.

"The man who kidnapped her had been hired by her
mother to sit with the child while she worked. He'd been
confined to a mental institution in Pennsylvania for most of
his teenage years...but the child's mother didn't know that
when she hired him.

"All she knew is that he'd lived in town for over a year,
in the house next door to theirs. He was quiet and well-
mannered and she liked him.

"She—the mother—paid him to take care of her daughter so she could work the night shift at a factory on the edge
of town. She was sole support for the two of them, and the
night shift provided a larger income."

A cold, hard knot formed in the pit of Rachel's stomach.
She knew what was coming and didn't want to hear it, but
couldn't seem to raise her hands to shut out the uneven
murmur of his voice.

"Everything was fine," Jake continued, recounting the
tragedy he'd lived with night and day for the past several
months, "for a while at least. And then, one morning,
she...Mary..." he dredged the name up from a well of
misery deep inside "...she went home and found her
daughter gone.

"But by the time I was brought in on the case, several
weeks later, Mary was only a shadow of her former self. You
see, the young man sent her pictures—"

"Stop it! Stop it!" Rachel dropped the razor and covered her ears with both hands.

"I'm sorry—I'm sorry!" Jake said quickly, raising both
hands flat against the door. "I didn't mean to upset you! I
just wanted you to understand...why I thought...what I
thought...."

The silence was so complete, Jake feared he'd lost her.
Maybe she'd gone out through the hall door and was even

now getting into her car to leave—and he wouldn't blame her.

A moment later, the clicking of the door's lock filled the vacuum of sound. Jake stepped back as the door swung open and Rachel stood facing him.

"What happened to the little girl?" she asked with shaking lips. The question had been plaguing her since she'd seen the headstone in the graveyard earlier that evening.

Like a stream of icy water, the words fell from his lips, drenching them both with the horror. "She died. I killed her." He offered no excuses nor explanations to soften the blow of his words.

"No!" Rachel shook her head, her lips working, but no further sound came from them. Her mind struggled to cope with what he'd said and to make sense of it.

Jake knew a moment of satisfaction at the shock he'd caused her. Now she'd leave.

"I don't believe it," Rachel managed at last, catching a fleeting glimpse of raw torment looking out at her from behind the man's eyes. True, she'd been frightened of him a little while ago, but that was because she hadn't understood why he was acting as he had.

Now, putting her earlier fear of him aside, she knew that what he had said didn't make sense. She couldn't make herself believe that this man was a killer of children.

"It's true," Jake assured her in an emotionless voice, turning away from the look of doubt on her pale face. She must believe him. He wanted her to know the real Jake Frost, the man he faced each morning, when he could stand to look at himself in the mirror. He wanted her to hate him as much as he hated himself, because then she'd go away and leave him to live in the hell he'd created of his own life.

Rachel hesitated before laying a fingertip on the rigid wall of his back and instantly felt the muscles bunch tighter. "Tell me . . . please, what really happened?"

Jake stepped away from her touch. Suddenly he didn't want to speak of it, but his knees felt too weak to carry him through the door and into his own bedroom. Turning slightly, he dropped down onto the closed lid of the toilet, letting his hands fall between his knees, and focused his gaze on the floor.

He didn't want to relive the manner in which he'd orchestrated Lacy Tolbridge's death. But, if anything could make this woman clear out fast, it was the realization that she'd come to the wrong man for help.

Jake cleared his throat and began to speak. "The case was already four weeks old when I was called in to work on it. I was in Washington at the time, finishing up another case. Gus—you met Gus—was in Texas. He called and told me to get here, 'yesterday.'

"I was on the next plane. I met Mary Tolbridge just after she'd gotten the last picture. The child had been beaten—" Jake turned his head aside and closed his eyes at the memory.

After a moment, he continued, "I spent a lot of time with Mary and I got to know... Lacy, through her mother. The woman lived for her child. You might expect a child with a mother like that to be spoiled, or smothered with all that attention. But from all I learned from the people who knew them best, that wasn't the case."

He broke off and stared down at his empty hands, at the white bandage encircling the middle of one.

His voice, when it came again, trembled slightly, touched by some emotion Rachel couldn't immediately define. "At first, this was just another case to me, but as I got to know the mother—and the child through her eyes... it became... something more.

"It took three weeks to track down Steve Craig, the kidnapper." His hands clenched into tight fists. "I found them about fifteen miles from here, at the farmhouse where he'd been born. His grandparents were native to this area.

"I decided to go in after her alone. I misjudged him from the very first—I was so confident I could talk him into letting Lacy go. He hadn't killed before...." Jake seemed to be talking to himself now as he muttered tautly, "I should have remembered that *everyone* is a potential killer.

"It was dark that night. I expected them to be in the house—they were in the woods. They saw me first. Lacy pulled away from her kidnapper and stood alone, facing me." His face worked as he remembered. "She was in a bad way. I told her not to be frightened, I was there to help her.

"She looked up at me with huge brown eyes in a face bruised and swollen almost beyond recognition...and smiled." He sounded mystified. "She smiled as if she knew why I was there and trusted me to help her."

Getting quickly to his feet, as though there wasn't enough space in the cramped room for the both of them and the burden of guilt he carried, Jake strode through the bathroom door into his bedroom and out that door to the hallway. Rachel followed on his heels.

"Craig was carrying a sawed-off shotgun." He spoke rapidly in short nervous bursts. "He didn't try to grab Lacy, or to threaten me with the gun. He didn't bother listening to what I had to say, either. He raised the gun and pointed it at Lacy.

"She didn't cower from him. She didn't even look at him. She just kept looking at me with those big brown eyes."

Jake shook his head. "Craig told me calmly that he'd shoot her if he saw me on the place again. He'd shoot her if he saw anyone at all on his grandparents' property after that night."

Rachel stared at the swiftly changing expressions on his face and when he didn't continue, probed gently, "What happened after that?"

"What?" he responded blankly.

"What happened after his threat?" she asked softly, knowing he needed to get it all out of his system.

Jake raised bleak eyes and whispered, "I got her killed. He warned me—but I didn't listen...."

"Tell me."

Jake stared into her face for a long time without answering, then turned and went into his room. He stood on the threshold looking around as though the place was unfamiliar to him, before finally moving toward the bed and sitting on its edge.

Rachel stood in the doorway watching him.

"I decided to kidnap her myself," he whispered almost beneath his breath. "I'd simply steal her from Craig, the way he'd stolen her from her mother. I was an arrogant fool."

All at once he looked up at Rachel with a puzzled expression twisting his dark brows. "Somehow he knew."

Rachel crossed the room and dropped down onto her knees beside him. She touched his knotted fingers with a comforting hand. Words were beyond her.

"As though he knew my plans before I knew them myself," Jake continued, "he let me get to her. He let me get her out of the house and into the woods—and then...he was just there, carrying a lantern.

"He didn't say a word, just set the lantern on the ground at his feet, raised the gun, pointed it at Lacy and..." Jake jerked his hands from her touch and buried his face in them.

"It wasn't your fault—" she offered.

"Don't tell me that!" He sprang to his feet and walked out of the room into the hallway again. Once there, as though uncertain where to go but feeling trapped, he stopped and stared down the end of the hallway, and then toward the stairs.

"It isn't your fault that she was shot—"

"He didn't shoot her," Jake answered in a distracted voice. "He shot me."

"You!"

"Yes...he broke her neck."

Rachel couldn't withhold a gasp of revulsion, but tried to cover it with her next words. "That's awful...but she wouldn't have stood a chance of getting free without you—"

"She didn't have a chance with me!" he snapped. "Don't you understand what I've been saying? I killed her! It was my decision and I did the one thing that was certain to get her killed."

"But...you can't blame yourself."

"No? Well who is to blame? Her mother, because she had to work to support them? The local cops because they couldn't find her? Steve Craig, because he was insane? Or me? The man who found her and let her die?''

He stepped in front of her and took her shoulders in a tight grip. "Look, don't try to rationalize what happened to me, okay? I've been through all that with the agency shrinks.

"A little girl died and she died because of *me*. I know that, and they know that. I accept the guilt for it, but I won't be responsible for anyone else dying.''

"What do you mean?" Rachel asked with a rising sense of uneasiness.

"I can't go on with this. I'm sorry, but I can't work this case. Tonight has clearly brought that fact home to me.''

"No!" Rachel jerked her shoulders from his grasp and took hold of his shirtfront with both hands, bunching it tightly. "You can't just walk away from us now. You can't!''

"I can!" Pulling her hands from his shirt, he threw them from him and turned on his heel.

"Then you'll be responsible for another child's death! As sure as I'm standing here—if you quit now—you'll be responsible for Amy's death!''

Jake's shoulders compacted rigidly, then fell. Taking hold of the newel post as though needing it for support, he murmured, "At least I won't be responsible for *both* your deaths.''

A slight sound caused him to swing round to face her. "That's right. I didn't finish my story. Mary heard about her daughter's death late that night. The next morning, they found her...sitting in the bathtub..." he stared hard at her, knowing she didn't want to hear what he had to say next, and continued " ... clutching a razor in one hand.''

"No—no—''

"It was too late. They couldn't save her.''

Rachel lifted a shaking hand to her mouth and whispered, "Oh, my God.''

Her look of aversion was too much for him. Jake turned away.

Now she'd go.

Rachel stood behind him, trying to cope with an image of herself and her own reaction under similar circumstances. She struggled for words, but nothing she could come up with seemed appropriate.

She finally managed to say, "You poor man."

Jake spun toward her. "Save your sympathy. I don't need it, and it won't change my mind."

Rachel looked into his icy, unresponsive eyes and prayed for guidance to say the right thing. "It wasn't your fault, even I can see that. If the child was treated as badly as you've said, I'm surprised she remained alive long enough for you to find her. I understand your need to blame some-one for her death—"

"You understand nothing. *Nothing!*" he yelled.

Rachel hesitated and then continued. "When both my parents became ill within a few months of each other, I was away from home for the first time in college. I had no brothers or sisters they could call on for help, and they hid their illnesses from me. When they died, I blamed myself for their deaths. I thought if I had only been there, maybe, somehow, I'd have been able prevent their dying.

"I grieved for them to the point of becoming ill myself. It took me a long time to realize they loved me and would have been horrified to think I blamed myself for their deaths.

"Guilt is something we all feel at the loss of someone we love. But it isn't healthy to let it take over and run your life. You must see that.

"Put them to rest, Jake." She stumbled over the unfa-miliar feel of his name on her lips. "Put your dead to rest and get on with living. There are still plenty of children out there who need you.

"You have a gift. Use it. Don't throw it away because you failed one time. Does a doctor quit when he loses a patient?

"Lacy is gone and so is her mother. I'm sorry for them. I'm sorry for you. But from what you've indicated they were good people. They wouldn't want others to suffer as they were made to suffer.

"Please," she urged, "don't quit now. Help those who still need you—help us—help Amy! Don't leave her to the same fate as Lacy...." Her voice became drowned with tears. "Don't abandon us now...please...."

Jake's eyes fastened onto her face with a stony indifference. She was willing to forgive him because she wanted something from him. There wasn't an ounce of sincerity in anything she'd said.

He was on the point of dismissing her plea out of hand when she blinked and a glimmer of light became caught by a crystalline tear hesitating on the tip of one dark lash. It hung there, suspended for what seemed like hours, before slipping gently to her cheek and gliding slowly toward her chin where it stopped to caress the edge of her quivering mouth.

Suddenly he wanted to believe her. With everything inside him, he wanted to believe what she'd said. He wanted to find the comfort she offered with her words...but he couldn't...he'd lived too long in the real world to believe in happy endings.

You couldn't wipe away years of accumulated pain in a few minutes with soft words. And yet the need to eradicate it from his life was there...waiting...but he just couldn't let go and believe.

"It's killing me," he whispered deeply. "It's eating me alive inside. I can't sleep—I close my eyes and see her face...see the smile she gave me that night...see the fear in her eyes change from hope...to acceptance...."

He swallowed tightly, and when he spoke again the anguish in his voice was like a live thing between them. "I was looking at her. I was lying on the ground, pain exploding inside me, looking at her. There was screaming and yelling—gunfire—and so much confusion. But, for a brief instant, we shared something...."

Jake's gaze lowered, as did his voice. "I knew I was dying...and it was like she knew it, too—knew she was about to die."

He was shaking all over. For the first time since that night, he was facing that instant when the world had careened to a stop, leaving nothing except himself and a little girl, facing each other, each forced to recognize the moment of their own mortality.

With a taut jerk of his head, his gaze fastened onto Rachel's swimming eyes, but his eyes had become unfocused as he plunged headlong into the past. "I couldn't move...but I could hear and I could see.... I saw her face...saw the light die out of her eyes the instant he grabbed her...."

Licking tears from her lips, Rachel asked, "Why didn't someone stop him? Didn't anyone, besides you, see what was happening?"

"It was dark and there was so much confusion. Craig didn't even try to run after he shot me. Gus shot him where he stood, with the shotgun still pointed at me. I guess everyone thought he was dead...but in the glare of the headlights...I saw..."

"I know, I know," Rachel murmured soothingly, putting her arms around him and pulling him close. How helpless she felt against his sorrow. Even knowing what he'd gone through, it was impossible for her to know exactly what he was feeling.

She, too, was eaten alive by the knowledge that she hadn't been able to keep the child she loved more than life itself from being ripped from her arms. But the child who tormented Jake had died. And whether he knew it or not, Jake had loved that little girl—perhaps not in the same way she loved Amy, but he'd loved her nonetheless.

Jake slowly became aware of the fact that he was being held in Rachel's soft arms. His next realization came as a shock. He wanted to stay there.

Gently, he slipped his own arms around her narrow waist, lifted his head from her neck and pressed her face against his shoulder. Now it was he who cradled her, but the feeling was the same. The sensation of being in the right place for the first time in his life flooded through him, taking away the sadness and guilt and momentarily filling the dark places in his soul with illumination.

Jake drew back to gaze into her face with wonder. A smile trembled on her lips—lips so sweet he couldn't resist.... It started as a tribute for the measure of peace she'd brought him after months of critical self-judgment. His lips brushed hers lightly, offering a surprisingly gentle caress, until he felt her lips open slowly beneath his.

All at once, his heart jolted and his pulse began to pound. A tingling sensation began in the center of Jake's body, filling him with a need he recognized in surprise.

Raising his lips, he gazed into Rachel's stunned eyes. A spark in her expression made him catch his breath. His mouth plunged toward hers, taking her lips with a hunger that left them both reeling.

Rachel raised herself blindly on her toes, opening her mouth and responding in a manner she'd rebuke herself for later. Her arms slipped up his shoulders and encircled his neck. She wanted him closer.

Jake's tongue explored the recesses of her mouth as he fit her soft curves to his hard body and an even deeper surge of potent hunger swept though him. His mouth moved hungrily over hers, drawing a profound response, and still it wasn't enough.

His hands cupped her derriere, molding her against the growing heat in his lower body. A small voice sounded in his head, telling him to beware, but he was beyond being able to heed its warning. His breath quickened. His hands moved slowly down her back, caressing all that he touched.

Rachel flowed into him, his gentle massage sending currents of desire pounding through her. Wave after wave of sensation flowed over her, taking her to new, dizzying heights. She'd never wanted anyone as badly as she wanted this man. *What was she thinking?*

Rachel froze in Jake's embrace. *She was there to get help to find her daughter, not to engage in a sexual liaison with this man!*

Jake slanted a kiss against the underside of her chin, heard a whispered moan and drew his tongue gently down her neck. It took a moment for him to realize the sounds she was making weren't sounds of pleasure, but of protest.

Drawing back, the hazel eyes glazed with passion, he looked down into her face. The expression of horror plainly written there, shocked him back to an awareness of what he was doing. Jake froze. Dropping his arms, he almost jumped away from her.

"I'm sorry..." He shook his head in confusion. "I don't know what..."

Rachel accepted the blame readily, anything to get them over this awkward and embarrassing moment. She didn't want to analyze what had happened between them, she just wanted to forget it. "It's all right. It was my fault."

"No." Jake shook his head and ran an unsteady hand through the tight curls. "It's my fault...I..."

"Let's just call it a night," Rachel suggested softly.

"Yes," he agreed readily enough, looking at her and looking quickly away. Backing away from her, he whispered, "Good night." His hand was on the doorknob to his room when Rachel suddenly spoke again.

"Tomorrow—"

"—will take care of itself," he intervened quickly.

Rachel wanted to protest but accepted his forecast with a slow nod. She was too exhausted to argue.

"No more razors in the middle of the night," he added abruptly, as she followed his lead and turned to her door.

Her glance touched his for a fleeting instant and she almost smiled. "No razors," she agreed. "And no more talk about leaving the case before Amy is found?" she added on a questioning note.

Jake stiffened and refused to meet her eyes. "I'll see you in the morning."

With the door closed between them, he leaned back against it and pressed the heels of both hands over burning eyes. *My, God, what had he done?*

Chapter 6

"What about my car?" Rachel asked, watching Jake push his suitcase across the seat of the dark red sedan.

Jake straightened, closed the door and leaned back against it. "I want to talk to you about that. I think it would be a good idea for us to travel to San Antonio in separate cars."

"Why?" she demanded instantly.

Jake darted a look at her set face. She wasn't going to like what he had to say, but he'd done some heavy soul-searching through the long hours before daylight and what he planned was intended for her sake as well as his own. "I've thought about it and I'll continue with the case, but I'd rather go on with it alone. I work better alone.

"You've been a big help in giving me information, but the rest is up to me. You can best serve your daughter by going home and preparing for her return."

"You're trying to get rid of me," Rachel accused rigidly.

"I'm a trained federal agent. I know how to handle myself in the field. You haven't been prepared for this kind of work. You're a schoolteacher . . . a mother."

"No," Rachel said with a stubborn shake of her head, "I won't let you push me out. I'm going with you, and I'm going to be there when you find Amy. If you won't let me travel with you, then I'll simply follow on my own."

Jake lunged away from the car and took hold of her shoulders in exasperation. "Didn't you hear a word of what I said last night? Your husband could be dangerous, not only to your daughter, but to everyone involved.

"Remember his threat? Just the sight of you could set him off. Do you want that? Do you want to be responsible for your own child's death?"

Rachel gasped at the brutal picture his words painted and tried to shrug out of his grasp, but Jake wouldn't let her go. The tender moments they'd shared in the middle of the night might never have been as he tried to make her see sense.

"You may not like the sound of that." His hands bunched her shoulders and drew her closer. "But you know it's the truth. Are you willing to risk your daughter's life, just to defy me?"

"*You* have nothing to do with my reasons for wanting to come along. I may be the only one who can save her," Rachel whispered through numb lips. "Have you considered that? It isn't Amy he wants to hurt...it's me. I'm not the great student of human nature you consider yourself to be," she continued with mild sarcasm, "but I know my ex-husband."

"Do you?" he asked in hard, cynical tones.

"I know my ex-husband well enough to know that the only way we may be able to get Amy away from him unharmed is if I'm there."

Jake peered closely into her face. "Are you saying, you don't think the threat he made is genuine? That he won't actually harm the girl?"

Rachel wished she could have the satisfaction of telling him that's exactly what she meant, but she knew it would be a lie. Didn't his words haunt her each night, slipping into her dreams and giving her nightmares? How many nights had she awakened in the past month with Amy's voice screaming, "Mommy! Mommy!" in her head?

"I'm saying, I'm going along, you can't stop me—that's what I'm saying," she answered with a final wrench that freed her from his disturbing touch.

Jake saw the determination in her set jaw and knew he was only wasting time. "All right." He gave in, but only temporarily. "We'll leave your car here and take mine. Yours should be safe enough if we drive it around back and leave it locked."

The trip started off in silence. Neither had much to say to the other. But as the miles sped by, the new undercurrent in their relationship, the one they'd done their best so far that morning to deny, was strong in both their minds.

Rachel's irritation with his high-handed, dictatorial manner took a long time to subside. When it did, she sidled a quick glance in his direction and was surprised by what she saw.

Until now, she hadn't paid any attention to what he was wearing. But now she saw that the stained jeans and worn sweatshirt were gone and in their place, he wore a dark blue suit, white shirt and dark tie.

On closer inspection she noticed that he must have trimmed his own hair because, if she wasn't mistaken, it was at least an inch or two shorter in the back. It still reached his collar, but went no farther.

She reached deep inside herself for a return of the outrage. She wanted to be angry with him, since it allowed her to vent some of the frustration she felt over Amy's kidnapping. But all she came up with was a memory of his face and the expression on it when he'd told her about what had happened to Lacy and her mother, and the anger just wouldn't materialize.

There were things she was beginning to like about him, like the way he gave her his undivided attention each time they'd talked about Gary, her ex-husband and their past life. Gary had always seemed preoccupied when she tried to talk to him after they were married.

There were also things about Jake that were starting to become familiar. Things she looked for...things she was beginning to find attractive...like the sleepy droop to his right eyelid . . . the way his hair grew to a widow's peak and the curl that kept flopping over onto his forehead . . . the cleft in his chin. . . .

Why was such an attractive man still single? That was only an assumption. He hadn't mentioned his personal life, so she supposed he could very well *be* married. Her glance flew to the hands firmly attached to the steering wheel. No ring. But that didn't necessarily mean anything.

She eyed her own hands folded in her lap and rubbed a fingertip across the gold band on the left one. She still wore her wedding ring, but only because of Amy.

Her thoughts filtered back to her first meeting with Jake. She recalled the way he'd turned toward her in the cemetery, standing so silent and still, his expression one of frozen dread. He'd looked as though he'd just seen a ghost. An uncomfortable thought flashed into her mind.

"Do I remind you of Mary Tolbridge?" she asked abruptly.

Jake's hands flexed on the steering wheel. "No."

"Not at all?"

"No," he answered stiffly.

She wasn't being insensitive. She knew he no doubt preferred to keep the memories of the woman buried in his subconscious, but that's what had turned him into a recluse. Getting him to talk about the woman might be just what he needed. "Was she a young woman? Her child was only four, so I imagine she couldn't have been very old."

"I . . . don't remember."

Rachel stared at his taut profile. There was something in his voice she didn't quite understand. Could he have been attracted to the woman?

"What kind of a person was she? I know you . . . admired her. Did she . . . like you, too?"

Jake shifted restlessly in his seat and threw an impatient frown in her direction. "Do we have to discuss this?"

"No, of course not, not if it makes you uncomfortable. But hiding from things never makes them get any better."

Rachel played with her fingers, a tight feeling squeezing her chest. Why wouldn't he discuss this with her? It wasn't as though they were complete strangers and she was prying into his private life for the sake of a cheap thrill. He'd shared his feelings with her early that morning.

"She was fair," Jake muttered softly.

"Was she attractive?"

Jake checked the rearview mirror, signaled a turn and pulled into the passing lane around another car, before replying. "Yes."

He could still see the lines of worry and premature aging around Mary's deep blue eyes, the hint of a dimple in her right cheek when she smiled, something she'd done rarely in the weeks they'd known each other. But once, a long time ago, she had been beautiful, of that he was certain.

"Were you in—"

"Look, can we let it rest?" He guessed what she was leading up to, and he didn't want the question between them. She had no right to ask.

Reaching into the inside pocket of his jacket he removed a pair of dark glasses with metal frames and shoved them onto his face. "If you need noise, turn on the radio."

Rachel took a deep breath and held it, the riotous confusion going on inside her throwing her completely off balance. She suspected there might be more to his relationship with the dead woman than he'd admitted. So who did he think he was, James Bond? Did he make love to all the women he encountered in his work?

Turning toward the window, she pretended an interest in the passing scenery. Why should what he felt for another woman bother her? He was only a public servant—isn't that what they called themselves?—a man she'd convinced to help find her daughter. Beyond that, they were simply two unhappy adults forced together on a journey neither wanted to make.

When his temper was finally under control, Jake shot the woman at his side a look from beneath partially lowered eyelids. She looked withdrawn. At this instant, she was probably telling herself how much she hated him and he couldn't blame her.

So far, she'd seen little of his nature to recommend him. And he knew his reaction upon finding her in the bathroom with a razor had terrified her. It bothered him, too.

He was a private person, one who didn't easily open himself to another. And the thought of what he'd admitted to this woman—the laying bare of his soul to her—made him cringe with embarrassment.

Nothing had been said between them about the scene in the hall since it had happened. But yesterday, stuck in the house most of the day because of rain, it had been there, all the time they were together, between them.

Jake stared at the road. What had happened to the hard-won control over his emotions he'd fought all his life to maintain? Sometimes, despite all his efforts to the contrary, he still saw too much of his parents in himself.

The open road, banded on either side by gently rolling hills, disappeared from his vision and another road took its place in his mind. He was very young, traveling by car with his parents. They had stopped to eat lunch and Jake had wandered off, following the trail of a happy family with a large, friendly dog on a leash.

He'd tagged after the family until they'd stopped outside the restaurant to let him pet the dog. After that, he'd gone back inside to find his mother and father but they were gone. The table where they'd been sitting was empty and had already been cleared.

Stunned, the four-year-old Jake had been terrified. They'd left without him! What was he going to do?

The friendly waitress who had waited on them found him crying in a corner by the bathrooms. After ascertaining that he was alone, she'd called the local sheriff.

It was evening, a long time after he'd told his tearful story to the sheriff, before his parents returned. Amid tearful hugs and cries of relief, because their little boy had been restored safely to them, Jake had looked into his mother's eyes and known the truth, and known, too, what was in store for him later. Jake would never wander off again.

Blinking the past from his vision, Jake reached for the button on the radio. In a moment of weakness, he'd revealed too much of himself to this woman, but it wouldn't happen again. No one must be allowed to get inside and know the real him.

No one ever had, except for Janet—and she was dead.

On the outskirts of San Antonio, Jake stopped for gas. Breaking the thick silence that had risen like a wall between them, he asked Rachel if she'd like to go home, while he kept the appointments. She refused, and they drove to the home of Charles Rothwell. The elderly man had been a friend of Rachel's since her marriage. He was also the former head of the English department that Gary Dryden had been a part of for several years.

Charles was now retired and in ill health. A nurse greeted them at the door and led the way upstairs to the old man's bedroom.

"Rachel." Charles held out a bloodless hand. Rachel moved quickly across the room to take it, holding it between both of hers as she sat down on the chair beside his bed.

"How are you, Charles?" she asked with sincere concern in her voice. She'd always liked the courtly old gentleman. She used to imagine fondly that this was what Gary would be like in later years.

"Not very well," he answered in uneven tones, smiling wearily. "At least, not if my doctor is to be believed. But it's all right." He patted her hands before pulling his loose. "I've never subscribed to the idea of living forever. We all have to go when we're no longer useful, to make room for the new generation."

The white brows rose, as his gaze became focused on the man standing behind Rachel's seated figure. "Now, who is this young man?"

"I'm Jake Frost, I spoke with your nurse on the phone yesterday. I work for the FBI." He shot a brief quelling glance at Rachel's upturned face, hesitated over the slight discrepancy in his true work status, and continued, "I understand you know Gary Dryden rather well, and I'd like to ask you a few questions about him."

Charles Rothwell turned his mud-brown eyes toward Rachel's solemn face. "I'm sorry, my dear. I heard what happened, of course." He shook his head. "You just never can tell," he murmured softly, "I had such high hopes for the boy. All other considerations aside, he's an excellent academician."

Jake opened a small spiral notebook and removed a pen from his pocket. "I understand you and Dryden used to play a weekly game of chess."

"Yes, that's right."

"So the two of you must have been rather close?"

"No, I wouldn't say—" Charles' words were interrupted by a sudden fit of coughing.

Rachel stood and stared at the man in alarm. Before she could do anything, the nurse who had ushered them into the room earlier came through the door and hurried toward the bed. Moving around Rachel's motionless figure, she raised the old man to an upright position.

"Can I help?" Rachel asked anxiously.

"Hand me the glass of water," the woman replied in calm tones.

Rachel handed it to her and the woman held it to Charles's blue lips once the cough had subsided. When he was breathing easier, she murmured something for his ears only and the old man shook his head and waved her aside.

"Sorry," he breathed unevenly. "I'm afraid I didn't quit smoking soon enough." As he smiled, Rachel noticed the pipe and tobacco pouch lying near an ashtray on the bed-side table.

"May we continue?" Jake asked, when it appeared he'd recovered.

"Yes, of course," Charles replied, giving Jake his full attention. "You were saying?"

"I was asking if you and Dryden were close enough to discuss personal things during your chess games?"

"No. Gary was never what you'd call an easy man to get to know. And in the last couple of years, if anything, he became more withdrawn.

"But, as I said, we were never really what you would call close friends. We simply enjoyed a good game of chess, and I kept a watchful eye on him at work."

"Was he good at chess?"

"Excellent player," Charles answered, "and a very good strategist."

"Is there anything at all you can add that might give me a clue about where he'd go if he was trying to drop out of sight with his daughter?"

Charles shook his head, leaned back against the pillows tiredly and closed watery eyes. "Why don't you speak to Marian Benning? They used to be quite close. There was even talk at one time of an engagement. . . ."

Rachel made a sudden move and the thin, blue-veined lids opened suddenly. The old man's gaze settled on Rachel's startled face. "Didn't you know?"

Rachel shook her head.

"Well, don't be upset, my dear, I can assure you, that whatever was between Gary and Marian was over a long time ago. Now they're simply friends."

"I'm not upset," Rachel replied quickly, "but I didn't realize...Gary never said...Marian has never indicated there was ever anything of a personal nature between them."

"Well, perhaps they weren't as close as I thought," Charles said, seeking to soothe her confusion.

"Yes, that's probably it," Rachel responded. She didn't want to upset the old man. He'd always been kind to her.

Outside, in the car, she failed to notice the sharp glance Jake shot in her direction. She was busy wondering how she'd been married to Gary Dryden for six years and never in all that time known he'd once dated Marian Benning.

"Have you changed your mind about wanting to go home?" Jake asked abruptly.

"No." She stared straight ahead. Nothing could keep her from attending this next interview.

Marian Benning was a woman in her mid-forties. She was a classically beautiful woman, one whose beauty age would no doubt improve upon. She was also a very generous woman who shared herself with all her friends.

Greeting them warmly at the door, she offered her hand to Jake and put a comforting arm around Rachel's shoulders. They moved down a long, elegant hallway and into a room bright with sunlight and fresh flowers.

Jake perched on a chair, but Rachel was led to a love seat and seated next to her hostess. As though at a prearranged signal, an older woman, dressed in black with touches of white at shoulders and collar, entered the room with a tray of tea and small sandwiches and cakes.

"I hope you like tea." Marian smiled, the perfect hostess, as she poured the tea, offering it around.

This time it was Rachel who conducted the interrogation and Jake let her. "We've just come from Charles's house." Rachel swallowed a quick sip of tea and spoke directly to her hostess.

"Poor man," Marian said with real distress in the cultured tones, "I must get over to see him soon. I understand it's his heart."

"Yes, he doesn't look at all well," Rachel agreed solemnly. And then, placing her cup and saucer on the table in front of her, she turned to face the older woman at her side. "He said something a little while ago that surprised me."

Marian eyed her curiously. "And what was that, my dear?"

"He said you and Gary used to date."

"Yes, that's right..." Marian broke off, a frown marring the attractive line of her forehead. "Didn't you know?"

Rachel shook her head, wondering what else she didn't know about the man who had fathered her darling Amy.

"I..." Marian lifted elegant shoulders and looked helplessly from Rachel to the silent Jake and back again. "It's true, Gary and I dated for a while...." She hesitated, gave a slight shrug and continued. "As a matter of fact, we had talked at one time about getting married."

"Married?" Rachel asked quickly. So, it was true!

"Yes. But..." The older woman broke off and looked down at the ring on her right hand for a long moment. And then, as though coming to a sudden decision, she met

Rachel's intent gaze and said, "Gary wanted something I couldn't give him—he wanted a child."

Rachel swallowed and concentrated on keeping the shock she felt from showing on her face.

Marian lifted a hand and made a graceful gesture toward the room around them. "Does this look like a house that would readily accommodate children?" Smiling without humor, she answered her own question. "I don't think so. And neither, I'm afraid, would this." She gestured toward her own self.

"I'm just not the motherly type, I'm too set in my ways. What's that old adage about an old dog and new tricks?" After a brief laugh, she sobered almost instantly and added, "Besides, my childbearing years are long past."

"He wanted to have a child with you," Rachel murmured wonderingly. Gary had told her he'd never considered the possibility of fathering a child until he'd met her.

Seeing the confusion in Rachel's expression, Marian leaned over and patted the younger woman's taut fingers in a gesture of comfort. "Gary just wanted to have a child," she corrected gently. "To be truthful, I think that's the only reason he began seeing me in the first place. I was the only unmarried female member of the staff under the age of fifty.

"When I told him my views on the subject of producing a family at this late stage in my life, he listened carefully, nodded, then left. We never spoke on the subject again.

"You see, there was no great love between us, and I don't think it particularly mattered to Gary who the mother might be, as long as she was well-bred and produced a healthy child." Recollecting herself, she exclaimed, "Oh . . ."

Marian put a hand to her lips and gazed at Rachel contritely. "I'm sorry, my dear. I truly didn't mean that the way it sounded."

"It's all right." Rachel smiled faintly. "I understand what you mean. I'm beginning to see that a wife was never what Gary wanted. I was only a means to an end."

Jake took over the interrogation at that point. Marian was very accommodating but had no real information for them. It seemed she knew the man, Gary Dryden, no better than

Charles Rothwell, despite what apparently was a long-standing relationship.

In the car once more, Jake kept his eyes away from Rachel's face as he asked, "Was Miss Benning a frequent visitor to your house?"

"We were very good friends. Marian is not a person you can know at a distance. She has a very giving nature. Despite her words just now about not being the motherly type, I've always thought she'd have made a wonderful mother. I often wondered why she'd never married, but didn't like to ask, because I didn't want her to think I was prying.

"When you asked for the names of people Gary was close to and I told you about Charles and Marian, I thought if anyone could tell you something about Gary that I didn't know, it would be one of them. They've known him since he first came to Harrisbrook College. But, now," she muttered uneasily, "I just don't know." Jake smothered any thought of sympathy for her and hardened his resolve to remain uninvolved with the people in this case. The woman at his side was only beginning to realize what he'd suspected all along, that she didn't know the man she'd called husband as well as she thought.

But Jake was beginning to know him, and a parallel between Gary Dryden and Steve Craig was beginning to form. Jake kept the thought to himself, remembering all too clearly what a quiet, seemingly pleasant, likable young man was capable of doing with cold-blooded deliberation.

Pulling into a parking place, Jake removed the dark sunglasses from his pocket and placed them on his face. Rachel watched his actions with a raised brow. The sun was watery at best and they were getting ready to go inside the offices of the college.

"I thought they only did that in movies?" she said.

"What?" Jake turned the opaque lenses in her direction.

"The FBI and those sunglasses," she replied brusquely. "Do you really think you're going to need them inside? They do nothing for your image."

"Sometimes it's advantageous to keep others from knowing what you're thinking. It keeps them a little off balance."

Wallace Anderson, the Dean of Harrisbrook College, was waiting for the pair in his office. It was Friday and he had an appropriations committee meeting to attend later that afternoon, but paperwork had kept him in his office until after lunch.

"So." Dean Anderson shook hands with Jake, noting the glasses with pursed lips, and withdrew his hand promptly. "We've never met, but I do recall your name in reference to a case you worked on a while back that made the headlines." It was obvious from his tone of voice that he wasn't a member of the Jake Frost fan club.

Jake stared silently at the man until Anderson dropped his eyes, shuffled some papers on his desk, then glanced up at Rachel. He had ignored her until now. "I'm sorry to hear about your daughter." She was not one of his favorite people, and she'd done nothing to endear herself to him by bringing the college bad publicity first with her divorce and now with the child.

"What, exactly, is it you think I can tell you?" Anderson asked the question of Rachel, but it was Jake who answered, drawing his attention.

"You may have information that can lead us to Gary Dryden and his daughter. I'd like to have a look at his file."

"I have only your word for who you say you are," Anderson said abruptly. "I haven't seen any identification."

"I don't have my ID with me at the moment, but you can call this number and the person at the other end will identify me." Jake wrote a series of numbers on a piece of paper from his spiral notebook and held it out to the other man.

Anderson hesitated a long time before taking the piece of paper, and when he did, he simply laid it on the desk without looking at it. "Do you have authorization to look at the college's private files? I believe it takes a search warrant for such a move," the older man said with satisfaction.

He was a past master at the art of staring down students and faculty members to get his point across, and though the dark glasses somewhat nullified his technique, he was determined to let this man know he wasn't impressed with his arrogance. He recalled, all too well, what he'd read about Jake Frost in the newspapers.

"I can get a search warrant," Jake rigidly. "But that takes time and I don't want to waste a lot of time taking unnecessary steps. However..."

He picked up Anderson's calendar from the corner of the desk, looked at it, and set it back down a little to the left of where he'd found it. Anderson followed the move with a frown.

"Now, if I do take the time," Jake continued, "then I'll probably want to make it worth the trouble." Picking up a stack of papers that Anderson had been going through for his appropriations meeting, Jake flipped quickly through it, restacked it neatly, and laid it on the desk where he'd found it.

"I'm sure there must be other areas here at the college that I can look into at the same time. Sometimes things have a way of getting away from you, and in my job I can't afford to have that happen."

Removing the dark glasses, Jake folded them and put them in his jacket pocket. Shooting Anderson a direct look, Jake added, "Being in charge of a big place like this, you must know how things like that can happen. Right?"

Anderson nodded, wondering what the man was getting at.

Jake glanced toward the desk and said, "I'll bet it takes a lot of paperwork—a mountain of paperwork—just to keep track of all those little things. Things like..." he leaned over and picked up the top paper on the stack he'd straightened, and looked at it "...departmental spending," he read. "Now that must involve a lot of time and meticulous work." He shot a quick glance at Anderson's suddenly immobile face. "I'll bet you have to depend a lot on the heads of different departments to keep track of what they spend on the tools they need for their classes. Sometimes..." Jake returned the paper to the stack "... I'll bet little things, like tracking down the expenditures on certain items—in the athletic department, for instance—must take a great deal of time and effort."

Rachel had been wondering impatiently where all this was leading, but when she glanced at Wallace Anderson's florid complexion and saw it become redder, she actually wanted to smile. Jake was on to something.

Wallace Anderson struggled with thoughts of the retirement house he was building on an island in the South Pacific. How could this man know?

"I will of course cooperate with the FBI, it's my duty as a law-abiding citizen," he emphasized for Jake's benefit, "but just let me make one thing perfectly clear. Gary Dryden was always an exemplary instructor, and no scandal touched his name while he was here."

"He kidnapped our daughter," Rachel put in, feeling her hackles rise. Anderson was a pompous ass and always had been.

"He is the child's father."

"The file, if you please," Jake reminded him firmly.

Anderson left the room without another word. Kidnapping, indeed! He didn't like giving in to the arrogant Mr. Frost, but if a hint of an investigation by the FBI over misappropriation of funds leaked out... He could see his dream house disappearing into thin air, along with his job.

Jake moved to the window and stood with his hands in his pockets staring out at the campus green. He sensed Rachel didn't like Wallace Anderson and he had no difficulty in understanding her reasons—

"How did you know?" Rachel whispered behind his right shoulder.

Jake shrugged, but before he could answer, the man, himself strode through the door. "Here we are." Anderson offered the file to Jake.

Jake took the file and sat down in a chair by the window. After a few minutes, he looked up. "It says here, Dryden has a mother living in Ft. Worth."

"Yes, that's right. She retired there after years as a public figure. She was, I believe, a concert cellist."

"M-mother?" Rachel asked with a frown.

"That's right." Anderson nodded.

"There must be some mistake—Gary's family are all dead."

"No, there's no mistake," Anderson corrected her with a small smile that looked polite on the surface, self-satisfied beneath it.

"I don't understand," Rachel murmured, looking from Anderson to Jake.

"It doesn't surprise me that Gary didn't mention his mother to you. When we employed him, he didn't mention any family to us, either. But we here at Harrisbrook College take pride in hiring instructors we're certain the sons and daughters of our generous benefactors will benefit by knowing.

"We want only the best and that's why we do a thorough and complete history check on our 'family,' as I like to think of the faculty. I can't think why Gary didn't want us to know about his mother. I was quite pleased to learn she was once a noted talent among concert circles. It's too bad she dropped suddenly from public view."

"What happened to her?" Rachel asked curiously.

"Oh…I wouldn't know. I just know from the report that she no longer performs and hasn't for quite some time," Anderson replied. "I suppose Gary thought that since she's still known by her stage name, we wouldn't be able to trace the relationship."

"Stage name?" Rachel asked.

"Yes, she doesn't go by the name Dryden. She was known as Alexandra Conroy-Wilkes."

"I want this file," Jake said abruptly, drawing the man's attention to himself and away from Rachel's stricken face.

"Well, I—" Anderson didn't know if he was within his rights to refuse the man, but he knew he'd like to.

"I'll see it's returned to you when I'm through with it." Jake rose, moved to Rachel's side and took her arm.

"Thanks for the help," Jake said over his shoulder as he ushered Rachel from the man's office.

On the steps of the building, Rachel stopped to look up into Jake's face and ask in bewilderment, "Why did Gary tell me his mother was dead?"

Jake shook his head, took her arm, and led her down the stairs. Wallace Anderson was no doubt standing at his window watching for them and he didn't want the man to have the satisfaction of knowing he'd given Rachel cause for anxiety.

"Come on, we'll discuss this over an early dinner. I need to study this file. There's a quiet little restaurant—"

"No." Rachel said quickly, "I want to go home."

Except for giving him directions, Rachel remained withdrawn after that. Jake respected her need for silence, despite the torrent of questions boiling just below the surface of his mind. For the first time they could be on to something, really on to something, that might lead them to Gary Dryden and his little daughter. But that something was proving hard for Rachel to adjust to, because it was in direct conflict with her understanding of her ex-husband.

Rachel had moved out of the house she, Gary, and Amy had lived in on campus and into a small bungalow on the opposite end of town. Even though it hadn't been lived in for a while, Jake was aware of its homey feel the moment he entered the front door.

After indicating where the bathroom was located, in case he needed it, offering him something to eat and drink, which he declined, and showing him to the living room, Rachel disappeared. When she didn't return after a while, feeling a vague sense of disquiet Jake went in search of her.

"This is Amy's room," Rachel said unnecessarily, sensing his presence behind her. She turned toward him, and he saw she was holding a stuffed animal in both hands cradled against her chest.

"Who's your friend?" he asked, indicating the animal.

"M-Mr. McNab," she answered fighting for control. "It's one of a pair, a boy and a girl, Amy got for Easter last year..." Turning with her back to him, she crushed the soft toy against her face and felt hot tears dampen its matted fur.

Jake hesitated on the threshold of the room. Instinct told him to go to her, comfort her, but some deeper, inner voice told him to get out. He was getting too involved in this case—*just like the last time.* He was too involved with Rachel Dryden, and she was a woman in need of a hell of a lot more than he could offer her.

Once Rachel managed to get her emotions under control, she turned to find the doorway empty. She found Jake in the kitchen. The doors to most of the cabinets stood open and Jake stood in the middle of the room looking slightly harassed.

"Problems?" she asked from the doorway.

He pivoted toward her, noting the traces of tears still on her cheeks, and glanced away. "I thought I'd make coffee." He ran a hand through his hair, standing the curls on end. "But I can't find a damned thing."

"It's here." Rachel entered the room and moved toward a shelf by the door. A tense silence enveloped them growing tighter with each step that took her closer to him.

"Take a seat." She tried to speak normally, thinking it would dispel what was suddenly in the room between them. "I'll make the coffee and something to eat." She began to arrange things haphazardly on the sink.

"Are you all right?" Jake asked softly.

Rachel nodded without speaking, felt a hand hover near her shoulder, closed her eyes and held her breath. If he touched her... An instant later, she drew an uneven breath and knew she was alone.

Jake stood in the bathroom looking into the mirror. Water dripped down the lines of his face and off a chin darkened by a day's growth of beard. The face looked the same, but what about the eyes?

He studied himself a moment longer before bending and dousing his face with cold water. He'd thought life was complicated *before* he met Rachel Dryden....

* * *

"Well, that's that." Jake put down the phone and closed the folder on his lap. "I've got an address for Alexandra Conroy-Wilkes in Ft. Worth."

They had eaten a meal Rachel had prepared while Jake studied the file from the college. Jake had asked a few questions and Rachel had told him again that Gary had told her both his parents were dead and he had no living relatives. His father had supposedly died a soldier during the Korean conflict, and his mother a few years later from ill health.

Now they knew at least a part of that story was false.

"What are you going to do next?" Rachel asked when he'd put down the phone and made a few notes in the blue spiral notebook. She stared at the book and wondered if the question mark, beside the word truthful, was still there.

"I'll get a motel room for the night and leave bright and early in the morning for Ft. Worth."

"*We'll* leave bright and early in the morning," she corrected gently.

Jake gave her a long look from beneath half-lowered lids, but remained silent. Gathering up his papers, he prepared to leave.

"Don't go," she said abruptly.

Jake stiffened.

She explained quickly, "There's no need to go to the expense of a motel. I have a guest room, and we can get an earlier start in the morning if we both leave from here."

What she said made sense. She was determined to go with him, and at the moment Jake was tired of the constant struggle between them. With a nod of resignation, he agreed to her suggestion.

Rachel showed him to the guest room. They decided to leave at six in the morning, and after an awkward goodnight, she left him alone.

Jake couldn't sleep. He needed to walk—walking was his salvation. Glancing at the face of the clock on the table beside the bed, he saw it was after two in the morning.

He sat up on the side of the bed. He hadn't bothered to undress, only to remove his belt and shoes. Replacing them now, he moved cautiously downstairs, not wanting to disturb Rachel's slumber.

A light in the kitchen drew him toward that room. He saw another light coming from a small room off the side of the garage. Jake stuck his head in the door and stood stock-still in surprise.

Though he hadn't made a sound, again she seemed to sense his presence. "You couldn't sleep either, huh?" Rachel asked, laying down the acetylene torch and removing the protective glasses.

"No," Jake answered, noticing the creases at either side of her face from the glasses. He entered the room slowly, looking around him in amazement. "Are these yours?"

"Yes." Rachel smiled at the look on his face. "I guess I didn't mention I was a sculptor—of sorts."

"No, you didn't. They're beautiful," he said sincerely.

The room was awash with color and light. It bounced and sparkled off a menagerie of glass birds in all shapes and sizes. Some were suspended on wires from the ceiling, some perched on the branches of a tree made of glass, and others rested on shelves lining the walls. There were other glass figures, too, Jake noted on closer inspection, but mostly they were birds.

"I thought you were a kindergarten teacher. I didn't know you taught shop."

"I am." She smiled. "And I don't."

"How long—" His arm swept the room.

"I've been making them since I was in high school. My mother was an ornithologist. She got me interested in birds because she collected small replicas, and the detail on many of them was wonderful.

"One day, I was at a shopping mall when a man was demonstrating how to make figurines of glass. I decided I wanted to try it." She shrugged. "This is the result."

"My . . . someone I once knew used to collect glass figurines. She had a whole shelf full, but nothing like this." Jake picked up a tiny, intricately fashioned, humming bird with pointed beak and green-tipped wings. "None were as beautiful as this."

"Thank you." Something in her voice drew his eyes. "That's Amy's favorite," she explained with a sad smile.

Jake replaced it carefully on the lip of the delicately shaped snapdragon and moved away. "You're very talented."

"It doesn't really take talent, just a steady hand and lots of patience." She indicated the swan she had been attempting just now and shook her head. "My hands aren't very steady at the moment."

Jake helped her put things away and clean up her work area. When they were finished, he said, "I don't think either one of us is going to get much sleep tonight. Maybe we should go ahead and get started."

"I think you're right," Rachel agreed.

It was six in the morning when Jake pulled into a rest park a few miles outside the city limits of Ft. Worth and stopped. Contrary to what she'd said, Rachel had slept most of the way.

Jake felt her head shift against his shoulder and glanced down at her sleeping face. He'd resisted looking at her since the moment her head had slid across the back of the seat and come to rest against his shoulder.

But he hadn't been able to deny the warmth that spread through him at the thought that she felt safe enough with him to relax and sleep. He wished he felt so secure in her presence.

It was moments like this that made him wish he hadn't quit smoking.

Chapter 7

Alexandra Conroy-Wilkes slid her eyes over Rachel's taut figure seated directly across from her and sniffed lightly. "So, you are the woman my son chose for a wife." There was manifest censure in the remark.

"A bit young for him, aren't you? And you say there's a child? This is the first I've heard of it. The child is his, I suppose?" The small dark eyes, behind wire-rimmed glasses, narrowed on Rachel's livid face.

Jake intervened quickly. "We've come to ask you some questions about your son, Mrs. Conroy-Wilkes. As I've already told you, your son has kidnapped his daughter—"

"Kidnapped!" The beady eyes snapped to his face. "How can a man kidnap his own child?"

"The courts entrusted sole custody of the child to the mother, because your son made threats against both their lives."

"Humph!" Alexandra snorted, shifting her weight in the chair. "Threats, did you say? Any threat *he* made you can safely forget all about. He's nothing but a spineless jelly-fish—just like his father." With an awkward flutter of one hand, she dismissed the whole idea as ridiculous.

"The fact remains," Jake continued, "your son is wanted for kidnapping."

"What do I know about that?" she complained abruptly. "I haven't seen or heard from him for the last eight years. He dumped me in this hellhole—" she gestured to her surroundings "—dumped me and forgot all about me. I don't know anything about the ungrateful whelp!

"I sit here, day after day, in this hellish contraption—" she slapped the arms of her wheelchair with arthritic hands "—barely able to get about by myself. Does he care? Of course not. Just like his father before him—he didn't care, either. He went off to war and got himself killed, leaving me alone with a child to raise.

"He deserved what he got," she declared bitterly, "and good riddance to him." Knotting a misshapened fist she shook it at them. "I gave up everything for him—him and his child! I gave up my career on the stage, gave up life with my aunt to bear his child. She was going to leave *me* everything—*everything*—do you hear? Until I went against her wishes and married *him!*"

"Mrs. Conroy-Wilkes," Jake interrupted in an attempt to bring her back to the subject at hand, "we didn't come to stir up painful memories. We came to ask if you'd heard from your son, and if not, then do you know somewhere he might go to get away from everyone?"

"I don't go by that name anymore," she informed him sharply. "And I know nothing about my son's whereabouts," she answered haughtily, looking him up and down as though he was some species of being she couldn't immediately identify.

"As I have already told you, I didn't even know he was married. He never writes or calls." A whining note entered the petulant voice. "I don't even hear from him on Mother's Day. After everything he put me through. Not a card. Not even a phone call on Mother's Day."

"You mentioned an aunt," Rachel said hastily. "Is that aunt still living?"

Alexandra favored the other woman with an exacting glare. "And if she is? You'll get nothing from her. She gave it all to *him*."

"Him?" Jake asked quickly.

"To Gary," the old woman answered as though he was a ninny.

"Where does this aunt live?" Jake asked, casting a swift glance in Rachel's direction.

"Live? In a nursing home," Alexandra answered in sudden satisfaction. "I put her there. She, and my conniving son, left me with nothing but this. An apartment! They raise the price, force you to buy it, and call it a condominium, but it's still nothing but an apartment!"

Her gaze turned inward. "Once, I had it all," she murmured softly. "Travel, fine clothes, jewelry, my music..." Her glance centered on the swollen knuckles of the hands resting in a heap on her lap. "Now...I can't even button my own blouse," she whispered bitterly.

"Alexandra," Jake recalled her to the present gently, "where is the nursing home located?"

"It doesn't matter," she answered in a louder voice, shrugging off the past. "She hasn't seen him since he left me here. She only took care of him that one summer—the summer I traveled in Europe—but that's all it took. In one summer, she stole his love from me—and he stole my inheritance."

"Just give us the name of your aunt and the address of the nursing home, please." Jake had his notebook open. A few minutes later, they were on their way out of the apartment.

"I hope you find him," Alexandra called loudly. "And when you do, tell him for me what an ungrateful bastard he is."

Jake knew Rachel had been upset by the interview, but didn't realize how upset until they were out on the street.

"My God, what a horrible old woman," she whispered aghast. "No wonder he's crazy—he takes after his mother.

"We've got to find him!" She grabbed hold of Jake's arm. "We've got to get Amy away from him. Did you hear what she said? He has money—"

"We'll find them. Don't worry." Jake patted her rigid fingers reassuringly as he helped her into the car, then closed the door.

She fixed worried eyes on his face after he'd climbed in behind the steering wheel, and asked, "But what if it's too late?" She clutched at his arm again, the fingers digging in deeply. "What if he takes her out of the country? If he has plenty of money—"

"We don't know that's true," Jake interjected quickly. "Alexandra is a recluse, probably living on a fixed income, and she's a very bitter woman. An inheritance, if it really exists, could mean anything—including nothing more than a few dollars."

"But he lied to me! Gary lied to me! He told me his family was all dead. And I never knew anything at all about an inheritance. What if he's making plans right this minute to leave the country? What if he's already gone?"

"He hasn't left the country. Now, calm down, we'll find your daughter, I promise." He loosened the deathlike grip on his arm and started the car.

"Yes." Rachel nodded, feeling a little calmer. "But we have to find them quickly! I don't trust Gary," she added fiercely, vividly recalling the dour face of the old woman they'd just left.

It didn't take long to find the nursing home. It was located in a small lakeside town east of Ft. Worth. The place didn't look like the home of a woman who'd had a great deal of money to leave to anyone. It was run-down and proved to be short of staff. And it took only a few minutes for Jake to ascertain that Beaulah Conroy would be no help to them. He had convinced Rachel to wait in the car while he went inside alone and he was glad that he had.

One look at his face when he climbed in the car a short time later, and Rachel's spirits plummeted.

"She's in a coma," Jake told her with a set face. "The nurse said she's been in one for a few weeks, now. The old lady is in her nineties."

"She knew!" Rachel charged, making an angry fist. "That old witch knew and didn't tell us!" Her eyes pleaded with him. "What are we going to do? We're running out of time! I was hoping—I thought we finally had something to help us. What do we do now?"

Jake's glance swerved toward the road. She was looking at him as though he had all the answers. And he didn't.

"I don't know," he said finally, driving toward the lake, giving her time to get hold of her emotions.

Jake glanced at her from time to time and guessed she was trying to stave off a growing feeling of depression by pure strength of will. He wished her luck. Depression had been his constant companion for too long.

They rode around until evening, then Jake found a restaurant on the northern edge of the lake and they stopped for a meal. The air was saturated with the appetizing aroma of fresh seafood, but when the food was set before them, neither seemed to have much of an appetite.

"You know," Jake began slowly, when the meal had been cleared from the table, "this isn't what you should be doing." He moved his cup around the table, keeping his eyes riveted on its slow progress. "You should be home—"

He jumped as Rachel's cup slammed against the table. Nearby diners paused to cast surprised glances in their direction.

"Don't start with me again," Rachel said through clenched teeth. "I've told you, I'm going with you. I'm going to be there when Amy is found!"

Getting to her feet, she crossed the floor swiftly and disappeared behind a door marked Ladies. Jake watched her go with a deepening frown.

She was teetering on the edge of a complete breakdown. She had a quick temper. This wasn't the first time he'd felt the sting of it and if she cracked, there was no telling what she might do. The realization did little to settle his own strained nerves.

A small voice reiterated a question inside his head. *Had she showed her temper to her little daughter?* As he recalled, his own mother had had a quick temper....

They were driving back toward town when Jake began looking for a place to spend the night. It was late and many of the motel signs had been switched off. That didn't leave much to choose from.

He finally found a place that hardly looked first-rate, but he was too tired by that time to care. Inside, he learned the only room available was a double, and though Rachel gave him a look at the news, she followed him inside and immediately threw her overnight bag on the bed near the door.

The brittle silence that had descended over them since leaving the restaurant was still with them. Within fifteen minutes, both were lying in bed in the dark. Rachel lay facing the door, her eyes on the two-inch gap between the curtain and window.

Jake lay in the bed near the bathroom, his eyes on Rachel's unyielding back. There was no question in his mind that sleep tonight would be as elusive as ever.

The muffled sound of voices, arguing, drifted to his ears. It was dark in the room, but a thin band of light showed around the edges of the door.

Sliding off the narrow bed, he moved slowly toward it. The doorknob felt cold in his hand. He twisted it, pulled, and stood on the open door's threshold. A light was on somewhere downstairs, but the hallway was dark.

Jake turned toward the room at the end of the hall. He opened his mouth to call out but heard voices again and turned to see two figures struggling at the top of the stairs.

"You're not taking him."

"Are you nuts? Get out of my way!"

"No! You—you devil! You're all devils in this house. I won't let you take him!"

"What are you—"

The tall figure ducked, threw his hands over his head and darted away from something the smaller figure swung at his head. All at once the tall figure gave a startled cry and stood

*with arms flailing, balancing on the edge of the stairs. With
a loud cry of protest, he fell backward, down the stairs.*

"Oh, my God!"

"M-mother? F-father?"

*"No, Jake, it's me. Come here—come here, honey. We've
got to leave. Right away. Hurry! Help me get your things."*

"There was an accident."

*Jake pulled loose from Janet's restraining hand and ran
to the head of the stairs. Down below, he could see a dark
form lying in a heap—just like his clothes looked when he
left them lying on the bathroom floor—at the bottom of the
stairs.*

*He held on to the banister and crept down the stairs, one
at a time, stopping every few steps to squat down on short,
stubby legs and look at what lay below. He was crouched on
the last step, staring at a growing puddle of red around the
man's head when she came for him.*

*"Come on, Jakey, we have to get out of here. If we stay,
the police will come and I'll have to go away."*

"No!"

*Four-year-old Jake tore his fascinated gaze from the
gruesome sight of his uncle's still form and threw his arms
around the woman's legs in protest. "No! No! I won't let
them take you away! I won't let them!"*

Jake sat up in bed with a start, sweat sticking his shirt to
his back, chest heaving. Turning toward the bedside table,
his eyes found the cracked face of the clock radio.

Two in the morning. He hadn't slept long.

Glancing toward the other bed, he saw Rachel lying on
her back, an arm thrown across her forehead. At least his
own disturbed sleep hadn't bothered hers.

He slipped his legs off the side of the bed, found his boots
in the dark, and hopping on first one foot and then the
other, pulled them on. Earlier, he'd forsaken the suit and
white shirt for the more comfortable jeans and sweatshirt,
and that's what he'd chosen to sleep in.

Grabbing his jacket from the chair in the corner, he
moved cautiously toward the door. He needed to chase away

the jitters this particular dream always caused with a brisk walk in the chill morning air.

Rachel opened both eyes as the door closed behind Jake's stealthy figure, and leapt off the bed. Sliding her feet into soft leather boots, she grabbed her jacket and made for the door. She didn't know where Jake Frost was headed, but she wasn't taking any chance on his leaving her behind.

If he had it in mind to slip away in the middle of the night because she wouldn't agree to go back to San Antonio as he wanted, he had another think coming. She was right behind him.

Easing out the door, she looked for and found the dark red sedan sitting exactly where he'd parked it. Nonplussed, she hesitated. If he wasn't leaving town without her, then where was he going?

Her eyes spotted his figure disappearing around the corner of the building and she hotfooted it after him. She knew he walked at night when he couldn't sleep, but instinct told her to follow him anyway.

Jake set a brisk pace, unaware he was being followed. A few blocks later, the lights and music from a country and western bar attracted his attention. It was Saturday night, and the place was rocking.

Inside, he took a seat at the corner of the bar and unzipped his jacket. Jake ordered a beer when the bartender came over. A cigarette was dangling from the corner of the man's mouth, and a cloud of smoke encircled his head. When he returned to set the beer down before him, Jake took a deep whiff of the smoke and sighed with remembered pleasure.

While he drank his beer, his eyes wondered leisurely around the room, finally settling on a waitress in tight jeans, western shirt with sparkling fringe at the shoulders and along the arms, cowboy boots, and a hat. With sudden enjoyment, he watched as she laughed and joked with a customer while taking his order.

Feeling his eyes on her back, she turned, spotted him at the bar, and smiled, giving him a broad, friendly wink.

Swaying in his direction, she stopped beside him to give her order to the bartender.

"You aren't from around these parts," she breathed in a soft, Texas drawl.

Jake lifted a brow and accepted her challenge. "What makes you say that?"

"You're too good-looking. I'd remember."

He smiled. "Buy you a drink?"

"Not now—too busy." The drinks she'd ordered were up, and she placed them on her tray. "I get off in an hour," she paused to lean toward him and whisper, "If you still want to buy me that drink, I'll meet you right here."

Jake watched her sashay away, frowning abruptly as he realized uncomfortably that there was something familiar about her. And then he knew what it was. She reminded him of Rachel. Taking a last swallow from his mug, he thrust a hand into his pocket, came up with a bill, laid it on the bar, and slipped off the stool.

Rachel shook her head at the waitress coming toward her, and slipped out the door behind him. She was furious. He'd been flirting with that woman!

She'd watched them talking and seen the smile light his face at her blatant invitation. Anger rose hotly inside her. He had no business drinking or flirting with women! He should be concentrating on finding her daughter!

Jake took a deep breath of fresh air and shook his head to clear it. What the hell was he thinking? That woman hadn't looked a thing like Rachel Dryden. Was he going out of his mind?

He'd better get his thoughts focused on the facts of the case and leave personalities out of it. Rachel Dryden was beset with worry about her daughter. And it was his job to find her—nothing more.

All he had to go on so far was the man's mother and the fact that Dryden had kept her existence a secret. And unless he could get past her anger and her own self-absorption, he'd never get anything useful out of her. He was going to have to interview the woman again, but this time, he'd keep the conversation on a level guaranteed to produce answers.

Hands in the pockets of his jacket, he moved down the deserted street in the direction of the hotel. He hoped Rachel was still asleep, because at the moment he didn't fancy answering questions about where he'd been.

As he moved through the dark, a feeling he recognized from old slowly seeped into his consciousness. His senses became more alert. He listened for certain sounds, and when he heard them, knew he was being followed.

But just to make sure, Jake made a quick dash around the next corner, then slowed to listen. The footsteps behind quickened, turned the corner, then slowed once he was in sight.

So it wasn't his imagination. Jake decided to find out who was tailing him. About midway down the block, he could see a shadow deeper than the rest. Hurrying toward it, he realized it was a space between buildings and quickly hid himself from sight. Quick footsteps followed, hesitated, then moved closer.

Jake darted out of the shadows, grabbed the culprit, taking him by surprise, and twisted both arms up behind his back.

"Okay, jerk, why are you following me? Talk!" He added pressure to the arms he already held at what he knew had to be a painful height and heard the resulting gasp with a sense of satisfaction. "Talk!" he repeated. "Why were you tailing me? What are you after?"

"I—I just wanted to know where you were going," Rachel admitted between gulps of pain. It felt like both her arms were being ripped from their sockets.

"You!" Jake dropped her arms and swung her to face him. "What the hell are you doing here? Don't you realize I could have hurt you?"

"*Could* have?" she asked indignantly. "Both my arms feel like they're broken."

"I'm sorry." Jake began to rub her shoulders, massaging the feeling back into them. "I thought I left you sleeping back at the motel. Why were you following me?"

"I..." The hard warmth of his hands had eased the pain and was now driving all coherent thought from her mind. "I wanted to see where you went." She didn't want to admit she hadn't trusted him.

"I thought you were asleep." Sensing something in her manner, he grasped her shoulders and drew her up against him, trying to get a look at her face in the dark. "Look at me."

Placing a hand beneath her chin, he tilted her face up to his. "You thought I was skipping out on you, didn't you?"

"I—"

"Don't bother lying! Women!" He threw her away from him and stalked down the street.

"Jake..." she called tentatively and then called in a louder voice, running after him, "Jake!"

What was she doing? She was alienating the only person she had to help her find Amy.

Jake slammed into the motel, took off his jacket and threw it on the bed. He was furious! And he had a right to be.

Rachel entered the room just moments behind him and closed the door softly, casting a look of apprehension in his direction. Easing slowly out of her jacket, painfully aware of the strength of his anger, she folded it neatly and placed it over a chair.

He watched her from the corners of his eyes. Damn her! Just look at her. Look at how innocent she seemed standing there with that vulnerable expression in her gray eyes. Innocent, hell!

Stalking into the bathroom, he slammed the door and locked it—*in an attempt to lock her out of his mind?*—and sat down on the narrow edge of the tub.

Damn her! Why did she do this to him? How had she managed in so short a time to get beneath his skin?

Right up until the day he'd met her, he'd prided himself on letting no one and nothing get below his guard. Except that one time...

He'd kept his pain over the mistakes he'd made to himself. Life had taught him that. He was safe as long as he adhered to one simple rule—no personal involvement.

Except that one time...

Lacy Tolbridge's face floated before his mind's eye.

He should have learned something from it. He thought he had. Yet, within twenty-four hours of knowing the woman on the other side of that door—despite his determination to the contrary—he'd become involved in her problems and spilled his own guts to her.

Damn her! Damn him!

He wanted no part of this churning feeling in his gut every time she was near—but it was there. He didn't want this anger and disappointment inside him, because she hadn't trusted him. But it was there!

He wanted to shake her, he wanted to slap some sense into her, he wanted to take her in his arms and... he blocked that thought from his mind.

Climbing restlessly to his feet, he stared at the four walls like a caged tiger. The walls began to contract around him. There was no room for what he was feeling in this small space... no room inside him for what he was feeling.

Taking a deep breath and letting it out slowly, he tried for control. He didn't want control! Running an impatient hand through his hair, he paced the room.

He didn't want control—he wanted to throw things! He wanted to break things! He wanted to destroy what was inside him, but he couldn't.

Jake took another deep breath and forced himself to relax, the fists knotted at his sides. He *could* control what he was feeling! He could crush the emotion Rachel forced him to feel. He could do it. He'd learned how to do it a long time ago, as a child.

Jake twisted a tap on the sink and doused his face with cold water, praying the roar of the water would blot the sounds in his head. It didn't work, so he lowered his head and let the running water try to wash them away. But the sounds were still with him, becoming louder all the time, and now there were images....

Grabbing a towel, he rubbed his head and buried his face in it. But the images only became more distinct...*his mother's face distorted with anger...his father...they were yelling at him—at each other—hurting him...hurting each other...*

And then it grew quiet...so quiet...except for the sounds of their labored breathing as they kissed—tore at each other's clothing...and made violent love.

"I'm not like that," Jake whispered aloud. "I'm not like them."

"Jake?" Rachel's voice snatched him from the past. "Are you all right?"

Lifting his head, he listened without answering. It was her fault. She was responsible for bringing the past back into his life. He'd been safe, sheltered from it all, until she came into his life, forcing him to remember. Because of her, pain was now his constant companion. Because of her he knew compassion. Warmth. Tenderness. Desire.

The bathroom doorknob rattled. "Jake? Are you listening? I want to talk to you. Will you please come out?"

The words had hardly left her mouth when the door swung open and Jake stood looking at her. But, now that she had his undivided attention, her tongue wanted to stick to the roof of her mouth.

"I want to apologize—"

"Don't bother." He brushed past her and walked to the center of the room. "It isn't necessary."

"It is," Rachel insisted, in no way pleased by the fact he was brushing this off—brushing *her* off—so lightly. She'd agonized over what to say, and now he wouldn't let her say it.

"Look..." He swung abruptly to face her. "During the past couple of days, it's become indisputably clear to me that it's impossible for us to work together." He was proud of the fact that his voice remained neutral.

"Over the years, I've grown accustomed to looking out for myself. I've forgotten what it is to share those instincts with a partner.

"I didn't want this job, I didn't ask for it, but you wanted me involved and whether I like it or not, I am. But I don't want . . . I can't deal with the responsibility of working with you. It would be better for both our sakes if you went home."

"No!" Rachel glared at him tautly. "You can't send me packing like some . . ." she floundered " . . . like some recalcitrant child! I won't go! Amy is my daughter—she's all I have. Don't you understand that?"

Jake shifted his weight, thrust balled hands into the pockets of his jeans and refused to back down. "I won't continue on the case if you don't agree to go home and leave me to it."

The passiveness of his expression irritated her beyond anything his anger could have caused. "How can you do this? Could you walk away if it were your daughter?" she demanded. "Could you live—go through the motions of living—each day, not knowing what was happening? Waiting for word of her safety . . . or death?"

Marching to within a foot of him, she stared up into his face. "You, of all people, should know how it feels to ache with guilt every single minute of the day." She paused. "Tell me, do you play the 'if only' game?" Something in Jake's eyes flickered. "I see you do. Well, so do I—every waking minute, I think, if only I hadn't gone to the store that night. If only I hadn't taken Amy along. If only I had been quicker—smarter—stronger."

Her nerves were at the snapping point. She swallowed the lump at the back of her throat and murmured thickly, "I should have been able to save her—*dammit*—I should have been able to save her from him."

Jake shifted his eyes to a spot above her head. He wouldn't change his mind. Nothing she could say would make him change his mind.

"The only thing keeping me going—keeping me sane—is being here with you, taking an active part in finding her. If you consign me to waiting for a phone call or the ring of the doorbell . . ."

By strength of will alone, she forced him to meet her eyes. "I'll die a little inside . . . every time the phone rings and it isn't her . . . every time there's a knock at the door and it isn't her."

She compressed trembling lips and shook her head, unable to continue for a moment. "Don't do this to me . . ." she finally gasped, closing eyes filled with a rush of hot tears. "Please don't do this to me."

Jake didn't realize he'd moved until he felt dampness beneath his fingertips. "Don't," he whispered. "Shhh. Stop crying . . . shhh . . . it's all right."

Rachel gulped and opened eyelashes stuck together by tears and in a blur saw him bending toward her.

Jake's hand slipped from her damp cheek to cup her trembling chin. He tilted her face gently up to his and wiped the tears from her cheeks with the other hand.

"Don't cry anymore," he murmured achingly and closed his lips over hers. Gathering her close, the hand at her chin slipped around to the back of her head, the fingers becoming entwined in the curls there, and urged her mouth more firmly to his.

His lips persuaded the first kiss from her, but those that followed, each one deeper and more ardent than the last, demanded a response. Fire and ice raged in his veins. One minute he flamed at the touch of her lips, her hips crammed against his, and in the next instant was shaken to his core with burning chills.

His lips and hands devoured her. The small voice of caution deep in his brain signaling for control was completely obliterated by the one urging release. The hand knotted in her hair, twisted her head so his lips could drain every ounce of passion from them.

The hand at her waist squeezed her body tighter, until their hipbones ground against each other. Jake jerked his mouth free for a quick breath, a gasping breath, before assaulting her lips once more.

He was soaring, his body was singing, vibrating with the pounding rhythm of the blood racing through his veins.

He'd never felt so alive! His heart thumped against his ribs, pounded in his temples and throbbed in his lower body.

Excitement rose with his acceptance of what he was feeling, kindling a deep hunger. He hungered for this woman like no other, hungered for the sweet taste of her lips, the feel of her soft skin beneath his fingertips, her naked body sliding hotly against his.

He'd never known this unbridled need to consume and be consumed by the sensations ripping through him and engulfing the woman in his arms. It frightened him! His need for this woman was the most frightening experience he'd ever had to face. He felt shamed, as though he'd been stripped of everything and stood naked before her...yet, he couldn't let her go.

For the first time in his life, he was taking a step without calculating the cost his self-control. And he felt complete—whole—as though he'd died and been reborn.

He felt like a child trembling on the threshold of life, with Rachel to act as his guide through the first steps. He was eager for those steps, yet, at the same time, afraid, because he could get hurt.

But Jake's passions had been repressed for too long. He had no real choice in the matter, because they would no longer be denied. Ignoring the part of him cautioning retreat, he leapt headlong toward the first stage with this woman in his arms.

Rachel felt his heat, returned his kisses and felt him mold their bodies close together, as close as their clothes would allow. Suddenly, a voice inside her cried for caution. *This was wrong!*

The feelings Jake was creating came as a shock to her—unexpected and scary. She'd never felt like this with Gary, never felt like this with anyone... until tonight.

She held back, fighting his touch, keeping her lips pressed firmly together to evade his seeking tongue. She didn't want this, didn't want to feel this terrible, seething need, this torrent of emotion he was arousing inside her.

But while she hesitated, a part of her whispered that these feelings weren't all that sudden. They'd been building since her first glance into Jake's tormented eyes. Eyes that could change in an instant from a sad lonely green, to deep stormy black.

What color were those eyes now? She didn't dare look.

"Let me go—" Wedging a hand between them, she created a narrow space and pushed against his chest.

"No," Jake responded in low, goaded tones, pressing her arms down between them and pulling her tighter against him. This had to be. There was no turning back now.

"Please." Rachel strained away from him. "You're frightening me. Let me go."

Jake loosened his hold but kept her locked against him. "Look at me," he whispered. "Look at me," he repeated when she refused to obey. She shook her head stubbornly, but Jake captured her chin and tilted her eyes to his.

Why this woman? Why now?

Jake's mouth hovered near hers, his eyes asking the questions his lips couldn't. But he found no answers in her eyes, only a reflection of his own confused state of mind.

She knew pain, but his pain went back much further than hers. It went back to the beginning of life.

Tomorrow he'd regret his lack of control, but tonight...

"What's that perfume you're wearing?" he breathed against the side of her neck, holding her head still while he took a deep whiff. "After you came to stay...I smelled it everywhere. Every time I entered a room I knew when you'd just left it."

"It's s-soap," Rachel whispered with closed eyes and clenched jaw, refusing to give in to the shivery sensations rippling down her body from the touch of his lips.

"I won't hurt you," he whispered with a catch in his voice.

"Rachel..." Her name throbbed on the air between them, driven from him by a need too great to resist. A mere thread of sound followed. "Don't hurt *me*...."

Rachel caught her breath and opened her eyes. All she could see was the curve of one shoulder and the tip of an ear, but she sensed an expectant quality in his sudden stillness. The words could have been an echo of what was in her own mind, but she didn't think so.

Suddenly, all thought of resistance left her. She'd been fighting herself every bit as hard as she'd fought him, but now she admitted that she wanted his touch—longed for it in fact.

Just for tonight, she quickly appeased her conscience, just for a little while. For tonight she'd pretend there was only the two of them in all the world and this unexpected feeling between them. Tomorrow she'd feel guilt, but tonight...

Closing her eyes, she lifted her mouth for his kiss. The kiss was slow and seeking, neither knowing what to expect from the other. She unlocked her lips and in a heartbeat it changed.

A shudder surged through Jake as he devoured her mouth with kisses. He drew her mouth into his own and rubbed his tongue against her lips, sending a message she couldn't help but understand.

Rachel felt weak. Jake's knees trembled.

"I have to lay you down," he panted hotly against her ear. Picking her up in his arms, he fell with her onto the nearest bed. His hands and lips were all over her, like a child going to the circus for the first time. He wanted it all—the excitement—the color—the sights and sounds—all at once.

His hands played over her eagerly, across the curve of her shoulders, over the fullness of breasts, down the curve of her hips and along the slender thighs. But her clothes were a barrier, an unwelcome barrier, and he was suddenly impatient to be rid of them.

Rachel helped him unfasten the buttons on her blouse. While she did that, he was pulling off her boots and socks, climbing off the bed and shedding his own. Standing in nothing but jeans, suddenly he paused to look down at her.

She was so beautiful it hurt to look at her. The pale pink blouse lay open revealing the cups of a white lace bra. While he watched, she shivered and pulled the blouse together, holding it in place, feeling suddenly shy as her glance encountered his emotion-bright eyes.

"Don't ever hide from me," he whispered abruptly with a soberness that surprised her.

"I...don't hide from people." Rachel met his glance and held it for long moments without moving. And then she raised up on her elbows and slipped the blouse off her shoulders.

Jake helped her and when she reached for the front fastenings of her bra, he was beside her on the bed. "No. Let me." The need for urgency had left him. He wanted this night to last forever.

He was close to her, so close he could see the look of fear she was trying her best to hide from him. As he eased the smooth material gently from each breast, his fingertips touched her flesh and he felt her shiver.

"What's this?" he murmured softly, running a light fingertip along a pale line on one smooth globe.

Rachel felt goose bumps raise on her skin. "A stretch mark," she replied in embarrassment. "It's from being pregnant." She raised a quick hand to cover herself. Gary hadn't liked looking at them because he felt they marred the perfection of her beauty.

"No." Jake caught her hand before she could block his view, moved it aside, and bent his lips toward the creamy skin. Taking his time, he planted kisses along the silvery line until he reached the puckered nipple which he took gently into his mouth.

Rachel closed her eyes at the first gentle tug on the sensitive flesh and bit her lip, letting the sensations his warm mouth created sweep away all feeling of embarrassment. After a moment she felt his lips leave the curve of her breast and move across her chest to close over the other puckered nipple.

By the time his head moved away, Rachel was clutching the sheet with both hands. Her eyes glowed with an inner radiance as he lifted his head and looked at her.

"Rachel..." Jake moaned, kissing her, licking her lips with his tongue, gliding a hand down her flat stomach to the snap on her jeans. "What have you done to me?" It was a cry from the heart.

"What have *you* done to *me?*" she countered, suddenly pulling him closer. Her fingers moved toward the zipper on his jeans. "Help me," she urged, and he did.

Soon they were lying naked in each other's arms, shoulder to shoulder and hip to hip. Rachel fastened her hands around his strong shoulders, slipped them down the muscular curve of his back and held him to her. She didn't want to talk anymore or try in her own mind to rationalize what was happening between them.

Tomorrow was time enough for that. Tonight, Jake Frost's burning passion had the power to block everything from her mind but the touching...the kissing...the loving....

Jake's mouth traveled slowly across her face, down the side of her neck to the hollow between her breasts and there he paused to lift his head. He met her glance and held it for a long feverish moment, but Rachel couldn't read the message in his dark, turbulent eyes. And then he blinked, leaned toward her and took her lips in a kiss so heartbreakingly tender, she felt her heart clench inside her breast.

Rachel took his face between trembling hands and kissed him back. The kiss burned with sudden urgency. She was ready for him, ready for him to fill her with his love.

But Jake held back, wanting to prolong their lovemaking. He kissed the smoothness of her stomach and beyond, teasing the sensitive skin of her inner thigh. And each touch of his hands and lips heightened her passion, igniting his own almost beyond endurance.

Rachel ran eager fingers through the soft dark curls covering Jake's chest and kissed him there. He in turn saluted her eyelids, lips, chin, both breasts, belly, and thighs. It was chilly in the room, but the heat of their combined desire could have fueled the whole city of Ft. Worth.

For the first time in his life, Jake felt truly alive and he never wanted it to end. He was like a drunk who hadn't had a drink in weeks. One sip of her wasn't enough. He wanted all of her—to know every curving inch of her lovely body.

He rode the sensations, flowed into them, gave himself over to them and let them direct his movements, much like a great maestro allows the music to flow through him and out the tips of his wand. Jake raised a hand, and the excitement inside him directed where to put it and what to do with it. He offered his lips, and they told him where to kiss. He vibrated with the pleasure of loving, as did Rachel.

He entered her at last, the veins standing out on his forehead, neck, and forearms as he moved against her in the age-old rhythm of love. Time became as nothing, while their combined moans of ecstasy filled the room.

Jake's arms began to quiver, his back to ache with strain, as his groin throbbed with the need for release. Lowering his head, his mouth sought hers, drawing every ounce of sweetness from it and into him. It renewed his strength. The muscles in his legs pumped like well-oiled pistons as he thrust his tongue into her mouth and dueled with hers.

Rachel's hands glided over the taut muscles of buttocks and thighs, pulling him to her, arching her back to his thrust as she returned his kisses with relentless passion.

They climbed, scaled the heights of sensation, reaching a fever pitch that shook them to the heart of their being. Suddenly Jake's furious movements slowed and then increased abruptly. Rachel felt everything gather inside her, as she grew tight, breathless ... waiting ...

All at once, Jake's head reared back and his body shook. He gave a final thrust as his body exploded and felt a low groan from the very depths of his soul push its way toward his lips, forcing him to clench his jaw in silent protest.

The air became filled with the sound of Rachel's unrestrained cries of fulfillment. Their bodies moved together, playing out the final moments of the act, but Jake's lips remained firmly closed, the sound of his joy locked somewhere inside them.

Exhausted, he unlocked his elbows and rested for a long moment against Rachel's heaving body. Finally, moving his lips from her curving breast, he moved and rolled onto the bed beside her. Gulping down mouthfuls of air, they lay silently touching, too overwhelmed by what they'd just shared to so much as look at each other's faces.

SILHOUETTE

AN IMPORTANT MESSAGE FROM THE EDITORS OF SILHOUETTE®

Dear Reader,

Because you've chosen to read one of our fine romance novels, we'd like to say "thank you"! And, as a **special** way to thank you, we've selected <u>four more</u> of the <u>books</u> you love so well, **and** a Victorian Picture Frame to send you absolutely *FREE!*

Please enjoy them with our compliments...

Senior Editor,
Silhouette Intimate Moments

P.S. And because we value our customers, we've attached something extra inside ...

EDITOR'S
FREE
GIFT
SEAL
THANK YOU

PEEL OFF SEAL AND PLACE INSIDE

HOW TO VALIDATE
YOUR
EDITOR'S FREE GIFT
"THANK YOU"

1. Peel off gift seal from front cover. Place it in space provided at right. This automatically entitles you to receive four free books and a lovely pewter-finish Victorian picture frame.

2. Send back this card and you'll get brand-new Silhouette Intimate Moments® novels. These books have a cover price of $3.39 each, but they are yours to keep absolutely free.

3. There's no catch. You're under no obligation to buy anything. We charge nothing–ZERO–for your first shipment. And you don't have to make any minimum number of purchases–not even one!

4. The fact is thousands of readers enjoy receiving books by mail from the Silhouette Reader Service™ months before they're available in stores. They like the convenience of home delivery and they love our discount prices!

5. We hope that after receiving your free books you'll want to remain a subscriber. But the choice is yours–to continue or cancel, anytime at all! So why not take us up on our invitation, with no risk of any kind. You'll be glad you did!

6. Don't forget to detach your FREE BOOKMARK. And remember...just for validating your Editor's Free Gift Offer, we'll send you FIVE MORE gifts, *ABSOLUTELY FREE!*

YOURS FREE!
*This lovely Victorian pewter-finish miniature is perfect for displaying a treasured photograph– and it's yours **absolutely free**–when you accept our no-risk offer!*

THE EDITOR'S "THANK YOU" FREE GIFTS INCLUDE:

▶ Four BRAND-NEW romance novels
▶ A pewter-finish Victorian picture frame

PLACE
FREE GIFT
SEAL
HERE

YES! I have placed my Editor's "thank you" seal in the space provided above. Please send me 4 free books and a Victorian picture frame. I understand I am under no obligation to purchase any books, as explained on the back and on the opposite page.

(U-SIL-IM-04/93) 245 CIS AH7P

NAME

ADDRESS   APT.

CITY   STATE   ZIP

Thank you!

THE SILHOUETTE READER SERVICE™: HERE'S HOW IT WORKS

Accepting free books puts you under no obligation to buy anything. You may keep the books and gift and return the shipping statement marked "cancel." If you do not cancel, about a month later we will send you 6 additional novels, and bill you just $2.71 each plus 25¢ delivery and applicable sales tax if any*. That's the complete price, and—compared to the cover price of $3.39 each—quite a bargain! You may cancel at any time, but if you choose to continue, every month we'll send you 6 more books, which you may either purchase at the discount price...or return at our expense and cancel your subscription.

* Terms and prices subject to change without notice. Sales tax applicable in N.Y.

For Rachel, Jake's lovemaking was an awakening experience that left her reeling. Nothing like what they'd just shared had ever been a part of her life.

As for Jake, he was too astonished to think at all. There had never been anyone even remotely in his life like this woman, with her ability to challenge his long-standing self-control almost to its limit.

The force drawing them together was very potent and raw. And it frightened them both, but on totally different levels.

Chapter 8

"Can we talk?"

Jake stood at the window holding the curtains aside, staring pensively into the darkness. At the sound of her voice, he glanced back over his shoulder to where she was lying beneath the blankets, on the bed near the bathroom door.

"I thought you were asleep."

Was that a note of irritation in his voice?

"Uh-uh," she murmured, folding the blankets beneath her arms and sitting up against the pillows. "You look exhausted..." Her voice trailed off, remembering exactly why he looked so exhausted, and she blushed a becoming shade of pink.

Jake gave her a sharp look, then went back to whatever interested him outside the room.

"Are you sorry?" she asked softly. She didn't have to explain; he understood perfectly. His answer was a slight shake of the head.

"Don't you ever sleep?" She couldn't leave it alone. He looked as though he carried the weight of the entire world on his broad shoulders and she thought maybe, if he shared his thoughts with her, it would help lighten the load.

Jake had turned off the light beside the bed so it wouldn't disturb her, and the only light in the room spilled from the partially opened bathroom door. It was enough for her to see the sudden stiffening of the muscles in his shoulders and back.

"Maybe I'm a vampire."

"You can joke about it?" she asked gravely. "Whatever drives you—drives you to the point of exhaustion—can't be all that funny." A sudden thought made her ask, "Is it the death of the child, Lacy, and her mother?"

With a spasmodic jerk on the drapes, Jake spun to face her, a shadow of anger tightening the shadowy lean jaw. She had no right to speak to him about something he'd told her in a moment of weakness.

She wouldn't be satisfied until she knew it all—every shameful secret in his past. He should never have started this. He should never have given in to the lust he felt for her and let himself go.

Rachel saw the anger but couldn't read beyond it. Her eyes moved over the growth of dark bristle covering his lower jaw and traveled slowly down his tall, muscular frame.

His body was bare except for the jeans riding low on his hips, the waistband gaping, showing a curl of dark hair. Out of the corner of her eye, she spotted the white of his underwear lying near the foot of the other bed, and her heart tripped a beat.

Jake rubbed an impatient hand across his chest, pulling her eyes toward the mass of puckered, star-shaped scars on his right shoulder and lower rib cage.

"Is that where you were shot?" she couldn't help asking.

The thought of his almost dying, even at a time when they hadn't yet become acquainted, squeezed her heart with terrible anguish. He was the only man she'd ever been to bed with besides Gary, yet he was little more than a stranger to her.

She supposed she ought to feel shamed by the knowledge, and the fact that it had happened now. But she wasn't

ashamed. She wished she had the courage to throw herself
into his arms and beg him to hold her, because that's the
only place she'd felt safe for a long, long while.

"Yes." Jake studied her with a lethal calmness.

She felt his stare and began to feel as though he wasn't
looking *at* her so much as *through* her. She squirmed and
felt something sharp poke into her hip.

Delving beneath the blankets, using the act to cover the
sudden uneasiness she felt beneath his unwavering stare, she
came up with a wide leather belt. Jake's attention immediately
became riveted on the belt.

"What is it?" she asked softly, looking from him to the
belt and back again. "What's wrong?"

Jake's eyes swerved toward her puzzled face, lingered a
moment, then dropped away. Moving stiffly toward the unoccupied
bed, he sat down. "I was kidnapped when I was
four years old," he said flatly.

"What?"

Climbing onto her knees, Rachel crawled toward the end
of the bed. She didn't know what to say. There were so many
questions she suddenly wanted to ask, but, somehow, at this
moment, they all seemed terribly inappropriate.

"How awful—I didn't know. . . ." And then she couldn't
help asking, "Is that why you have nightmares?"

Jake threw her a questioning glance, and she explained
hesitantly. "A little while ago, before you went out, you
were thrashing around on the bed . . . you cried out."

Shaking his head, he muttered, "I'm sorry if I disturbed
you."

"No!" Rachel slid off the bed in quick protest, wrapping
the sheet around her, and then stood undecided. She
wanted to touch him but sensed he wouldn't welcome her
touch.

"I wasn't sleeping, and even if I had been, it wouldn't
have mattered," she assured him earnestly, and then, after
a slight pause, asked gently, "Do you want to talk about
it?"

"No, I don't want to talk about it," he whispered tiredly.
And then he did. "When I was four years old, my nanny

took me from the house where I lived with my parents. During the kidnapping, my mother's younger brother was injured. The nightmares revolve around the accident involving him."

"Was your uncle badly injured?"

Jake shrugged.

"How long were you separated from your family?" She wanted to put all the pieces together that made up this man, and feel as though she really knew him.

"A lifetime." He almost sighed. "I was a grown man when my mother—when Janet, the woman who kidnapped me—died suddenly from a stroke. It was then that I learned about the kidnapping, from papers she'd kept hidden in her personal belongings."

"And were your parents shocked at your return after so many years?"

"They were dead by that time, killed in an accident."

"Oh, I'm sorry. Your uncle?" she asked tentatively.

"I don't know." He shrugged. "I didn't see any sense in going back after learning my parents were gone."

There had been so much tragedy in his life. If only she dared take him in her arms. "I wish there was something I could say. I feel ..." She lifted one hand in a helpless gesture, secured the slipping sheet with the other hand, and then, aching for his loss, asked, "How can you do this? How can you deal with the kidnapping of others every day of your life?"

"Therapy," he muttered, getting to his feet and moving around her toward the bathroom.

"Jake," her voice stopped him. "Maybe you should go back and see your uncle. Talk to him about what happened. You were a child. Surely, you had no part in the accident. Perhaps seeing him would stop the nightmares."

Jake turned slowly to face her. Rachel took a quick step back at the frigid expression in his storm-tossed eyes. "The accident was his fault! Janet didn't mean to hurt him. If he hadn't ..." He broke off, shaking his head. "Why am I talking about it? It doesn't matter," he muttered, "none of it matters now."

"But it does," Rachel whispered beneath her breath, watching his figure disappear into the bathroom, "it matters very much to you."

Jake closed the door and stared down at his bare toes. What a muddle. What a hell of a muddle. There was nothing he'd like better than to go back through that door and bury himself in the woman, letting the world and all its damned trouble go to hell in a hand-basket.

With her, he could forget his past, become free for the first time in his life. The sudden realization that *he could have loved her,* astounded him. It superceded all logic and reason and burned its way into his brain.

He'd never expected that. He'd never intended it to happen.

But it didn't really matter. It was too late for him. It had been too late before they'd ever met. His parents had cursed his life when he was too young to do anything about it, and he'd completed the job all on his own.

He hadn't told her about his parents. He couldn't. He didn't want to see her face when she knew the kind of people he came from. But he hadn't been able to prevent the flashbacks in his own mind, just now, while they were talking. He'd seen strobelike images of his mother and his father, their faces contorted with rage, and their unhealthy passion. And, then, he'd seen himself...with Rachel.

"So—you're back. I expected it."

"Did you?" Jake asked, giving the woman's pinched face a long, ruminating glance.

The note of triumph in Alexandra Conroy-Wilkes' voice edged his already uneven temper. Since last night, he'd kept a firm distance between himself and Rachel.

A chasm as wide as a continent lay between them at his instigation and he made no move to breach it. He told himself it was for her own good and tried to ignore every glance of unhappy confusion she cast in his direction.

Alexandra smiled sourly. "She didn't tell you anything, did she?"

"How long have you known your aunt was in a coma?" Jake asked coolly.

Alexandra raised an eyebrow at his bluntness but answered with a shrug, "A few weeks."

"You mentioned an inheritance. What, exactly, does that entail?" Jake asked abruptly.

"Money and property."

"Property?" His brain was once more seething with possibilities.

"That's right." She eyed him with a calculating expression twisting the puckered skin around her eyes. "But don't bother asking—I don't remember all the places Beaulah owned land. She got funny in her old age, decided she didn't trust the banks with her money, and started buying property all over the country."

"So, you don't really know how much money your son— I believe you said it was your son—inherited?"

"I have no idea how much money was involved, but in any case, owning land is as good as having money in the bank. Even Beaulah, senile as she was, knew that."

"When did Gary come into this inheritance?" Rachel asked suddenly.

Until now, she'd remained silent, puzzling over Jake's sudden change in behavior. But, all at once, an unpleasant idea began forming in the back of her mind, and she had to know if there was any basis for it.

The older woman made it clear she didn't like Rachel's intrusion into the conversation. Her eyes veered slowly toward the younger woman's face and she took her time answering.

"A while back."

Rachel swallowed dryly. "How long a while?"

"Let me see. . . ." Alexandra lifted a hand to her brow in pretended concentration and stared at the ceiling. "How long did you say you've been married?" She darted a pseudo-casual glance at Rachel's face.

"We're not married any longer," she answered with light emphasis, "but your son and I were married nearly six years."

"And your daughter is how old?" the old woman took pleasure in asking.

"Four. She's four years old."

Alexandra nodded as though her suspicions had been confirmed. "I understand the papers were signed at the same time I was given this condominium by my oh-so-generous aunt," she sneered. "That was about eight years ago. The papers stipulated that everything went to Gary upon her death—"

"But your aunt isn't dead," Rachel protested quickly.

"Might just as well be," Alexandra answered callously. "There was a stipulation in the will that said something about the will being validated when it became apparent that Beaulah could no longer understand what was going on. I don't know the legal term for it. Anyway, it meant Gary got everything *before* she died."

"And do you know when she officially became designated incompetent?" Jake asked softly.

"Should have been years ago, before Gary even got around her," the old woman answered tartly, "but it was only about six weeks ago. I got a letter in the mail from my aunt's lawyer—he's been my lawyer for years, too, and has kept me informed of what was happening with her estate."

Jake felt Rachel's stunned glance, but kept talking to Alexandra. "Is there someone from whom we can obtain a list of these properties your son now owns?"

"You mean you want the name of my aunt's lawyer?"

"Yes."

The old woman hesitated, glanced at Rachel from beneath half-lowered lids and asked abruptly, "What's this child called?"

Rachel blinked. "I beg your pardon?"

"The child," the other woman said impatiently, "what's her name?"

"Amelinda, Amelinda Lucille," Rachel responded softly. "Gary chose the names. But I call her Amy."

"Amelinda was my mother's name. She was Beaulah's baby sister, but there was so many years between them Beaulah was more like a mother to her than an older sister.

She named my mother, you know what the name means? It means beloved.

"All her life, my mother lived as Beaulah dictated. That included marrying my father, the man Beaulah chose for her.

"Beaulah never let me forget that—right up till the day I married Gary's father. After that, Beaulah would have nothing to do with me—not even after my husband left to go to war—not till that one summer, the summer I took Gary to her. I was prepared to beg her to keep him, while I went on tour, but I didn't have to."

The old woman pulled at a crease she'd worked into her skirt and stared at Rachel. "Gary was the spitting image of my mother. What does your Amy look like?"

"Her father," Rachel murmured through stiff lips. "She looks very much like her father."

Jake hovered near Rachel but didn't touch her. "The lawyer's name?" he asked briskly.

"There." Alexandra pointed shakily toward the desk in the corner of the room. "You'll find a card with his name and number on it there."

Jake found the card, thanked the woman for her help, and turned to escort Rachel from the apartment.

"Wait!" The old woman's strident tones halted them at the door. Jake sensed Rachel gathering herself for another attack. They turned as one.

"That summer Gary spent with Beaulah . . . well, he changed. I can't put my finger on it . . . but he was different after that.

"One thing I do know, he kept pestering me to let him go live with Beaulah. He talked about her like she was his mother instead of me." She hesitated a moment before continuing. "He talked a lot about my mother after that, too. She died when I was little more than a child myself, and he never knew her, but he talked as though he did. It gave me the willies.

"I knew, then, that Beaulah had filled his head with the same sort of obsession about my mother that she'd had herself. My mother was a beautiful, delicate creature with a voice like a nightingale. I do remember that much, and I loved her and missed her.

"But Beaulah's house was a shrine to her. There were pictures and items that had belonged to my mother all over the place. It wasn't healthy, and that was why I wouldn't let Gary stay with her again, even though she saw fit to visit us really often after that.

"I thought for a while that she kept coming around because she realized she was getting old and wanted to reconcile her differences with me. But it wasn't me she wanted—it was my son. She wanted to possess him, just like she possessed my mother."

Working the deformed fingers of one hand through those of the other, she stared down at them sadly. "I wasn't a very good mother, I admit that. But Beaulah...what she wanted to do to him—to Gary...to smother him with the past...was just plain sick."

She looked at Rachel for the first time since their meeting without malice. "He kept talking about the house they lived in that summer. I never saw it, but I know it was near a river."

"Where?" Jake asked tensely.

Alexandra glanced at him as though she'd forgotten he was even in the room. "I don't know the name of the river, but it was somewhere near Nacogdoches."

"Thank you," Jake answered for Rachel because she seemed beyond speech, and they started for the door.

Rachel was already through it when Jake turned back to the old woman. There was nothing malicious about her now. She made a pathetic picture, her body twisted and knotted with crippling arthritis, sitting alone, in the middle of the large room.

"Is there anything you need?" he asked abruptly.

Alexandra took a deep breath, hesitated, then shook her head. "No—nothing."

Grasping the wheels of the chair with difficulty she began to turn away. The only thing she truly wanted he couldn't give her. No one could. She wanted her music...her youth....

* * *

"What do you think?" Jake swung his glance in Rachel's direction. She hadn't spoken a word since they'd left her ex-mother-in-law's apartment. They were driving through Ft. Worth, through a portion of the freeway known to the locals as the Mixmaster, headed toward Dallas.

"Six weeks ago. He inherited all that property and money six weeks ago. Only two weeks before he kidnapped Amy," Rachel replied in a weak, tremulous whisper. Turning to him, she asked, "Do you think he was planning this all along? Do you think he'd have taken Amy away from me, even if we hadn't gotten a divorce?"

"I don't know." Jake shook his head. He had his own ideas about the man, and they involved a loose screw in the guy's head, but Rachel was already upset enough. "I think we should head for Nacogdoches."

"But what about the other properties?" Rachel protested. "Alexandra said her aunt—Gary rather—owns property scattered all over the country."

"You're right." Spotting a gas station he drove off the freeway and pulled up to a pay phone.

Rachel watched him place the call. Her thoughts were chaotic. She couldn't comprehend Gary's true motives for anything he'd done in the last couple of years. Had he wanted a child so he could put her in his dead grandmother's place? Rachel shivered. The idea was repugnant.

She heartily condemned Gary for taking her daughter, but until now, she'd considered it the act of an angry man, trying to get back at her. True, she'd considered him possessive of Amy to the point of being obsessive, but now...

Now she was faced with the realization that he may have been using her all along in some twisted scheme of his own to bring back the dead in his daughter's image. She'd called him crazy, but this... this was too horrible to even contemplate. Poor Amy!

"I just spoke with Gus. I gave him the name of Beaulah Conroy's lawyer. He'll get hold of the man and get us an address in Nacogdoches. He'll also get staff started checking out any other property the aunt may have had."

"We don't have to wait here, do we?" she asked, suddenly anxious to start the real search.

"No. I'll stop somewhere along the way and call in again."

They were in heavy traffic heading out of the city when Rachel spoke again. "What makes you think Gary is in Nacogdoches?"

"His mother thinks he is."

"But she doesn't know him!" Rachel insisted. "He's deceptive. Maybe that's what he wants her to think."

Jake threw her a brief glance. "Maybe you're right. But—"

"If Gary was so taken with the place, why didn't he settle there once he was grown? Why did he wait until now?"

Rachel's jacket was open. Jake saw her picking nervously at a loose thread on the black sweater she wore beneath it. She was strung out, and it was partially his fault.

She shouldn't have been at that last interview. The innuendos her ex-mother-in-law had made were guaranteed to give anyone the willies—and then there was his own part in upsetting her.

"I don't know that he has," Jake said, quickly terminating the vision of her lying naked beneath him. "I'm only following a hunch." A hunch brought about by the thought that maybe the reason Gary hadn't returned to the place before now was that he didn't yet have a daughter.

Rachel looked unconvinced, so without mentioning that last idea, he tried to explain. "Look, Gary hid the fact of his mother's existence. He thought we wouldn't find out about her, but we did. That was his first mistake.

"He thinks his past is still safe from us and that means he won't be expecting anyone to be this close to him. And that's another mistake he's made. He'll make more, and when he does—we'll have him."

He eyed her critically. "I know all this is hard on you. If you'd rather wait—"

Rachel shot him a withering glance, and he swallowed the rest of what he'd been about to suggest. The atmosphere between them became frigid as the car merged onto the interstate and headed southeast, toward Nacogdoches.

Rachel sat hunched on her side of the car, considering what they might find if Gary actually was in Nacogdoches. And Amy—what condition would she be in? The child had loved her father. Surely, he wouldn't hurt her....

Perhaps not physically, but what about emotionally? Rachel was beginning to realize she had no idea of what her ex-husband was capable, or the way in which his mind worked.

The memory of his shy smile flashed into her mind, followed by his hate-filled eyes the night he'd shoved her onto the road and threatened Amy's life. How could he have so completely fooled her—and for such a long time?

Rachel slanted an uneasy glance at Jake's stern profile. Was she making the same mistake twice? Was she letting her emotions shape this man into the image of what she wanted him to be, instead of seeing him as he really was?

Jake didn't pick up on her troubled thoughts. He was lost in an unhappy reverie of his own. He was thinking about another time, another child, and the mentally unbalanced man who'd kidnapped her. A sick feeling began to churn in his gut. As his hands grew cold, the palms stuck to the steering wheel with sweat.

Darting an uneasy look at the woman beside him, meeting her probing stare, he wondered what she was thinking. Was she, too, beginning to wonder how he'd handle the inevitable showdown with her ex-husband?

"Are you hungry?" The lights of the city were coming into view.

Rachel sat up straighter in the seat and shook her head. "I'll just be glad to stretch my legs."

Jake nodded. "Let's get a place to stay for the night first, and then, if you change your mind, we'll get something to eat later."

The Round-Up Motel was expensive. Jake felt like he owed Rachel that, after the accommodations she'd suffered in silence since their first meeting.

This time there was no problem getting separate units and from the look on her face, he figured she was as relieved as he felt about it. They separated immediately.

Jake took a long, hot shower, then hunted down a Chinese restaurant that served excellent tea. He took the drink and a sack of food back to the motel.

"You like Chinese?" He held the sacks up for her inspection when she opened the door at his knock.

"Yes, I like Chinese food," she answered, moving back so he could enter the room.

They ate heartily, Rachel displaying an appetite she hadn't showed up to now. When the carton was empty, she laid down her chopsticks and took a long sip of hot tea, watching Jake deftly maneuver the last of the Peking duck to his mouth.

"You're very good with those." She indicated the chopsticks.

"I learned the art of eating Chinese food from an elderly man I met in Hong Kong."

"You've traveled in the Orient?"

"I spent some time over there."

"Did you travel for business or pleasure?"

"Both."

He began to gather the empty cartons and stuff them in the brown paper bags. It was obvious he didn't want to discuss his travels with her.

"That was very good." She eyed her own empty carton with a rueful eye. "I was hungrier than I thought. Thank you," she added with a smile.

"You're very welcome."

He glanced up, and for a split second she could have sworn a smile hovered around the corners of the firm mouth. A sudden sound from outside shattered the fragile moment. The remote expression he'd worn since coming out of the bathroom last night was once more rigidly intact on his rugged face.

"Have you been able to reach Mr. Davison?" So far, his attempts hadn't met with success.

"Yes. And I wrote down the address he gave me. I also learned there isn't any money. What was left of it—what Beaulah Conroy didn't use to purchase land—was used up a long time ago on medical bills."

"So Gary hasn't any money?"

Jake threw the paper bags in the trash and took his seat at the table. "I think we have to consider the possibility that your ex-husband will go back into teaching."

Rachel looked startled. "Teaching?"

"Yes. It's what he knows best. He won't want to draw undue attention to himself by attempting a new line of work. He's a teacher, and that's what he'll do, if he needs money."

"But what about the property? If there's as much land as Alexandra said, it has to be worth a great deal of money."

"True, but first, he has to sell it."

"Teaching," Rachel mused. "You mean it's going to be as easy as that? We just go to the school board and find him?"

"I doubt it," Jake answered indulgently. "He's probably changed his appearance, and he won't be using his real name. It isn't hard to get falsified documents."

"You mean he'll be using an assumed name?"

"Probably."

"I don't care how many different names he uses, or what kind of a disguise he's wearing, I'd know him anywhere. Let's get started. We can start calling members of the school board right now—"

"Whoa—wait a minute." She was rummaging around in the desk looking for a local telephone book.

"What?" She cast an impatient glance over her shoulder as she straightened with the blue and white book in one hand.

"We can't go waking up people at ten o'clock at night to ask if they know a teacher who fits the general description of your ex-husband. We'll get a whole lot more cooperation if we wait until morning."

"I suppose you're right," she agreed reluctantly. "But it won't hurt to get a list made of the schools in the area, so we can get a early start."

They wrote down every possibility: colleges, junior colleges, elementary schools, middle and high schools, private and public. It was close to midnight when Jake set a cup of coffee on the table in front of Rachel.

"I don't know how good it'll taste, it's instant. The package was in the drawer over there, and I used hot water from the bathroom sink."

"Thanks." Rachel took a sip, made a slight face, and took a large gulp of the lukewarm brew. Looping a strand of hair back behind one ear, she set the cup down and stretched. "Oh—"

"What's wrong?"

"A crick in my neck." Turning her head this way and that, she rubbed at the back of her neck.

"Let me." Jake was behind her. "Hold your hair out of the way," he murmured softly.

"No, that's all right—"

"Take hold of your hair," he said with quiet emphasis.

Rachel twisted the mass of curls in a bunch with one hand and held them atop her head. Taking an unsteady breath, she waited for his hands to begin kneading the soreness at the back of her neck. After a few moments, her eyes drifted shut.

Warmth and a sense of well-being spread through her. The gentle motion of his hands gradually worked their way down toward her lower neck and across to her shoulders.

Rachel felt the tension slowly drain from her body. And as her muscles relaxed, so did her mind. Giving herself over to his skillful hands, she let her thoughts float amid clouds of tranquillity. Her head began to nod languidly on her shoulders.

"Loosen your sweater."

The low, husky tones sent a sudden shiver of awareness surging through her. For a moment she couldn't move, and then, as though in a trance, she raised a hand to the top of the three buttons down the front of the sweater and loosened the first one. Her fingers moved again, continuing until the sweater lay open to the tops of her breasts.

Jake's position behind and above her gave him a perfect view of her creamy breasts and the shadowy hollow between. A jolt of desire hit him, so strong his hands tightened involuntarily on her shoulders, hurting her.

She moaned. He whispered, "Sorry," and loosened his grip. But the feeling moving through him was so intense that the sensation of his jeans rubbing against his flesh caused him immediate embarrassment.

He floundered. His hands stilled. Rachel moved as though to turn toward him and Jake hurriedly began to knead her flesh once more.

"Tell me about your daughter," he managed in a sterile voice.

"What would you like to know?"

He was beginning to get himself under control. All he had to do was concentrate on something besides the fresh, clean scent emanating from her body—the sight of her breasts— the feel of her soft skin....

"Whatever you want to tell me," he answered quickly, causing her to frown at the uneven sound. Again, she made as though to turn toward him and again he held her in place with the rhythmic movement of his hands.

"Well," she began, "you know what she looks like from the pictures I've shown you. You know she has dark, curly hair and large dark eyes. What you don't know is the way her eyes crinkle and almost disappear in her cheeks when she laughs, or that she has a tiny scar at the corner of her mouth—"

"Scar?"

"Yes, she fell and cut her lip when she was first learning to walk. It left a scar. There's a scar about an inch long on the back of her head, where hair won't grow—"

"How did she get that?"

His voice sounded odd. "She fell out of a swing in the park—"

"Were you with her when it happened?"

"Yes, of course I was."

"Then, how did it happen?"

"I was just turning to answer a question from a friend, and she fell. I remember how upset I was, because she was wearing a new, white dress and there was blood everywhere."

"You were upset about her dress?"

"Yes, it was a birthday present and the blood wouldn't come out."

"Did you take her to the doctor?"

"Doctor? No, it wasn't that serious. Head wounds bleed a lot, but that doesn't make them dangerous, at least that's what the doctor said when I called him. He told me to watch her to make certain she didn't have a concussion and keep her quiet the rest of the day."

"But you didn't take her in to be examined?"

"No—" Rachel sounded uncertain.

"Did she get . . . hurt, a lot?"

"A lot?" Rachel frowned. "No, no more than any other child her age."

He didn't have a child. He couldn't know what it was like, having all that responsibility. You couldn't run to the doctor every time a child fell down. She tried explaining a little of what it was like, being a parent.

"When she was three, she went through a period where I thought I was going to have to padlock all my cabinets, or else tie her hands together and tie her to the bed at night.

"She would get up in the middle of the night and take everything out of the cabinets and pile it all in the middle of the kitchen floor. The doctor said she was hyperactive and put her on medication for a while."

"I imagine that must have been very frustrating for you."

"It was."

"Did you ever . . . spank her?"

"Sometimes . . ." All at once she felt uncomfortable beneath his hands and became aware of a kind of tension transmitting itself from him to her. Pulling away, she swiveled around to face him. "Why do I feel like I'm getting the third degree?"

Jake shrugged, dropped his hands, and moved away.

"What is it you want to know?" she demanded, becoming suddenly angry, following him with her eyes. "If there's something you want to ask, come right out and ask it."

When he didn't answer, and kept his back to her, something clicked far back in her mind. "You think I abused her," she accused in a shattered voice. "You think I deliberately hurt my own child? My God ... my God ..."

A feeling of guilt stabbed at her. She looked at Jake's rigid back through a glaze of tears.

Was it that obvious? Had he looked into her heart and found the guilt buried there?

"Did I? Did I abuse her?" She bit her lip painfully, trying to hold back a sob. "I smacked her hands sometimes, when she got into things she shouldn't. And sometimes, I was sharp with her, when things were ... getting bad between her father and I. And I made her eat vegetables she didn't like, because they were good for her."

A hot tear rolled down her cheek, hesitated on the curve of her upper lip, then rolled into her mouth. *And worst of all*— "I couldn't stop her father from taking her. He hit me—shoved me from the car. She was crying ... I can still hear her crying—"

"That's enough!"

Jake was across the room, pulling her from the chair and into his arms. He held her, feeling her body tremble against his, heard her wracking sobs, and heaped coals of fire on his own head for bringing her to this.

"I'm sorry," he murmured against her hair. "I'm sorry. I know you're a good mother. I know you are. Don't cry anymore. I was a bastard to suggest—"

"No—I wasn't a good m-mother ..." Rachel hiccuped. "If I'd been a g-good mother he'd have never got his hands on my little girl. It's my f-fault he has h-her."

She pulled away, eyes bordered with tears, to look up into his face and ask with a dreadful anxiety, "What am I g-going to do? How can I live with myself if he ... h-hurts her?"

Chapter 9

Jake felt Rachel stir against him. With gentle fingers he brushed the hair back from her face. She'd cried herself to sleep in his arms after his bungled attempt to determine the kind of mother she'd been before the kidnapping.

Why did he search so hard to find something to denigrate her in his eyes? Was he afraid to admit that she might be the genuine article, a good mother?

One thing was certain, she loved her child very much. He didn't know if that meant she was a good parent or not. In his lifetime, he'd seen a lot of pain and sadness visited upon people in the name of love.

He had no idea whether his own parents had loved him. And he didn't know if he'd ever loved them. During the time he'd been in their care, he'd been too frightened of them to think about love. Love was a commodity he had little acquaintance with—except for Janet. It always came back to Janet.

Looking back now, he wasn't even certain she'd done him a service by taking him from his parents. The damage had already been done. He was so confused about everything....

It had been easier when he was four years old and didn't know the differences between his life and that of other kids his age. A time when he didn't know that all boys and girls his age weren't whipped until the skin on their legs, buttocks and back was one solid welt of burning pain. Or that other children were allowed to watch television, and had birthday parties and friends over to play.

And it wasn't until Janet that he'd learned what it was to taste chocolate—and how he'd paid for that new experience. But he'd thought it worth it at the time, just as he'd thought all the other experiences Janet had introduced him to in the next six months had been worth the beatings and harsh words he'd had to endure afterward.

He'd been young, but not too young to learn cunning that year, and he'd kept secret what he and Janet did during the day when both his parents were at work. There were no happy times spent around the dinner table in his house, talking about what everyone had done while they been apart that day.

And when his mother learned about the picnics and the ice-cream cones, Jake had paid for it, dearly. But, he'd kept that to himself, too, kept it from Janet. Instinct had warned him that if Janet ever found out about what his mother and father were like when she wasn't around, he'd lose her. And he couldn't take that chance.

Gradually, however, little things became known to her. And the day she kept him in bed, because his mother had informed her he had a cold and wasn't to get up, she'd discovered the terrible truth.

She discovered that he lay on his stomach in bed, because he couldn't stand to lie or sit on the painful bruises covering his back, buttocks, and legs. He'd had to plead with her, cry and beg her not to go to his parents, because he knew that somehow they'd get rid of her if she did.

His fear had finally gotten though to her, and Janet had promised she wouldn't say anything about what she'd seen, but he knew she did. Later that night, he heard a row between his parents about it. His mother had wanted to get rid of Janet immediately, but his father had urged caution.

What if she went to the authorities? he'd asked. At the time Jake hadn't understood the meaning of the word authorities, but whatever it was, it had made his mother keep Janet on as his nanny, and that's all that he'd cared about.

Rachel hiccuped in her sleep and Jake held her closer, trying to picture her as a mother. Could he see her beating the child, Amy, with a belt? No, he couldn't. Nor could he see her denying the child the joys of childhood like picnics and birthday parties.

But it was so hard to judge. His parents must have had friends who genuinely thought *they* were good parents, too.

What kind of a family life had Rachel, her daughter and husband enjoyed before the man's sickness began to make itself known? Had they done things together? Vacations? Visited the zoo?

Jake stroked the side of Rachel's neck absently, staring at the ceiling, thinking about the zoo. It was the last outing he and his parents had made together before Janet had taken him away, and the reason he had been confined to bed that morning.

They had gone to the Indianapolis Zoo for the day. It was an attempt at proving to Janet their family was a normal one. She'd been brought along to keep an eye on him, so his parents could enjoy themselves without worrying about his getting lost.

The day had been warm and sunny, a typical Indian-summer day in mid-September. Jake was looking forward to the outing with excitement. He'd never been to the zoo, and he wanted to see if the animals really lived outside of cages just like people, the way they did in his picture books.

His mother and father were both in good spirits. They were smiling and laughing and that made him feel good, too, even though he knew his mother's mood could change in an instant. He'd been extra careful to see that he did nothing to upset her. He'd been careful not to spill anything in the car, to keep his feet off the seats, and not to chatter during the long ride.

But he was so excited, it was hard to sit still. His mother and father had been talking about getting a dog. They wanted it for security, but Jake remembered the lovable sheepdog he'd wandered off to pet a while back and envisioned something along those lines.

As they left the car, Janet tentatively suggested that she and Jake go off on their own and meet his parents at the gate at a prearranged time. Jake's mother had informed her curtly that she and Jake could not wander around the zoo at will. She had been brought along for the purpose of keeping him with them. They would stay within sight of her and her husband.

At first, Janet had made a great effort to comply with the command. She pointed out the animals and made an effort to tell Jake a little bit about each one. But his parents weren't interested in his enjoyment, and gradually, he and Janet had fallen behind.

When Janet realized what had happened, she began to panic. It wasn't herself she was concerned about, but she'd discovered by now, that though Jake's mother might be cold to her, she was downright cruel to the little boy.

The only reason she hadn't left was Jake. She'd grown to love the little boy and couldn't simply walk away, leaving him to the woman's mercy. She was shortly to learn just exactly how cold and calculating the woman could be.

She and Jake were apprehended by the police as they neared the front entrance to the zoo, and Janet learned she had been accused of kidnapping. His mother had hysterically insisted the police be called when she realized her son and nanny were no longer in sight, crying that she just knew her baby had been taken away to be held for ransom.

Janet and Jake were taken to the police station. Jake's mother had been taken to the hospital, prostrate with grief.

At the police station, Janet explained what had happened, and then had to explain again, when Jake's parents arrived to identify the two. Everything was cleared up, but Janet saw and understood the triumphant message at the back of the older woman's eyes. It was very clear—she won and she would always win against the likes of Janet.

It might well have been that incident, Jake realized now, that had put the idea of the kidnapping into Janet's mind.

But, it didn't matter now—that was all in the past and everyone involved, except for himself, was gone.

Eyes burning with exhaustion, he blinked, rubbed a hand across his closed lids, and wished it was as easy to forget as he constantly told himself it was. But the memories had a way of invading his mind and turning up in what sleep he could manage to find.

Rachel stirred, murmured something in her sleep and rolled against him, putting an arm across his chest and a knee over his leg. A moment later, she was once more deeply asleep.

Resting his chin against the top of her head, he tried to still the longings beginning to stir at her intimate touch. Out of the blue, he found himself wondering what a child of theirs would look like.

The thought stunned him. He'd never before considered becoming a parent. Knowing the disaster of his own childhood, parenthood was something he shied away from, even in his thoughts. But now, suddenly, he found himself trying to picture himself as a father. Would he be a good one?

Shifting his arm beneath Rachel's head, he glanced into her serene countenance and seriously considered the possibility. Would he enjoy spending time with his child, taking him or her fishing, to baseball games, to the movies?

Or would he turn out like his own parents? That thought alone should have been enough to wipe the idea from his brain. But once seeded, it grew.

If Rachel were the mother...

Of its own accord, Jake's arm tightened around Rachel, bringing her closer. Turning onto his side, he slipped a knee between both of hers, drawing closer to her warmth. Her breath mingled sweetly with his as he gently eased toward her.

He knew he should go to his own room. He'd let things get out of hand between them once already, and all it had done was to confuse him even more. Yet, for a little while, she made him forget....

He studied her mouth. It was so innocent-looking in sleep. He strained toward her. He needed her. A hand cupped her jaw, skimmed along the smooth line of her cheek, tested the silkiness of her hair, and came back to touch the fullness of her bottom lip.

His glance dropped to the front of her sweater and lingered on the pale skin of her breasts. Dipping his head, he brushed the tops of both breasts with a gentle caress.

Rachel stirred against him, murmured something he didn't catch and licked her lips. Jake's eyes followed the movement of her small pink tongue and felt excitement stir anew.

Bending quickly, he touched the moistness on her lips with the tip of his own tongue. Rachel's eyes fluttered as he drew away to look down at her face.

"Is it morning?" she formed the words lazily.

Jake shook his head.

"Is something wrong?" she asked, slowly becoming more alert.

Again he shook his head and Rachel's glance concentrated on the expression in his hazel eyes. They were changing, turning a deep sea-green. Her glance moved from them to his lips. She faintly recalled dreaming that he had kissed her.

Her eyes were moving back up to his when all at once his face became an indistinct blur. His mouth covered hers hungrily while the arm beneath her locked her to him. After a moment the hunger gentled and his lips played with hers, caressing them slowly, drawing from her every ounce of sweetness she was willing to give.

Rachel's body began to tingle. She was conscious of every inch of his long frame nesting intimately against hers. And when his knee moved, she caught her breath and pressed closer.

Of their own accord, her arms slid along his hips, up his chest to his shoulders, smoothed the muscles there, then moved around to slide through the hair at the back of his neck. Her lips parted willingly for his tongue, tested and matched its explorative touch.

Jake's palm covered one puckered nipple as he eased her gently over onto her back. His lips traveled to the underside of her chin and along her throat to the open collar of her sweater.

"Take it off," he whispered against her mouth.

Rachel eased the sweater up to her shoulders with Jake's help and then pulled it from her head. Her hands went to the front fastening of her bra while her eyes met his and asked a question.

His answer was plain to see. She loosened the bra and slipped it from her body. Jake took it from her and dropped it to the floor.

In minutes his clothes along with the rest of hers had soon joined it. They lay in each other's arms. Their movements were slow. They took time to explore, to arouse, to give each other pleasure.

Outlining the tips of her breasts with one finger, Jake leaned suddenly forward and kissed the taut nipples, rousing a melting softness within her. Rachel arched her body to his lips, raked her hands down his back and pulled him against her.

"Now," she moaned, "make love to me now."

"I am," he whispered against her moist skin, trailing kisses to her flat stomach, dipping his tongue into the hollow of her navel and feeling her shiver against him. "I am...."

His hands skimmed her hips and moved up the inside of her thighs. Set aflame by his touch, Rachel quivered with the heat of desire, then shivered as though encased in a sheet of ice.

He entered her slowly and the world exploded in waves of pure ecstasy. His lips captured hers, his tongue entered her mouth and his hands palmed both breasts, working their magic on all of her at once.

The feelings became so intense Rachel moaned between kisses, alive with sensation, melting, flowing, dissolving into him. She drove to meet his passion, stroked his tongue with hers, held him tight within her, and quivered with elation. She'd never felt like this, never felt anything remotely like this in all her life.

Heat rippled beneath Jake's skin, shot in flames from his fingertips, from the tip of his tongue, from his whole body. He became liquid with it, swirling and eddying within the bounds of his frame, pouring into the woman beneath him, joining with her, until they became one.

Suddenly he tensed. For a moment his body stilled, as if not even his heart beat, and then it was like a live thing let loose inside him that had to be free. He moved, and the whole world came crashing down on top of him. He was caught in a vortex, eddying, spinning, whirling, out of control.

Lifting his head from Rachel's mouth, he drew breath into burning lungs and cried out. Gone was his control. He had to let loose what he was feeling, or he'd explode. The sound echoed around the room, mingling with Rachel's cries of delight.

At last he relaxed, breathing in short, sharp gasps, and lay against her, feeling his heart thunder against his ribs. Nothing, not even the last time they'd made love had been so...soul shattering.

Jake lifted himself away from Rachel to lie on the bed at her side with closed eyes. The blood rushed through his body as he continued to feel a sense of exhilaration—and of defeat.

The harder he tried to ignore the truth, the more it persisted. His passions were strong, too strong for him to control, and they centered on this woman.

He'd never been a man of...passion. The word evoked nauseating pictures of his parents.

Despite the kind of work he'd chosen, Jake had always considered himself a pacifist, a man who measured his feelings in terms of what was right and what was wrong. Again, he blamed Rachel for his inability to control his emotions whenever he was around her, and he knew that as long as he stayed within her circle, it would only get worse.

Jake awakened slowly and focused his eyes on the ceiling. For a moment, he didn't know where he was and realized with a shock that it was because he'd slept so soundly.

Memory surfaced. He was in his own unit at the motel, and suddenly panic rose up in him. He remembered the night before and the lovemaking. This growing need for Rachel Dryden, and the ferocity of his passion, unnerved him. He tensed, feeling a swift, compelling need to get away from her—but he couldn't, not until his job was finished.

Dragging himself from bed, feeling a weakness of limb that embarrassed him, knowing its source, he strode into the bathroom. There, he gazed at himself in the mirror, shocked by what he saw.

For the first time in months, there was a notable lessening of the desperation he'd grown accustomed to seeing in his eyes. The lines around nose, eyes and mouth appeared less severe.

Holding on to the sink with both hands, he dropped his head and closed his eyes to shut out the sight of his own face. What was she doing to him? He knew he should be glad of the changes, and part of him was. But the old fear as bitter as gall was still with him—would always be with him. *What if he turned out to be like his parents?*

After a while, when he thought he had himself in hand, Jake showered, shaved, and then examined the stitches on the palm of his hand. The skin was knitting. He changed the bandage, trying hard to ignore the ghost of Rachel standing at his shoulder, studying the cut with a horror she tried hard to hide while she attended to the hand.

Throwing the roll of bandage and unused tape into his bag, Jake wiped the image of the woman from his mind. Everything came back to her, since he'd met her. It always seemed to come back to *her.*

What was he going to do when this case was over and she was no longer a part of his life?

A couple of hours later, Jake made his way to her room carrying a carafe of coffee. During his absence, Rachel had awakened, showered and dressed.

"Good morning." She greeted his surly expression with a tentative smile. "And thank you for the coffee."

Jake's reply was a grunt. He sipped his own coffee without quite meeting her eyes. The events that had taken place in this room last night were too recent and too disturbing for him to be comfortable with her there.

"Are we ready to get started?" she asked with an enthusiasm that irritated Jake all to hell. She seemed totally unaffected by what had recently taken place between them. It had been a momentous occasion for him—he wasn't certain exactly in what manner, but he knew that, somehow, it had changed him—and the fact that she appeared no different, angered him.

Tearing his glance from her eager face, Jake took no little pleasure in replying, "I have to make an official call on the local sheriff before we can do any investigating in his town. It's protocol," he explained a moment later, expecting an objection, and much to his surprise, getting none.

Since it was close to noon on a Sunday morning, Sheriff Benjamin Langly wasn't easy to find. The office was closed and the emergency radio dispatcher next door said he'd gone to church with his family. The woman suggested they might go have breakfast and return later, but after one look at Rachel's face, Jake told her they'd stick around and wait.

Two hours later, when a tall man, dressed in jeans, shiny boots, a dress shirt and suit coat, wearing a black Stetson, walked through the glass door with another man dressed in the traditional beige uniform of the sheriff's department, Rachel knew immediately that the taller man must be the sheriff. There was an air of command about his militarily correct figure that made his position unmistakable.

She hung back, intimidated by the man's stern mien, listening to him and Jake talk, offering nothing herself. While their voices registered somewhere at the back of her mind, Rachel studied Jake.

Something was different about him this morning, but she couldn't quite put her finger on it. This new perception of the man warred with her fear that Amy was slipping away from her. She knew she ought to be concentrating on nothing but her child, because the longer Amy remained in her father's custody, the more Rachel feared losing her forever. But something unexpected was happening between Rachel and Jake, and she couldn't seem to stop it or slow it down.

Jake introduced himself to the sheriff, apologized for calling him out on a Sunday, then broached the subject of his missing credentials. "If you'll call this number in Washington—" Jake handed him a piece of paper "—my identity will be confirmed to your satisfaction."

Ben Langly accepted the paper and excused himself to go to his office to use the phone. When he came back, he returned Jake's look and said, "Well, you're who you say you are, but that doesn't tell me what you want from me."

"I'm looking for a man by the name of Gary Raymond Dryden. He's wanted for the kidnapping of his four-year-old daughter. Mrs. Dryden—" Jake indicated Rachel "—was awarded sole custody of the child during a recent divorce. Dryden has made serious threats against both his ex-wife and his daughter's life.

"We have reason to believe he may be in Nacogdoches, possibly using an assumed name. The man has a background in education, and I figure he'll probably stay in teaching, if he decides to go back to work.

"We're in town because there's a piece of property located somewhere near here that he's recently inherited. He could be living there with the little girl."

"Where's the property?" Sheriff Langly asked.

Jake took the spiral notebook from his pocket and read off the address to the man.

"That's quite a ways out—about halfway to the town of Alto and right on the Angelina River. How did you come into town—down the El Camino Real?"

"I came down Highway 21," Jake responded.

"That's it. Hell, you probably passed the turnoff to the old Conroy place on your way here. I grew up on a ranch near there. Not much in the way of civilization."

Jake nodded his agreement, remembering the last twenty-five miles before reaching Nacogdoches. The few houses they'd passed along the way had mostly been abandoned.

"You know," Sheriff Langly said thoughtfully, "there's an unfinished development out that way, about ten miles from the lake. A builder from out of town bought up the land and started it a few years back, then he went bust before it got off the ground, and it's been sittin' there, nothin' but an eyesore and collecting trouble ever since.

"Every now and then," he explained, "we get a few winos and vagrants out that way. They like to use the place to sleep off their drunks. Trouble is, fire's a real hazard in this country, and they don't much care where they drop a match. So, we try to keep an eye on the place.

"If you don't find your boy at the house, you might try giving that place a once-over. Or I can send a couple of deputies out that way—"

"I'll check it out," Jake said quickly, "we want to keep a low profile. In the meantime, here's what I have on Dryden." He handed the sheriff a file. "There's a photo inside. He's been on the run with the child about a month, so he may have changed his appearance somehow."

Sheriff Langly took the folder and studied Gary Dryden's photograph. He began to read the particulars and after a moment, still reading, walked toward the other side of the room. Jake watched him motion for the deputy he'd arrived with, give him some quick instructions, and hand him the file.

"Is he going to help us?" Rachel asked suddenly at Jake's elbow.

"He'll help us," Jake replied, turning toward her.

"I've got the ball rolling," Sheriff Langly spoke from behind Jake's shoulder. "But it is Sunday, you know, and most folks go to church and then with friends and family for a big Sunday dinner. You won't get much done around here before Monday morning."

Rachel looked as though she wanted to protest, but Jake nodded his understanding of the situation.

"I'll send a picture around to all the schools Monday morning and ask for information concerning anyone who fits the description," Sheriff Langly said. He looked at Rachel and asked, "Is there anything we need to be know about your daughter, ma'am?"

Rachel looked blank and the sheriff explained, "She hasn't any medical conditions that might require a medical team on standby?"

"No. She's perfectly healthy," Rachel assured him.

"The warrant?" Jake asked.

"I'll have a judge standing by—"

"What warrant?" Rachel interrupted, looking from Jake to the sheriff.

"A third-degree felony warrant will be issued for your husband's arrest," Sheriff Langly explained. "It can only be issued by a judge, but it can't be issued until we actually have your husband within sight."

"Caution your deputies to be very circumspect around the schools," Jake said to the other man. "I don't want Dryden to know we're closing in and manage to slip through our fingers before we get him in custody. His four-year-old daughter's life may be at stake."

"I'll warn them," the sheriff promised.

"Excuse me, sir." The young deputy stood at the man's elbow. "Here's the file. We've made copies of all the documents."

Langly took the file and handed it to Jake.

"Thanks." Jake held out his hand and the other man shook it. "Mrs. Dryden and I will take a trip out to the Conroy place and we'll check around the abandoned housing developement, too."

Langly nodded, picked up a pencil, and began to draw a series of lines on a piece of paper that quickly took on the appearance of a map. "This should get you to there."

Jake took the map, glanced at it briefly, then folded it and put it in the inside pocket of his dark blue suit jacket. "Thanks."

The sheriff nodded and watched them move toward the door. "Oh, by the way," he called halting the pair, "you got a number where I can reach you?"

Jake gave it to him, and they left.

"Monday morning," Rachel protested once they had left the sheriff's office, "that's a whole twenty-four hours away. Gary could be long gone by then—with Amy!"

Twenty minutes later, Jake turned down a dirt road bordered by trees on one side and the brown, swollen, Angelina River on the other. The trees were all crowded together and even without the cover of leaves, made the forest appear dense.

Rachel stared at their bare branches as they slid by the car and felt a chill spread through her. "I don't like this place," she murmured, on a mere thread of a whisper.

Jake heard the comment but made no reply. His attention was concentrated on his driving, because he didn't want a broken axle or a flat tire. Over the years the road to the house had been narrowed by thick overgrowth, and deep ruts caused by years of neglect now cratered its surface.

The house was a large, sprawling, two-story Queen Anne replete with towers, turrets, arches, chimneys and bay windows. At one time it might have looked majestic, but now it looked old, worn-out, and just a little bit sinister.

The windows were boarded up, and the porch sagged. Jake doubted anyone had been inside it for a long time, but he couldn't afford to dismiss it without an inspection.

"You getting out?"

Rachel gave the house an apprehensive glance from eyes shaded with disappointment and shook her head. Somehow, she knew Gary wasn't here.

Half an hour later, Jake resumed his seat behind the wheel.

"Well?" she asked when he didn't immediately offer a observation.

"Someone has been here, but I can't tell how long ago. There's a lot of junk inside, old furniture and drapes and things. But not much else. And it doesn't look as though anyone has actually stayed here, except, maybe overnight to get in out of the rain."

"I knew it," she muttered softly.

"Still, I think I'll have Sheriff Langly put a man out here, if he can spare one, just in case."

Their next stop was the aborted housing development. There were only three actual structures, houses that had been abandoned in the final stages of completion. Others had been laid out and foundations poured, with holes left where the pipes for water and sewage would have gone, but no buildings existed. You could see streets had been planned, but all that remained were strips of hard packed earth, ravaged by the elements.

Jake drove down the nearest street where the three houses stood a few hundred yards apart. "You stay here," he instructed this time, "and lock the doors."

Rachel did as she was told, uneasy about the somber tone of his voice. What did he expect to find? For the first time, she wondered if he had a gun.

When he returned, she scooted across the seat and unlocked the door for him. "Well?" she asked anxiously.

"There are signs that someone has been here recently, but I seriously doubt it was your ex-husband. There were cheap wine bottles all over the place and a half-burned blanket."

"Gary doesn't drink," Rachel said tonelessly, while Jake backed the car out and drove carefully onto the highway.

It was a shadow of her formerly eager self who watched the lights of the motel come into view.

"What about something to eat?" Jake asked as they pulled into the space in front of Rachel's room.

"I'm not hungry," she replied dismally. Glancing up at the clouds on the horizon, noting that more rain appeared to be on the way, she added, "I think I'll take a nap. This weather isn't good for much besides sleeping."

Jake watched her climb from the car, fit her key in the lock and close the door. Was she blaming him because they hadn't yet found a trace of her ex-husband?

The thought of sitting alone in his room, staring at the television, or the four walls, held no appeal. After making a quick call to the sheriff to tell him what they'd found and suggesting he have someone keep an eye on the old Conroy house, Jake decided to take a walk.

His walk took him past the Old Stone Fort Museum located on the Stephen F. Austin University campus. It had been the combined home and business of one of East Texas' most famous smugglers, Antonio Gil Ybarbo, during the 1700s.

Jake paused beneath the trees and contemplated the stone structure. In its time, it had served as a trading post, the seat of government, a prison and a fort. The first two newspapers published in Texas had also been published there.

He might have gone inside, just to take his mind off his troubles, but it was late Sunday evening and the place was closed.

He resumed his walk and his thoughts returned to the woman he'd left brooding behind a locked, motel-room door. What would happen once her child was found? The question aroused old fears and uncertainties. What would he do? How would he handle the showdown with Gary Dryden?

A cold knot formed in the pit of his stomach as a pair of trusting blue eyes flashed into his mind. Jake's steps quickened. Fear gnawed at his insides. What if he was faced with an unreasoning man determined to make good the threat he'd made against the child's life? Could he stop him?

Jake moved along the street at a faster pace. The precarious hold he'd been able to maintain on his emotions wobbled. He couldn't handle it—he couldn't handle the thought of another child dying because of him!

If only she hadn't come to him. If only he hadn't agreed to listen to her! He was almost running now, hurrying to get away from his past, from the mistakes he'd made, from the memories that still haunted him.

If only . . .

All at once Jake's steps slowed. *If only . . .* The words rang in his mind. Rachel had mentioned the if only game she played in her head, and now he realized he was doing it, too.

Rachel's guilt was only in her mind. There had been nothing she could do to save her daughter from being taken by her ex-husband. Jake wished his own guilt was so easily propitiated.

But he knew the nature of his guilt, and nothing could save him from it. Not even a woman with long brown hair, a madonnalike beauty, and a gentleness he was beginning to crave more than life itself.

Chapter 10

Jake with Rachel at his side, made the rounds the next day, going from school to school, showing Gary's picture to teachers, school custodians and even school bus drivers, asking the same question. "Have you seen this man?"

But the answer was always the same. No one had seen a man of Dryden's description within the school system, either now or in the past. And then, at a small junior college, they struck pay dirt.

"May I see that photograph again?" Myra Templeton asked with narrowed eyes. She was the college staff coordinator and knew all the instructors on the school's roster by sight.

Jake handed it to her. "Take your time, and remember, he could look a little different now. He may have cut his hair, or changed the color of it and he could be wearing glasses."

"What about a beard?" the older woman asked thoughtfully. "Did he ever have a beard?"

Jake looked at Rachel and she shook her head. "It's possible that he may have decided to grow one."

He could feel excitement trembling just below the surface and got a quick grip on it. This was the first person who'd asked for a second glance at the photograph.

"Does that strike a familiar chord?" Jake asked the petite brunette studying Dryden's picture closely.

"Yes." Myra nodded and removed the square reading glasses from the tip of her nose. Dropping them to hang from a black cord around her neck, she peered up at Jake. "I think I know this man."

Rachel's fingers found Jake's elbow and squeezed it. "Does he—the man you know who looks like this picture—have any children?" she asked tautly.

Myra studied Rachel for a moment without speaking. "I believe he does." She looked at Jake. "You understand, I don't know him from the school here, but from church. He attends the same church I attend. I just saw him, yesterday, at the Sunday evening service."

"Alone?" Rachel asked quickly. "Was he alone?"

"I'm not certain. But I do remember that he spent quite a long time speaking to our pastor after the service. He's always doing that," she added with a waspish note entering her frail voice. "He plants himself in front of the door and makes anyone who wants to have a word with Reverend Jasper before leaving the church wait until he's had his say.

"It isn't like he's a long-standing member of the church or anything. Just because he gave a small sum of money..." She broke off to look at Rachel and say, "It really was a very small sum of money, you know," and then continued, "for the addition of another Sunday-school room. But that doesn't make him a saint.

"I always thought those who went about God's work were supposed to do it with a silent tongue in their heads—but not him. He got right up in church and told everyone what he was about. And that's a sin, if ever there was one committed."

She shook her head. "But, poor Lionus—Reverend Jasper," she quickly corrected, "is such a good man. He doesn't see the wickedness of others, even when it's right beneath his nose.

"He's a widower, you know, and since his wife died, I'm afraid he's too trusting. I've said it before and I'll say it again, he needs someone to look after him. A man like that, a good man like the Reverend Jasper, shouldn't be troubled with the likes of someone like—" she lowered her voice "—*that man.*"

"Do you know where he lives?" Jake asked as a gentle reminder of why they were there.

"You mean the man in the photograph?"

"Yes."

"No," she responded after a moment's hesitation, "I'm afraid I don't." She handed the picture back to Jake.

"Would this Reverend Jasper know the man's address?"

"Well, I suppose he might."

"Do you have the reverend's number?"

"Yes," she answered slowly.

"What about the name of his church?" Jake asked when she offered nothing more. "We could pay him a visit and ask him in person."

"Yes," Myra agreed haltingly, "you could do that. The church is the Sacred Cross, and it's located on the corner of Birchwood and Elm streets. Lionus, Reverend Jasper, lives alone in the stone house directly behind the church."

"That's great. Thank you for your time, Mrs. Templeton." Jake offered his hand. "It's been a pleasure meeting you."

"Yes, and that's Ms. Templeton," the woman murmured vaguely, accepting a handshake from Rachel's cold fingers. "But, you know..." She hesitated. "I could be mistaken... I mean, I'm not positive the man I've told you about is the one you're looking for."

"That's all right," Jake said, beginning to walk toward the door. "We'll check it out."

"B-but... if I'm wrong..." She followed, looking suddenly apprehensive. "You won't—"

"If you're wrong," Jake said with a shrug, "you're wrong. There's no crime in that. Thank you for your time."

Ushering Rachel out the door and into the hallway, he hurried toward the entrance of the building. The momentary excitement he'd felt upon first hearing the woman's identification was fast receding.

He glanced toward Rachel and saw a look on her face that plainly said she was positive they were within moments of finding her ex-husband and child. But Jake doubted it. It was all too obvious that the woman had a grudge against the man who took up too much of the wonderful Reverend Jasper's precious time.

A short while later, he and Rachel were standing on the porch of the parsonage behind Sacred Cross Church. A middle-aged man whom Jake assumed to be the Reverend Jasper opened the front door after the doorbell's first ring.

"You must be Agent Frost," the man said in a beautiful baritone as he offered his hand to Jake and invited both he and Rachel to enter his home. "Myra Templeton called to warn me you were on the way," he explained with a smile. "I'm Lionus, and you are?" he looked at Rachel.

"Rachel Dryden," she responded, offering him her hand.

"And your first name is..." the Reverend Jasper turned to Jake, standing silently with a dour expression on his face.

"Jake Frost."

"Well, Jake. Call me Lionus—both of you, please. And now that we have that settled, let me take your coats."

Once the coats were in the closet, he motioned for them to follow him through the living room to a hallway that led to the kitchen.

"I hope you'll excuse me for being in my shirtsleeves," he said to Rachel, "but I was just about to sit down to a bite of supper." He gestured to a table spread with fried chicken, potato salad, corn on the cob and baked beans.

Jake sniffed the appetizing aromas and felt his stomach growl in protest. By his calculations, it was close to twenty-four hours since either he or Rachel had eaten a meal.

"Please," the other man was saying, "won't the two of you join me? As you can see, there is plenty. My parishioners are very generous with their time."

The lady parishioners, no doubt, Jake added with silent scorn, the *single* lady parishioners, like Myra Templeton.

"Oh, no..." Rachel was shaking her head. She couldn't eat a bite. She was too worried—and excited—to feel anything so mundane as hunger.

"Well—" Jake responded, his mouth watering at the thought.

"Come," Reverend Jasper said, removing plates from a cabinet, "I won't take no for an answer. We can talk afterward."

A little while later, Jake sat back in his chair, feeling replete after a meal the likes of which he hadn't known in years, and studied Rachel's animated face. She was actually smiling as she discussed the art of glassblowing with the older man.

He switched his attention from Rachel to the Reverend Jasper, and watched him laugh at a description Rachel had just made of her first attempt at producing something you could recognize as a bird. A rare man indeed, Jake thought, with hidden skepticism. Con artists had the same ability to bamboozle the unsuspecting public with a show of interest and friendship.

"So," began the reverend, gentle blue eyes turning suddenly in Jake's direction. "What is it that *you* do for relaxation?" he asked curiously.

Jake shrugged. "I read—"

"And walk," Rachel put in abruptly, meeting Jake's eyes.

"And walk," he repeated, holding her glance.

Lionus gazed from one to the other and a smile lifted the corners of his generous mouth. "Tell me, now that we've filled our bellies with good food, what has brought you from Myra to my door with such serious faces?"

"My daughter," Rachel said before Jake could reply. "We're looking for my daughter. She's been kidnapped by my ex-husband and the woman from the college, Ms. Templeton, thought you might be able to help us."

Lionus frowned, or came as close to it as his good-natured countenance would allow. "And why did the good lady, Myra, think I'd be able to help you?"

Jake slipped a picture from the folder lying on the table beside him and handed it to the other man. "She tentatively identified this man as a member of your congregation."

Lionus studied the photograph for a long time without speaking. "I'm sorry," he said directly to Rachel, "but I don't know this man. I've never seen him before now."

"You're sure?" Jake asked intently.

"Yes, I'm sure. If I had, I'd be only too glad to help you."

"What about the man Ms. Templeton saw you talking to at the church yesterday? She seemed convinced he was the man in this picture."

"I'm sorry, but that just isn't possible. I've known the man to whom she referred for most of his life—"

"She said he hadn't been a member of your congregation all that long," Jake cut in suspiciously.

"That's true, he has only recently found his way to God, but that doesn't alter the fact that he hasn't left this town since the day he was born. And he certainly doesn't have a charming wife like this young lady." He smiled encouragingly at Rachel. "Nor does he have children."

Jake looked toward Rachel. She'd pushed away from the table, a stricken look on her face.

"Please, could you direct me to your bathroom?" she whispered tautly. The food she'd eaten had risen to the back of her throat, choking her.

Lionus pointed the way and then turned to find Jake on his heels. "No." He shook his head gently at the younger man. "Let her have some time alone. She needs to deal with this disappointing news in her own way."

Jake hesitated, as though he might ignore the man's words, but Lionus touched his arm and whispered, "She's a strong woman. She'll be all right, son, I promise."

Pulling his arm from the man's touch, Jake resumed his seat. Lionus moved about the kitchen, very much aware of the other man's tension and the numerous glances he threw toward the door.

"Here." He set a cup of coffee before Jake and sat down to a cup of his own.

After the first sip, Jake glanced at the man with a raised brow. "Jim Beam?"

Lionus smiled faintly and took another sip from his own cup. "That's my secret—what's yours?"

At first Jake thought he was making a joke, but when he looked directly into the other man's eyes, he realized he was serious. "I don't know what you mean."

"No?"

"No," Jake replied curtly.

"Only God can read what's written in a man's heart, but it isn't hard to see what's written in his eyes."

"Experience," Jake replied stonily, "that's what you see. Life is a great teacher."

"And so is God—"

"I'm sorry," Rachel apologized suddenly from the doorway. "I didn't mean to be so abrupt. I'm afraid I was counting too heavily on your being able to help us," she said to the reverend.

"It's all right my dear. Come join us in a cup of coffee."

Jake watched curiously as Lionus got up to pour Rachel a cup. Lionus glanced at Jake as he set the cup before Rachel, and as though guessing what was in the other man's mind, he smiled and shook his head in answer to Jake's unspoken question.

"Now, my dear, tell me about your little girl."

For the next hour, Lionus drew Rachel out about the child and the strangeness of her marriage after the child's birth. And in a little while, Jake noted with amazement, the tension had slowly seeped out of Rachel's face and body.

"I want to thank you for listening to me," Rachel said shyly. "I know we've taken a great deal of your time, and I really wish you would let me help with the dishes—"

"No, no," Lionus said, shaking his head, "it gives me something to do in the evening before I settle down to read my Bible."

"I think it's time we left the good reverend to his Bible," Jake interposed, getting to his feet.

"Yes," Rachel agreed, giving Jake a strange glance, but following his example in preparing to leave.

Lionus led the way to the hall closet where their coats were hanging, and stood watching as they put them on. At the door Rachel paused. "I just want to say, I know we're strangers, but I feel as though I've known you for a long time. Your congregation are very fortunate to have you as their pastor."

"I've never met a stranger." Lionus laughed as he held both her hands in one of his and squeezed them gently. His gaze strayed over her shoulder to rest on Jake's impassive face. "But in my work," he added pointedly, "I've met a great many who are a stranger to God."

His glance shifted back to Rachel. "If you don't mind, my dear, before you leave, I'd like to offer a prayer for the safe return of your little Amy."

"Yes, please," Rachel replied, bowing her head.

When the prayer was done, Lionus held Rachel for a moment in his arms, saying gently, "Remember, we're all God's children, but He watches out particularly for the little ones. Your daughter is safe in His hands."

Feeling comforted, Rachel nodded and moved down the steps. Jake halted and looked back when he felt the other man's hand on his arm. "If you ever want to talk ... about anything ... you know where I live."

Jake jerked his arm stiffly from the man's light touch and whispered harshly, "You lied to her, *Reverend*. He doesn't look out for *all* the children."

Before the other man could offer a rebuttal, Jake was running down the steps to join Rachel at the car. Inside he was seething, but outwardly, he appeared calm. Rachel had found solace in the man's words, and he wouldn't take that away from her despite his own thoughts on the matter.

Jake reached for the telephone on the second ring. He hadn't been sleeping, just lying awake, staring at the ceiling, thinking and smoking.

On the way back to the motel, he'd stopped on some pretext or other and bought a package of cigarettes, concealing them from Rachel. And after he'd left her in her room, he'd wandered the streets looking for that elusive sense of peace she appeared to have found in Lionus Jasper's practiced words of comfort.

He'd never been a religious man. He found it impossible to put his faith in some all-powerful, mythical being who was supposed to protect the whole world, but who left innocent children at the mercy of people like Steve Craig, Gary Dryden—and his parents.

Did the Reverend Lionus Jasper really believe all that religious stuff? Was he so cut off from the world around him that he didn't see what people were doing to each other every day of the week? And where was his God while all that was going on?

"Hello?" His voice sounded raw from the cigarettes. There were only two left in the pack.

"Is this Frost?"

Jake recognized the sheriff's voice instantly. He sat up on the side of the bed. "Yes, this is Frost. What have you got, Sheriff?"

"Maybe nothing. But one of my deputies came across someone at the high school who remembers meeting a substitute teacher a week or so back who fits the general description of our man."

Jake switched on the lamp beside the bed, grabbed his pen and notebook and began making notes.

"Thanks a lot," he said when the man was finished speaking. "I'll let you know what I find out."

"Well, it isn't a solid lead, but it's a start. By the way, are you packin'?"

"No." Jake had sent his weapon along with his badge by courier to Gus when he'd dropped out of sight months ago.

"Come by the office, and I'll fix that," Langly said before ringing off.

Jake dialed the motel operator and asked for the time. He thanked the man and replaced the phone. Six o'clock. He wondered if it was too early to awaken—

"Jake?" A knock sounded at his door. "Are you awake?"

Jake was on his feet, opening the door before the second knock. "What's wrong?" he asked quickly, pulling her inside, scanning the parking lot behind her.

"Nothing." She pulled away and glanced toward the telephone beside the bed. "I thought I heard the phone ring." She looked up at him expectantly.

"You did. It was Langly. We have a lead. But don't go getting your hopes up," he warned quickly, seeing the light spring into her eyes. "It's only a lead, and not a very good one at that."

But Rachel refused his warning. She'd been living with constant fear for her daughter's safety but since meeting the Reverend Jasper last night, she'd been certain they'd find something soon.

"Let's go," she demanded instantly. "Come on. What are you waiting for? He might get away!"

"We're not going to find your ex-husband," he reminded her. "We're simply going to speak with a man who *might,* have seen and spoken to him—a week ago."

"A week ago?" she asked falteringly, some of her enthusiasm waning.

"That's right, a week ago. And I'm warning you, that's all it is, just a lead. It could turn out to be nothing. This man we're going to see may on second thought decide that the person he was referring to looks nothing at all like your ex-husband.

"Remember Myra Templeton? She *wanted* to find something wrong with the man who took up so much of her precious Reverend Jasper's time. This could be something similar."

The animation slowly left Rachel's face. She stared at him coldly. "Why are you doing this?"

"Doing what?"

"Why are you trying to take what little hope I have from me?"

"I'm not—"

"Yes," she insisted sadly, "you are. I thought you understood how I feel. But you don't, do you? You don't understand at all, because you've never known what it is to be a parent.

"You should spend some time with Reverend Jasper. I think talking to him might help you get over your pain at the death of the little girl, Lacy, and her mother."

"Hah!" Jake snorted. "I don't need any sanctimonious sermons from the good Reverend Jasper," he added caustically.

But Rachel only shook her head, the clear gray eyes clouding with pity. "Is there no one or nothing you believe in? Where do you go when you need comfort?"

"I don't go to a bottle!"

"And what makes you think the Reverend does? It isn't a sin to drink a little whiskey in your coffee." At the look of surprise on his face, she explained, "I saw the bottle sitting on the counter. He didn't try to hide it—and in any case I smelled it on your breath last night in the car.

"Jake..." She took a step toward him, a pleading look on her face. "Wasn't there ever a time when you believed in something? I know it must have been painful, being taken from your parents and then finding they had died just when you were about to be reunited with them, but—"

"Painful!" Her words stung, unleashing something terrible inside him. He rounded on her suddenly. "You think I felt pain at being taken from *them?*" he asked, advancing toward her angrily. "It wasn't pain I felt—it was joy! I was glad to be taken from them!"

Rachel backed away from him in surprise edged with fear. "I—I don't understand—"

"No," he agreed readily, "you don't. You make quick judgments about me without knowing all the facts."

"What..." She licked dry lips and asked, "What are you talking about? I don't judge you—"

"No? Well, let me tell you something, *my dear*," he sneered, repeating the reverend's words. "Not all children are cherished by their parents in the same way. My dear mother used to beat me regularly with a leather strap that had a wide brass buckle—while my father watched."

Speaking over Rachel's sudden gasp, he continued, "It excited the both of them. They were turned on by violence. Sometimes they knocked each other around instead of me to get their kicks."

Rachel's eyes widened in horror. Nothing he'd told her to date shocked her as much as this. "Oh...Jake..."

But he wasn't finished. "When Janet came to stay," Jake continued, turning so he didn't have to see the expression on her face, "things changed a little for the better, because Mother was afraid Janet wouldn't understand her need to punish me. I heard her discussing it with my father.

"But the reprieve didn't last long. There came a time when Mother couldn't contain herself any longer. One day, Janet saw the marks. When it happened again she discussed it with my uncle.

"He told my parents, and Janet was almost fired. Except...I think they were afraid to fire her. Child abuse wasn't as well publicized thirty years ago as it is today, but there were a few groups fighting against it. And Janet could tell things...things my parents didn't want told.

"They were lawyers with lots of money. They had friends in high places. They didn't want their little, harmless...perversions, known by others."

"Why didn't this...Janet, take you to the authorities?"

"Janet Frost—her name was Janet Frost."

"Then your name isn't—"

"Yes, it is!" Jake insisted forcefully. And then in a quieter voice added, "My last name was legally changed years ago." He moved restlessly around the room, wishing he'd never started this. He hadn't intended telling her about his parents.

"Tell me about when you and Janet left your parents' home."

"House," Jake corrected in a dead voice. "It was a showplace for their wealth—never a home.

"That night, as I said, they were both out of town on business. When they discovered they weren't going to make it home as planned, they called Janet and told her they were sending my uncle to get me.

"My mother didn't want to leave me alone overnight with Janet. I'm certain she knew how Janet felt about her, and she might even have been uneasy about what Janet might do if given half a chance. As I remember, Janet was never cowed by my mother's sharp words and icy demeanor."

"But what about your uncle?" Rachel asked when he paused. "Did he know—did he condone what they were doing?"

"He knew all right. He just didn't care. But Janet did, and she must have been waiting for the right moment to do something about it. That night, after my mother's call, was her chance.

"Unfortunately, my uncle arrived before she could get me away. They argued and there was a struggle...my uncle was injured."

Jake stood in the center of the room staring at the carpet, seeing another carpet stained red with blood. "I remember sitting on the steps above him and looking at the pool of blood. There was so much blood...all around his head."

"Was he badly hurt?" Rachel murmured softly.

Jake shrugged. "According to the newspaper articles I read, he's in a wheelchair because of some problem with his spine as a result of the fall. But I didn't know that at the time. Frankly, I don't think I really gave a damn. He'd never showed me any affection.

"The only one who ever did was Janet, and when she told me she was going away, I was terrified by the thought. She said she had to go, or they'd come and get her—put her where I'd never see her again.

"I was only four, but she was the only person who had ever treated me with kindness, and I was determined that no one would take her away from me. We left that night. I don't remember much about the trip, except I think I remember standing in the cold for a long time and then getting on a bus.

"I must have slept most of the journey. When I awakened, Janet told me we were going to live in Texas. Her family had originally come from Texas a long time ago. We lived there for the next eighteen years."

"Did you never...think about your parents?" Rachel asked tentatively.

"No—as a matter of fact, I forgot all about them in time."

"What happened to Janet?"

"She died," he answered solemnly. "One day, a few days before my twenty-second birthday, she had a stroke. I was in college. She died instantly."

"Was she kind to you all those years?"

"Kind?" He pinned her with a glance. "She was the only real mother I'd ever known."

"You loved her?"

Jake stared at his hands. The stitches were beginning to itch. "Janet never married. She worked two jobs to pay for my college education, took care of me through childhood illnesses...corrected me when I needed it...and praised me when I did something worthwhile. She was my mother.

"When she died like that...so suddenly...I couldn't believe it...she was only forty-two.

"It was a couple of weeks after the funeral before I could go back to the house. A neighbor woman, a friend of Janet's, offered to help me go through her things. We were going through her personal belongings, when I found a box of old letters."

Rubbing a hand around the back of his neck, Jake shook his head. "I'd blocked everything from my mind—the accident—my parents—the beatings—during those eighteen years, it had all become nothing more than a bad dream I had sometimes in the middle of the night.

"The things in the box brought it all back. Like a door suddenly thrown open, my past rose up to confront me. It slapped me in the face."

"What did you do?" Rachel asked when he didn't continue.

"I got on with the rest of my life."

"You..." What about grief? When did he give himself the time to grieve for all that he'd lost? "What did you do with your—with Janet's—things?"

"I went through the box alone and read everything. It seems Janet had a guilty conscience about the kidnapping. She tried twice a year, every year, on Christmas and my birthday, to write to my parents and let them know I was alive and well."

He grinned caustically. "She never mailed any of the letters."

Now she understood the tone in his voice. Jake felt that somehow Janet had betrayed him, because, though she had taken him away from the cruelty of his parents, she'd had a guilty conscience about it.

"About the time I was fourteen she stopped writing the letters. I found a newspaper account of both their deaths in a plane crash early that year."

"Oh, I'm sorry."

"Don't be." He faced her. "They were strangers to me. The only thing I remember clearly is the beatings."

"And your uncle?"

Jake shrugged.

"Didn't you go back and let him know you were alive?"

"Go back? To my uncle?" he asked with a sardonic laugh. "Not hardly! In his own way, he was just as guilty as my parents. He knew how they treated me—saw the marks on me—and he never lifted a hand to stop it."

"But...maybe you should go back and see him—for yourself," she added quickly, seeing the look on his face. "Do it for yourself, Jake, so you'll be free of it—free of all the pain and bitterness inside you—"

"I have nothing to say to my uncle that he'd want to hear," Jake replied in harsh tones. "Things are better left as they stand."

Suddenly he wanted to get out of the room and away from her. He had that naked feeling again, the one that said he'd been stripped bare before her eyes.

Going into the bathroom, shutting her out, he lingered as long as possible before going back into the next room and facing her again. She was standing by the door, looking out the window.

Rachel turned quickly at his entrance. "Why do you wear that?" she asked, eyeing the wide leather belt he was slipping into the loopholes on his jeans, with aversion.

"As a reminder," he answered without meeting her eyes.

"A reminder? I wouldn't think you needed one," she said with meaning.

"It's not to remind me of the past—it's to remind me of the future and what I won't ever become."

"And what is that?" she probed gently.

"A replica of my parents."

Chapter 11

Rachel shot an uneasy glance in Jake's direction as he studied the address written on a slip of paper and then looked for it on a city map. His face remained impassive as he started the car and moved from the parking lot near the sheriff's office onto the street. She had no idea why they'd made a stop here, and Jake wasn't talking. He'd been silent and avoided eye contact with her since leaving the motel a little while ago.

An abundance of jumbled thoughts and questions was running through her mind. She was anxious about this new lead, fearing that it, too, might turn out to be a wild-goose chase, but she was also concerned about Jake.

He was becoming important to her. She wasn't certain exactly what that meant, but she worried about him. She worried about the way he had brooded over the death of Lacy Tolbridge and her mother and the fact that he'd kept that pain and the pain from his childhood all bottled up inside.

If he didn't loosen up, some day he'd explode, or cave in under the strain. The fact that he'd told her a little about it was a good sign. But then immediately afterward, he'd gone right back to keeping her at a distance, raising his defenses as though ashamed that he'd spoken to her about it.

Another thing bothering her was his inability to admit that he had cared deeply for Janet, that he had in fact loved her like the mother she had apparently been to him. Rachel didn't for a minute doubt his love for her, but did Jake realize it?

And what, if anything, did he feel, for her? Did he care for her at all? Or was their coming together nothing more than a momentary release for him?

She recalled his whispered vow that he wouldn't hurt her and his own entreaty for her not to hurt him. Is that all he expected from people—from life? Pain? Did he view everyone with suspicion?

Look at his opinion of the Reverend Jasper. How could he have called such an obviously genuine man of God, sanctimonious? And a hypocrite?

Rachel wished she could see Jake's uncharitable behavior toward the preacher as a manifestation of jealousy because she had liked the man, but it took a giant stretch of the imagination for that. In truth, she didn't think Jake had allowed feeling for anyone to get beneath his barriers since adulthood—except, maybe, Lacy and her mother. And she wasn't certain now if it was feeling for the child and her mother that had driven him to seek sanctuary by removing himself from the world—or the fact that he'd discovered he was human just like the rest of the world and made mistakes, too.

Her own feelings about the sudden attraction between the two of them were mixed. She rationalized it during the day by telling herself it was nothing more than two people's need for comfort at a particularly trying time in their lives.

But sometimes, when they were alone together, when he looked at her—when he touched her—she yearned to have him touch her more intimately. She yearned to have him bring her alive, the way only he could when they made love.

A part of herself scolded her soundly for the feeling, telling her she should be thinking of nothing but Amy and getting the child back safely. And warning her of the mistake she'd made with Gary.

But another part, the part Jake had awakened with his lovemaking, told her what she felt was good and that it was all right to feel this way. And that's what she wanted to believe.

Could she be falling in love with the man? The thought should have come as a shock, but it didn't. Despite the harrowing experience with Gary, she'd known love as a child and she wasn't scarred inside as Jake must be.

She believed in happily ever after—for most people, at any rate. But she believed, too, that you had to work for it. It wasn't something that came to you automatically. Her mind wasn't closed to what was happening in the world around her—she saw the death and disease and poverty, but she saw the good things, too. Just as she saw the good in Jake and her heart wasn't closed to the idea of falling in love—

"We're here." Jake turned into a large, crowded parking lot and began looking for a place to park.

Those were the first words he'd spoken since leaving the motel, and though she tried, Rachel couldn't see beyond the mask of his face to gauge his mood. She turned her gaze from Jake toward the large gray stone building they were about to enter and felt the tension rise inside her. Would they find her ex-husband here?

The same dismal silence that had accompanied them on the short drive from the motel stayed with them as they abandoned the car. Hurrying across the parking lot through a sporadic rain, they slowed to climb the front steps of the sprawling high school.

A student led them to the principal's office where a tall, thick-waisted man with a wide grin introduced himself as John Hargraves, the principal, and shook hands with Jake. He then told the boy to get Mr. Parker and the young man left, closing the office door behind him. Hargraves offered them both a seat, noted that they preferred to stand, and remained standing himself.

"One of Ben Langly's men came around with a picture yesterday," he explained to Jake, "and we passed it around in the teachers' lounge after school.

"Adam—that's the man you're going to be talking to— wasn't here yesterday, so he didn't see it until today—"

Someone knocked on the closed door and Hargraves called, "Enter."

A short, balding man with an apologetic air and wire-rimmed glasses entered the room. The principal introduced the man as Adam Parker, mentioned that he'd go get them all a cup of coffee and left them alone.

"Well, Mr. Parker," Jake said, offering his hand, "I understand you may have some information for us."

"Y-yes...that is...I don't know if I do or not." The other man accepted his hand and shook it limply while shooting a nervous glance in Rachel's direction. He gave her a slight nod, an incomplete smile, and returned his attention to Jake.

Gesturing for the other man to take a seat, Jake waited until he was comfortable and then asked, "You were shown a picture that you tentatively identified as someone you knew, is that right?"

Parker smoothed a hand along the side of his thinning blond hair and nodded, qualifying, "I don't actually know him but . . . I think it might be him."

"Him?" Jake asked quickly, causing the man to give a startled little jump.

"Y-yes—the man in the picture."

"Dryden?" Jake asked.

"No . . . that is . . . that isn't the name he gave me."

"And that was?"

Rachel looked from Parker's apprehensive expression to Jake. When had he put on the sunglasses? Certainly, he didn't think he needed to intimidate this little man?

"I...don't remember." Parker peered up at Jake's opaque stare, slid a glance in Rachel's direction, and swallowed, grinning nervously. "I'm sorry." His hands were gripping the arms of the chair.

"That's all right, Mr. Parker." Jake removed the glasses, folded them and put them in his pocket. "May I call you Adam?"

"Y-yes—of course."

"Well, Adam, can you tell me where you met the man you identified from the photograph?"

"In Morris. That's a town in the next county," he explained. "I work there in the elementary school three afternoons a week—teaching art—that's why I didn't see the picture until today." He looked from Rachel to Jake. "I was teaching at the elementary school yesterday."

"Then you saw him yesterday?" Rachel asked quickly.

"N-no, I didn't." Seeing her sudden look of disappointment, he added, "I'm sorry."

"Does this man, the man you think looks like the man in the picture, live in Morris?" Jake asked.

"I don't know, he didn't say. And I didn't ask," Parker added quickly. He didn't know what Dryden had done, but he didn't want to be associated with him in this man's mind.

There was an aura about the man questioning him—Hargraves had said he was FBI—that made Parker greatly fear getting on his bad side. "I never saw him before that day," Parker explained. "It was a Wednesday, if that helps. He was substituting for another teacher who was ill."

"Can you describe him?"

"Well..." Parker frowned down at the tips of his shiny brown shoes. "I guess he was about five nine or ten, because that's about my height and we were on eye level. He was a little heavier than me, so he must have weighed..." he looked at Jake, then quickly shifted his glance back toward the floor "...maybe a hundred and seventy pounds."

"Hair color?"

"Black—but it wasn't styled like it is in the picture I saw. It was cut short on top—a flattop, I think they call it."

"Eyes?"

"Blue—and he wore glasses, dark-framed glasses. I remember, because they kept slipping down his nose while we talked and he kept pushing them back up."

"What about scars?"

Parker looked startled. "I don't recall any scars—should I?"

"No. Anything else?" Jake asked.

"No."

"What about a ring?" Rachel asked abruptly. "Was he wearing a wedding band?"

Adam Parker hesitated, then shook his head. "No."

"What about a family," Jake fired the question at him, "did he mention having a family?"

"N-no."

"Then what did you talk about?" Jake asked in exasperation.

The other man looked ill at ease. "N-nothing, really. I went to get a cup of coffee before my class started and...he was just there. We exchanged greetings—talked about the weather—" He shrugged.

"Did he mention if he lived alone?" Jake persisted.

"No." Parker shook his head. "Sorry."

"Give me the name of the school where you met him." Jake had his notebook open.

"Sam Davis Elementary."

Jake took a picture from his pocket and held it out to the other man. "Is this the man you saw?"

Adam Parker studied the photo carefully. "Except for the hair and the glasses..." He hesitated, studied the picture closely, and then confirmed, "Yes, it's him."

"You're sure?"

Parker glanced at the photo again. "Yes, I'm sure."

"Thank you, Mr. Parker, for your help." Jake shook hands with the man, apologized for taking him away from class, and watched as he left the room with a noticeable air of relief.

Turning to Rachel as the door closed behind his narrow shoulders, Jake said quietly, a note of triumph in his voice, "We've got him."

"Do we?" She responded without the enthusiasm he'd anticipated. "He was here a week ago, but he could be long gone by now." Despite her brave assurance a little while ago that they were about to find her daughter, she was suddenly afraid to hope.

"I don't think so," Jake responded in neutral tones. "And in any case, now that we have something to go on, we can trace him even if he has left the area."

"What happens now?"

"Now, we simply have to make a telephone call to the sheriff and let him set up an appointment for us with a member of the Morris school board. We find out if anyone there recognizes your ex-husband's picture, and then we find out who was doing substitute teaching on Wednesday of last week and see if any of those people recognize him."

The principal still hadn't returned, but Jake used the phone in his office to call Sheriff Langly.

"It looks promising," he told the other man. "Can you set up a meeting for me with a member of the Morris school board?"

"Sure, when?"

"Soon as possible. We'll leave right away. How far is the town from here?"

"About half an hour's drive," Langly responded.

"Make the call. We'll wait right here till we hear from you."

John Hargraves seemed to have disappeared. While Jake and Rachel waited, Jake tracked down two cups of black coffee and brought one to Rachel. Rachel took a sip, made a face, and Jake almost grinned.

"It definitely isn't anything like yours," she said with a tiny smile.

Their eyes met over the rim of the foam cup. "So... my coffee has made a lasting impression on you."

That wasn't the only thing that had made a lasting impression on her, Rachel thought as she swallowed hastily and looked hurriedly away. Suddenly the room felt too warm.

Twenty minutes later, the phone rang and it was the sheriff. Doctor Richard Schyler, head of the Morris school board, would be waiting to speak to him as soon as he could get there. Langly gave Jake directions and rang off.

On the way out of town, Jake stopped at a fast-food restaurant, remembering they hadn't eaten any breakfast. He didn't touch the sandwiches he'd bought, but drank two cups of strong, black coffee, hoping the caffeine would thaw the frozen lump of ice beginning to fill his insides.

The horizon was once more darkened with storm clouds, and a matching silence enveloped the car as they swept along the highway amid the stark reality of a wet, Texas fall, and on to whatever awaited them in the next town. And as the miles sped by, the chill inside Jake grew.

It was getting close. His hour of reckoning was almost at hand. Now was his chance to make amends, to rectify all the mistakes he'd made in the past. The thought did nothing to inspire him. He was getting a second chance—but at what cost?

Very aware of the woman at his side, Jake made an attempt to turn his thoughts in another direction, but found it impossible. How long could he hope to ignore the fact that the child involved this time was hers?

The realization only made the whole thing worse. He wasn't certain what his feelings were for Rachel, but he knew that whatever they were, they shouldn't even exist. Had he learned nothing in the past six months?

Rachel took a bite of roast beef and chewed methodically, staring straight ahead. She didn't taste the food, and each bite seemed to grow larger as she chewed.

They were close, she could feel it! Excitement bubbled below the surface—but it was an excitement edged with dread. She wouldn't only be seeing her daughter...she'd be seeing Gary again, soon, too.

"Do you mind?"

Jake's sudden deep tones routed her from the depths of dread and caused her to eye him questioningly.

He lifted a cigarette and asked, "Will it bother you if I smoke?"

"N-no—go ahead."

Jake placed the narrow white cylinder between firm lips, pushed the lighter in on the dash, and when it popped out, held it to the tip of the cigarette. Taking a long pull, he replaced the lighter and took the cigarette from his mouth.

Rachel watched the smoke drift through his nostrils and form a white cloud around his head. "I didn't know you smoked."

"I don't."

The reply made sense to her. She wished it didn't. And she wished, suddenly, that she, too, smoked. Maybe it would ease the churning sensations skittering around inside, making her feel ill.

Now that Jake had reminded her of his presence, she couldn't seem to concentrate on anything else. She watched him take another long draw on the cigarette and hold the smoke inside before letting it out through his mouth.

What was he thinking? He looked so calm. Was he worried at all about seeing her ex-husband?

No, of course he wasn't. He was used to it. It was his job to hunt down people like Gary...but, then, did anyone ever get used to what Jake was about to face?

Stupid question. If he'd been used to it, the deaths of the woman and child the last time wouldn't have affected him as that they had.

The seconds ticked by and a new sensation began to transmit itself to her. She glanced at the rigid planes of Jake's face, the inflexible fingers on the steering wheel, and realized he was coiled as tightly as a spring.

So, he wasn't as calm as she'd thought. Were his thoughts paralleling hers? Was he thinking about Gary? About Amy? About the last time?

Focusing her attention on the road, she took a hurried sip of coffee, fighting the tiny spark of fear at the back of her mind. The spark had been started the day she'd visited the cemetery and seen the two graves. But it was being fanned by a question that had been growing inside, ever since Jake's subsequent explanation about their significance in his own life.

What would he do if he was faced with a crazed man, one who threatened her daughter's life? Would he be able to get Amy away from Gary without getting her hurt—or killed?

Trying her best to beat down the growing fear, Rachel reminded herself that she trusted Jake . . . didn't she? *Didn't she?*

Of course she did! He wouldn't do anything that would hurt her child—*but what about the last time?* a small voice whispered. *The last child he tried to save had ended up dead.*

But that was different, she argued. *How?* That man had been demented . . . *like Gary?*

Gary is Amy's father . . . and he threatened to kill her and himself, too.

"Talk to me," Rachel said abruptly, unable to stop the voices arguing inside her head.

Jake spared her a glance, saw the uncertainty, the hint of desperation in her eyes, and wondered if the same look was in his own.

"You know," he promised softly, "I won't do anything that will jeopardize your daughter's life."

Their glances met and held for a long, heart-stopping moment, before she whispered unsteadily, "I know."

She just wanted this to be all over with, Amy back in her arms, and the two of them safe in their home in San Antonio.

And what about Jake? What would happen to this thing between them, when Amy was safe and Gary was in custody?

Nothing had been mentioned—no words had been spoken between them of . . . love. *Did she love him?*

Rachel's lids slipped down over her eyes. A slow heat crept up her neck. He was watching her and even though he couldn't read her mind, she couldn't help the embarrassment washing over her, making her feel hot and uncomfortable inside.

What would Amy think of Jake? Would he make a good father? Rachel's face burned hotter at the idea of his being Amy's stepfather. He hadn't even mentioned seeing her again, how could she consider the possibility of . . . anything else?

"Are you finished with that?"

Rachel stared at him blankly. He was looking at her hands. She followed his eyes to the half-eaten sandwich she was currently mangling.

"Yes," she responded slowly, putting the empty coffee cup into the sack and rewrapping the partially eaten sandwich. Jake took the sack from her and threw it onto the back seat.

"Are we about there?" She couldn't stand her thoughts any longer, nor could she stand the idea of being confined in this small space with the man at her side for much longer.

Jake glanced at the odometer. "Another ten miles."

"Do you think it's him?" There was a note of apprehension mixed with excitement in her voice. Only ten miles, after a month of not knowing where Amy might be, what was happening to her, or if she was safe and in good health—to be within ten miles of her at last.

"Yes," Jake answered solemnly.

Rachel folded her hands in her lap and squeezed the fingers tightly together. "What...have you thought about how...what you're going to do when we get there...when we...when you come face-to-face with him?"

Jake's stomach constricted into a tight hard knot. Here it was, here was the doubt he'd warned her she'd one day feel. He'd known it was coming—and still it was a shock.

Stubbing out the cigarette in the ashtray, he swallowed and shook his head. "I won't know how to handle the situation until I know what the situation is," he answered tightly.

"Do you think—"

"We're here," Jake cut across her words with a sense of relief. She was asking questions he'd been asking himself during the ride. He didn't know how he'd handle the child's release. He didn't know how he'd handle himself.

"Come on."

The offices of the school board were located in a modern four-story office building at the end of the main street of town. Jake and Rachel were showed inside Dr. Schyler's office by a trim, middle-aged secretary.

Once the amenities were over, Richard Schyler asked briskly, "You're certain Conrad Wilkison is the man you're looking for?"

"I won't know that for certain until Mrs. Dryden positively identifies him," Jake replied carefully.

"Well, he hasn't been with us long, but he came with excellent references. And I've heard nothing but good things about his teaching methods in the short time he's been employed with us. It will be a shame to lose him," the older man added with real regret.

"He's wanted for kidnapping." Jake's eyes looked hard at the other man's face.

"But, I understand he is the child's real father," Schyler suggested carefully.

"That changes nothing. The mother has legal custody—"

"You don't understand—" Rachel began, only to break off as Jake took her arm in a firm grip.

"The address?" Jake prompted with stony emphasis.

Richard Schyler gave them both a long, searching stare. A moment later, he left the room without speaking again.

The minutes seemed like hours while they waited for his return. Rachel stared at the framed certificates on the wall behind the man's desk. Jake stood staring out the window.

"You should have worn your dark glasses," she said, in a nervous attempt at humor.

Jake's broad back tensed. That sounded very much like a slur against his handling of Schyler. Keeping his eyes on the falling rain, he focused on one thought—soon it would all be over.

"What's taking him so long?" Rachel demanded abruptly. "We've been here a long time."

"Relax, it's only been a few minutes." The words were meant to soothe, but there was a tension about them that hung like a cloud over their heads.

"You don't think he's gone to warn him, do you?" she asked with dawning horror. She could see her child slipping away.

"No. He's probably gone to check my credentials."

"He doesn't want to help us."

"I know."

Rachel slowly drew closer to Jake. Despite everything between them, there was an inherent strength about his hard figure that attracted her like a moth to a flame. She needed something solid to hold on to, and Jake was there.

Her shoulder touched his and something bumped against his wrist. Jake felt cold fingers slip inside his and his hand closed warmly around them.

"Here we are." Dr. Schyler returned carrying a slip of paper. "I made you a copy of his address."

"Thank you." Jake reached for it with his free hand, retaining his hold on Rachel. They held hands all the way to the car.

"Is it far?" she asked hesitantly, watching him frown at the paper in his hand.

"It isn't located in town, it's about twelve miles from here. Someone has written down directions on how to reach it."

They were five miles from town, amid a vast expanse of hills, brush and little else when the car gave a sudden jerk and veered sharply toward the right. Jake corrected the move and felt the car buck beneath his hands.

Rachel gasped, grabbing for the arm rest. "What is it?"

Jake whispered a curse beneath his breath. "I think we have what is known as a flat tire."

"Flat tire! But we can't—"

"Yes," Jake corrected her succinctly, pulling onto the shoulder of the road. "We can. We do."

"Be careful!" Rachel cautioned as the car bumped over a rock and onto wet grass. "The shoulder is soft. What if we get stuck?"

"Don't look for trouble," Jake said between clenched teeth, "we've got enough on our plate as it is."

"What do you mean?"

"I mean, I don't think I have a spare."

"What?"

Rachel couldn't wait in the car. Even though the rain had started again and fell like sharp pellets of ice on her uncovered head, she climbed out and followed him to the back of the car.

"It's flat," she stated the obvious. "How could you start out on a trip without first checking your spare tire?" she asked impatiently, staring into the trunk at the flattened tire.

"I wasn't exactly expecting to take a trip," he reminded her caustically. Why did women always state the obvious?

"But it's only common sense to make sure you have a usable spare." She gestured wildly with her hands. "Look where you live—it's miles from *everywhere*. What would you have done if you'd had a flat way out there?"

"The same thing I'm going to do right now," he told her, slamming the trunk. "Get back in the car."

"But—"

"Do it!"

Rachel raised her chin haughtily, gave him a cold stare without moving an inch, then, having made her point, turned stiffly away. Marching to the passenger side of the car, she climbed inside and slammed the door.

Men, she fumed silently. How could this be happening? They were so close. . . .

Jake climbed in beside her and started the engine, though he didn't immediately move the car. "Look," he said finally, staring straight ahead, "I'm sorry about the flat. I know you're anxious about getting to the house—"

"He could be getting away—while we sit here, talking, Gary could be leaving with Amy and. . ." She didn't say it, but the rest of the sentence was obvious. He was to blame.

"I didn't put the damned nail in the damned tire," he shouted. "And why would Gary suddenly leave here? He has no idea we're on to him."

"What about that man, Schyler? He liked Gary, he could have warned him, while we waited in his office," she protested.

"He didn't warn him."

"How do you know?"

"I just know."

Rachel opened her mouth to make a scathing retort and closed it without speaking. He didn't understand. He didn't understand at all.

Without waiting for a reply, Jake turned the car around, and putting the two right tires on the paved shoulder, moved slowly forward. He didn't like the delay any better than she did, but she didn't seem to understand that, and he was too angry to try to explain it to her.

They hadn't gone more than a mile when a tractor trailer streaked past, shaking the car with its tail wind. Air brakes sounded suddenly and the blare of a horn followed.

Jake's eyes darted to the rearview mirror. The trucker was laying on his horn and motioning out the window for Jake to stop.

Rachel turned in the seat to look behind them. "What does he want?" she asked in bewilderment.

"To help us, I hope," Jake muttered softly.

Stopping the car, he got out and ran back to speak to the truck driver. Rachel watched them talking. Jake nodded and shook his head. A moment later, the truck began to back up as Jake ran toward the car.

"He's going to take me to a town up ahead a few miles," Jake panted. "I'll either get the flat fixed, or buy a new tire, whichever is quicker. Do you want to come along?"

"No. I'll stay with the car."

Jake hesitated. He didn't like the idea of leaving her alone on a country road with very little traffic, but he didn't want to take the time to argue with her, either.

"All right. Lock the doors and stay in the car. I'll be back as quick as I can."

Rachel spent the next hour scrunching down in the seat every time a vehicle went by, peering over the edge of the doorframe, watching for Gary. Chances were slim that he'd actually drive past while she sat there, and she had no idea what she'd do if he actually did, but still, every time a car popped the hill in either direction, she made it a point to wipe the glass and try to get a glimpse of the driver.

All at once, she saw a vehicle crest the hill and head straight for her. It crossed the road pulled up directly in front of Jake's car, and stopped. Bright lights flashed through the windshield almost blinding her. Rachel felt her insides tighten in apprehension.

Twisting in the seat and shielding her eyes from the glare she tried to see the vehicle more clearly, but the windows of Jake's car were steamed with fog. Rolling down the window, she stuck her head outside. It had started to rain again and her head was soaked in seconds, but she saw a beat-up orange truck sitting on the shoulder in front of the car.

All of a sudden the passenger door opened and Rachel gave a little scream. She'd forgotten to lock the doors like Jake had told her.

"It figures," Jake said in a tone of resignation.

Rachel breathed a quick sigh of relief, pulled her head back inside and rolled up the window.

"Mike—" Jake motioned toward the car up ahead "—came with me from the station. He's going to help change the tire. I had to buy a new one.

"We should be finished in a few minutes. Do you want to wait in the truck until we're done?"

Rachel stared at the rain dripping into his face from the end of a curl hanging over his forehead, and felt her heart lurch.

Jake wiped at the rain impatiently. The end of his nose looked pink, and his lips looked dry and cracked from the cold, and she was so glad to see him she wanted to throw her arms around his neck and hug him.

"If it's all right," she replied in a low voice, "I'll just stay here."

"Right. We won't be long."

Jake nodded and climbed from the car. Ducking his head into the collar of his jacket, feeling the cold rain slide down the back of his neck, he hurried toward the back of the car to help the man, Mike.

Rachel closed her eyes and leaned her head back against the seat, feeling the cold rain splash her hot face. It was impossible to stay mad at him....

"You're getting wet."

Rachel gave a slight jerk, opened her eyes and looked to her left. Jake was sitting on the seat beside her.

When had he gotten in the car? Surely, he hadn't been gone long enough to have changed a tire.

"Ready?"

Rachel nodded and rolled up the window, realizing with a shock that she must have dozed off. She was appalled at the idea. How could she have fallen asleep at such a crucial time?

"It happens to the best of us," Jake suggested mildly.

"What?"

"Giving in to stress."

Something warm covered her icy fingers where they gripped the edge of the seat. Jake squeezed her hand gently, then released it.

Rachel shot him a puzzled glance. Would she ever come to understand him?

Chapter 12

Jake turned off the pavement onto a winding dirt road bowered by pine trees and drove slowly, keeping careful watch on the road up ahead. He had no idea if there were other houses along the road, but didn't want to chance a collision with a vehicle that might come roaring around a curve at any minute and crash head-on into them. And, too, he was looking for something.

Rachel felt the breath become static in her lungs as they neared the house. With a growing sense of aggravation, she wondered why Jake was driving so slowly. She wanted to rush right up to the house, confront her husband, and get Amy away from him.

All at once, Jake pulled off the road and drove in among the trees. Small branches scraped the sides of the car as he drove several yards into them before stopping.

Rachel looked at him in amazement. Where was the house? "Now what?" She sighed, unconsciously whispering, "Is there something else wrong with the car?"

"No." Jake glanced at her caustically before pocketing the keys and sliding from the car. Bending to peer at her before closing the door, he said, "From here, I go on foot.

You stay in the car. It's still raining and I won't be gone long."

"Right." Climbing from the car, she stood beside it and stared at him defiantly.

"What are you doing?"

"I'm going with you."

"I told you to stay in the car."

"And I've told you, more than once, that I'm going to be there when we find Amy," she answered stubbornly.

"This could be dangerous."

"All the more reason for me to be there, to protect Amy."

The rain plastered his hair to his head as he stood with rigid jaw and stared at her hostilely. For a moment he toyed with the idea of dumping her in the trunk and locking her in there. He'd do it, too, if wasn't for the thought of something happening to him and no one finding her until it was too late.

"All right," he said irritably, "but if I say drop, you better be on all fours in a matter of seconds. You got that?"

Rachel wiped rain from her face with icy fingers and nodded.

"Let's go."

They wound their way through the trees, keeping low, with Jake in the lead. After about five minutes, the house came into view.

Catching an occasional glimpse of it through the trees, Rachel stared at the somber structure and shivered. As it grew steadily closer, and though it seemed silly even to her, she couldn't help feeling that as they watched it, it watched them, too. Trying to shake off her thoughts, she forced herself to remember this was only a house—and Amy could be somewhere inside.

When they were directly behind the house, Jake took up a position that enabled him to see both sides of the building and part of the drive leading to it. It was a one-story structure with a screened-in back porch and no garage or outbuildings. And it appeared large enough to house about six or eight rooms. Dryden could be hiding in any one of them.

Jake put his mouth against Rachel's ear to make himself heard above the sound of the rain and said, "You stay right here—don't move from this spot, no matter what happens. Understand?"

"Where are you going?" she whispered apprehensively.

"To get a look at the front. I don't see a car from here, but I can't see the front of the house. Stay right here," he mouthed again, pointing a finger at the ground, as he moved away.

Rachel flicked a nervous glance toward the house and when she looked back, Jake had disappeared. Pulling her collar closer around her neck, wishing she'd worn a hat of some kind, she hunkered down behind the cover of the bush and kept her eyes glued to the windows at the back of the house, looking for signs of life from inside.

It wasn't what you'd actually call dark, but it was getting later all the time and if anyone was in the house, they'd soon have to resort to turning on a few lights. Shooting a pensive glance in the direction in which Jake had disappeared, Rachel's head swiveled slowly to peer into the trees and the gathering darkness behind her. Feeling suddenly very vulnerable, she prayed Jake would be all right and that he'd return—very soon.

Jake worked his way around the perimeter of the house, staying hidden in the cover of trees. So far, he hadn't seen a sign of life. There wasn't a vehicle parked near the front of the house, but a car could be hidden anywhere along the road as easily and as quickly as he'd hidden his own.

He was methodically taking all the precautions he'd been taught, making certain all his moves were careful and well-thought out. This time, unlike the last, he'd know the place was secure before going inside.

When he'd learned all he could from the outside, Jake made his way back to Rachel. With a sense of relief, he saw that she'd done as he'd said and stayed put. Apparently she hadn't heard his silent approach, because when he touched her lightly on the shoulder, she gave a startled jump and opened her mouth to scream.

Jerking her back against him, Jake's hand covered her mouth before she could utter a sound. An arm across her breasts pinned her to him, and with his cheek alongside hers, he whispered, "Relax, it's me."

Rachel went limp. She made a quick recovery, but Jake held her for a moment longer, needing to feel the reassurance of her body pressed to his. Closing his eyes and sliding his lips against the side of her neck, he took a deep breath of the essence that was Rachel and found added strength for what lay ahead.

When he released her, Rachel looked closely at his aloof expression. Had she only imagined the momentary touch of his lips against her neck?

"I took a good look around," Jake said, "and I didn't find anything."

"You mean he's gone?" she asked in quick alarm.

"No, that's not what I mean. I mean it looks as though no one's at home. I'm going inside."

She stood up, ready to dash toward the door and demand an entrance. "Well, what are you waiting for? Aren't we going inside?"

"Yes, I'm going in," Jake answered with a trace of exasperation, "but not through the front door."

"Let's go."

Staring at her intently, he said, "I said, *I* was going inside. You are going to stay right here—just in case."

"You mean in case he's in the house?"

But Jake wasn't listening to her, he was moving away. Rachel followed quickly, grabbing his arm. "I want to go, too. You need me." She hunted around in her mind for a reason and came up with, "If there's evidence Amy has been here, how will you know without me to identify it?"

It was a valid point, but her safety was his responsibility, a responsibility he didn't take lightly, and so he persisted. "I'm sorry." He shook his head. "It isn't safe. What if your ex-husband is hiding inside? One sight of you could set him off. Your life could be in danger."

"That's a chance I'm willing to take." Her eyes pleaded with him for understanding. She shook his arm in agitation. "I have to take that chance for Amy.

"Besides, what if he isn't inside? What if he's hiding out here somewhere, watching us right now. Would I be safe out here, alone, while you're in the house?"

She was right, he couldn't let her out of his sight. "All right, but you do exactly as I say, you hear?—*exactly* as I say."

Rachel nodded.

"Come on."

Together they moved closer to the house while Jake's sixth sense kept tuned to their surroundings. He studied the screened-in back porch. There were two windows visible, one to the left of the back door and one to the right. Blinds were pulled over them so he couldn't see inside, but there was an unmistakable aura of emptiness about the place.

With one last all-encompassing glance, Jake moved boldly from cover, pulling Rachel behind, and hurried toward the porch. Resting against the side of the house, nerves stretched tight with tension, he waited, listening.

When nothing happened, Jake reached up and tried the porch door. He couldn't believe it when the door opened readily beneath his touch.

A few seconds later, he stood with Rachel close behind him, leaning against the white painted wall of the house. Looking up at the window directly above their heads, Jake made a quick decision. Going in through a door could be dangerous if the house was occupied. He had no way of knowing if Dryden was armed, but he didn't want to chance flying bullets with Rachel and a child on hand.

Besides, if he went in through a window and the place was empty, should Gary show up while they were inside, he'd have a quick, undetectable, means of escape. Withdrawing a large pocketknife from his jeans, he worked at the window, prying the screen loose. Now, he could move the window back and forth in the sill, but it still wouldn't lift.

Jamming the long blade of the knife into the paint at the bottom of the sill, he drew it back and forth with difficulty, breaking the paint loose. Then he pried hard on the window, first at one end and then the other.

As he suspected, the window wasn't locked. Most people didn't think to lock windows, despite the fact they never failed to lock their doors. Tugging on the wood, rocking it back and forth to loosen the paint on the frame inside, he managed to raise it an inch.

Rachel stood with arms wrapped around her chest, staring into the deepening twilight, fearing her husband's sudden return—if he wasn't hidden somewhere inside—and wishing Jake would hurry things along. Glancing up as Jake began shoving against the bottom of the partially opened window, she asked peevishly, "Don't you carry a set of skeleton keys or something? Wouldn't it be easier to go in through a door?"

Jake ignored her to continue with what he was doing and in a relatively short span of time the window stood open.

"Is this legal?" Rachel asked with a sudden attack of conscience, staring at the open window. "Don't we need a search warrant or something?"

She didn't want to take the chance that Gary could get set free on some legal technicality so he could try something like this again. She wanted him put away for a long, long time.

Jake gave her a measuring look, turned her around and boosted her through the window. She landed on her feet, finding herself in what appeared to be a laundry room, minus appliances. In fact, the room was totally bare, except for a clothesline with two clothespins pinned to it. On further examination she spotted a shovel, a rake and a hoe standing in a corner near the door.

By the time Jake had followed her through the window, Rachel was already halfway to the door. "Come on," she said anxiously, filled with a kind of reckless courage now that they were actually inside and her daughter might be near. "Let's see what's inside."

Jake took quick hold of her shoulder, halting her abruptly. Moving around to the lead, he put her firmly behind him. A moment later, he was reaching for the door's knob.

"Jake wait!" Rachel touched his shoulder quickly. "What if Gary is inside waiting for us? What are you going to do? Do you have a gun?" The questions spilled from lips that were suddenly unsteady.

This was it—this was what she'd been waiting for ever since the night Gary had brutally thrown her from the car and driven off leaving her alone in the dirt, crying over the loss of her child and the fact that she hadn't been able to stop him.

She wanted him to be here, she wanted to see him put in jail. She wanted to tear him limb from limb with her own bare hands—but she was terrified of him and that strange look of madness she'd seen in his eyes that night, too.

And then, too, all at once she didn't know if she could trust the man at her side. Could she rely on him to get her daughter out of her ex-husband's clutches, without bringing her to harm?

She *wanted* to trust him....

"I don't need a gun to look around inside," Jake replied shortly, taking her hand from his arm and drawing her along behind him.

He didn't need to be a mind reader to know what she was thinking; his own thoughts were mirrored in her troubled glance. "Let's find out what's inside before we worry about how to handle it." He tried to sound calm and matter-of-fact and to stem the crushing tide of disappointment flooding through him at this, her first sign of distrust. "Stay close and don't make any noise."

They moved through the door and directly into another room. Jake halted abruptly, shielding Rachel with his body from a possible attack by anyone hidden within the room.

Rachel moved up close behind him, trying to see around his shoulder. They were standing in a kitchen that looked as though it had never been used. Everything was neat and tidy. The table, countertops and sink were clean and bare, leaving no visible indication that anyone lived there.

"What do you think?" Jake asked Rachel.

"Gary is a neatness freak. This looks like him. My workroom at home, where I do my glasswork, drove him to distraction."

On the move again, they left the kitchen and stepped into a hallway. "Let's try that door." Jake motioned toward the door immediately in front of him.

Hiding his own uneasiness, he gripped her shoulder momentarily, before again placing her behind him as they moved on. Jake's gut instincts were telling him they'd found their man.

The first door he opened led into a walk-in pantry. A few canned goods lined the shelves along with a popular brand of cereal and a box of powdered milk.

"That's Amy's favorite cereal!" Rachel couldn't keep the excitement out of her voice as she pointed to it with a shaking hand.

"It's mine, too," Jake said shortly.

From the shelves' contents, Jake deduced that whoever lived here either needed to make a visit to the grocery store, or they weren't planning on staying here long. He kept the observation to himself.

The next door they tried led into a bedroom. The furnishings, a full-size bed, a dresser, a small nightstand with a lamp, and a wooden rocker, were utilitarian and impersonal.

Jake motioned silently for Rachel to move back against the wall and crossed the room toward another door. Throwing the door wide, tensed to spring forward if necessary, he relaxed in relief. The room proved to be a bathroom and it was empty—except for a disposable razor, a can of generic shaving cream, and a man's comb and brush, lying on the sink.

"He's here," Rachel declared solemnly over his right shoulder, staring at the white porcelain sink.

"Do you recognize something?"

"No, but I know he's living here—I feel it in my bones."

They left the room and moved down the hall toward the living room. It looked like the rest of the house. The papered walls were bare of pictures and the furniture bare of adornment.

Jake stepped around a couch set near the door and moved up to a small desk, sitting beside a nearby window. He began in turn going through each drawer methodically. A sudden cry from another part of the house first froze him, then caused him to whirl quickly about and scan the room for Rachel. She was gone!

"Rachel—where are you?" he called softly, instantly fuming inside. He'd told her to stay with him!

"Rachel," he called again in a slightly louder voice, listening carefully, but hearing no reply. By now his jaws were clamped tight with anger at her blatant disregard of his instructions. Did she think this was a game?

And then, another thought slithered into his mind, bringing with it a sudden sharp bite of fear. What if Dryden had been in the house all along, hiding as they went through the rooms—waiting until he could get Rachel alone? What if he had her right now?

The sudden spurt of anxiety spreading through him like a breath of icy wind solidified into a feeling Jake recognized. At whatever cost to himself, he determined coldly, he'd see that Rachel and her child came to no harm.

Jake quickly found his way down a long central hall that divided the house into two separate parts, hugging the wall as he moved cautiously forward, keeping a close eye on what was ahead as well as behind. Coming to an open door, he moved slowly forward, tensed for an attack, and peered around the doorframe into the room.

"Rachel?" He looked for signs of a struggle and saw none.

She stood alone in the center of the room, her back to him, head bowed over an object she held to her with both hands. Turning slowly at the sound of her name, she gazed at him with saddened eyes, yet he could see a strange kind of elation in their depths, too.

"I've found Mrs. McNab." Holding out what appeared to be a faded pink bunny with long floppy ears, she took a step in his direction. "It's her—it's Mrs. McNab."

Jake looked blank.

"Don't you remember the stuffed animal you picked up at my house? Well, this is the other half of the pair. Remember, I told you there were two of them, a boy and a girl?

"Amy got them for Easter last year. She named them Mr. and Mrs. McNab, after her Sunday school teacher and the woman's husband."

Rachel rubbed the furry creature a bit desperately against one cheek. "She loved this one the best, because she said it looked exactly like the real Mrs. McNab." Her eyes darkened with the remembrance. "She had Mrs. McNab with her the night Gary took her."

"You're sure?" Jake asked with quiet emphasis, stepping fully into the room.

Rachel turned the bunny over and holding its cotton tail aside for his inspection, said, "See those stitches? I made them, myself, because she was losing her stuffing and Amy wouldn't go to sleep at night without her."

Jake glanced from the toy to the room's contents. Unlike the other rooms in the house, this one was filled to overflowing. He bent to pick up a jack-in-the box and look at the painted face of the clown weaving back and forth on a spring.

"What the hell is all this?" he asked, looking around the room.

It was filled with toys. There were dolls in billowing lace dresses, clowns in colorful suits and caps, a brass drum complete with lithograph picture, a miniature china tea set that looked like the real thing, a small rosewood piano with yellowed ivory keys and a rare collection of doll's furniture and appliances from another era. He hadn't seen anything like this since the night he and his best friend had gone upstairs into his friend's attic to look for a place they could smoke without getting caught by his parents.

This was the only room he'd found in the whole house stamped with any kind of a personality—and it was bizarre in the extreme.

"What in the hell is all this?" Jake repeated in momentary confusion.

"My daughter's toys," Rachel replied hollowly.

Jake jerked his head in her direction. From there he looked toward the cracked and peeling face of a nearby doll, the mildew-stained dress of another. Picking up a broken teacup, he held it out to her. "This—this is what you give your daughter to play with?"

"No. It's what Gary has given her to play with."

Darting suddenly across the room to the open closet, she jerked the door back on its hinges and said, "Look!" Pulling out dresses made of gingham, cambric and batiste, designed in styles of nearly a century ago, she held them up for him to see.

"These don't belong to Amy." She let go of the dresses and hurried toward the dresser. Jerking open a drawer, spilling nightgowns of fine lawn and stockings made of wool onto the floor, she added, "And neither do these!"

Jake stared blankly at her impassioned expression.

"Don't you understand?" she asked in growing frustration. "Take a look around this room. These furnishings belong in a museum." Snatching an item from a nearby shelf, she whirled to face him.

"Here!" She advanced toward him, shoving the thing at his face. "Look at this and then tell me what you think."

When Jake made no immediate move to take what was offered, Rachel grabbed his hand and pushed it into his fingers. Wondering if she'd finally cracked beneath the strain, Jake brought the object slowly toward his face.

"This isn't Amy...."

"No," Rachel agreed grimly, "take a look at the back."

Jake flipped the framed photograph over. The words printed on the back had faded with time and were now almost illegible, but he managed to decipher them. Amelinda Lucille Conroy, aged six, nineteen-hundred and sixteen.

"Don't you see what he's done?" Rachel asked with horror crowding her voice. "He's trying to make Amy take the place of his grandmother. My God," she whispered brokenly, "he's trying make my baby over into the image of a dead woman."

Finally Jake understood, but he was more concerned at the moment with Rachel's frame of mind than with her absent daughter.

He replaced the small portrait and took Rachel into his arms. "It's all right," he reassured her somberly. "We'll get her away from him before he can do her any lasting harm. She's very young. Once she's back with you she'll forget all about what's happened while she was with her father."

"Are you sure?" she asked brokenly.

Gathering her close, resting his chin atop her head, he stared at the room with unseeing eyes. "Yes," he replied with conviction, recalling his own past all too clearly, "I'm sure."

Rachel pulled loose after a moment and wiped the tears from her eyes. Bending to pick up Mrs. McNab, she smoothed a finger along the faded silk ears.

"I'm so confused. I don't know what to think, how to feel." She grew visibly taut, her hands squeezing the pink rabbit. "One minute I hate Gary with everything that's in me—and the next . . . I pity him."

Her eyes found Jake's face. "He's crazy, he's really crazy, isn't he?" she asked softly.

"Yes," he answered gently, "I'd say he was."

She nodded, clutching the rabbit against her.

"I need to make a more thorough examination of the house," Jake said gently. "Do you want to come with me?"

"No, I think I'll stay here for a while."

Jake turned at the door and glanced back at her. She was standing in the center of the room, rubbing her cheek against the toy's soft fur. As he rounded the door, he heard her whisper in broken tones, "Oh, God, Mrs. McNab, if only you could talk. . . .

"*Amy—where are you?*"

Chapter 13

Jake left Rachel and moved back through the house searching for a telephone. He needed to call Sheriff Langly and bring him up-to-date on the situation they'd found and to get backup before Dryden returned with the child.

His search led him through the living room, into the man's bedroom, through a formal dining room without furniture, another empty room that was probably used as a bedroom and back into the kitchen. Rachel found him there, going through cabinets and drawers.

"What are you doing?"

"I have to get hold of Langly and tell him to get the warrant." Slamming a drawer shut, he turned with his hands on his hips and stared around the room a little desperately.

"No phone?"

"Does it look like it?" he snapped irritably. Dammit! Now what?

"Come on, I'll help you look. Maybe you just missed it."

He wanted to tell her that was highly unlikely. He'd been in every room and looked through every nook and cranny the house contained, to no avail. But he didn't—he accepted her offer without protest, because he didn't want to cause her needless alarm. But as for himself, first there had been the flat tire to delay them and now no telephone. He was starting to get a nauseating sense of déjà vu....

In the next few minutes he and Rachel retraced his earlier footsteps looking in all the likely places, and some unlikely ones, for a telephone. "That settles it." Jake sighed, standing in the kitchen with drooping shoulders.

"What?" Rachel asked with a frown. "That settles what?"

"One of us is going to have go back to town and call Sheriff Langly." He eyed her pointedly.

His meaning was clear. She knew which of one of "us" had been elected to go.

"No," she said stubbornly, starting to shake her head. "I won't leave. I'm not budging from this house until I have Amy with me."

"I understand how you feel—"

"No—you don't!"

"I know you're afraid your ex-husband might return, somehow suspect we've been here, and leave with your daughter. But, without the warrant, we haven't a legal leg to stand on. One of us has to go—"

"You do it!"

"And what if Gary returns after I leave? He's living in a fantasy world where there's no telling what he might do. If nothing else, that room where your daughter sleeps proves how dangerous he could be to you."

"And that's exactly my point," she caught him up swiftly. "Have you forgotten the threat he made against Amy? If I leave, and you're left here alone, he might do anything. You're a stranger, not only to Gary, but to Amy as well. No..." She shook her head decisively. "You go phone Sheriff Langly—besides, I wouldn't know what to say to the man—and I'll stay here."

Jake crossed the room and took hold of her arm. "You don't have a choice in the matter. You go and I stay—that's the way it works."

Grasping her elbow firmly, he hauled her with him from the kitchen to the laundry room.

"Why can't we use the door?" she asked as he ushered her toward the window.

"There's a chain on it. He'd know someone had been inside if we leave it unfastened."

At the window, expecting her to try something, Jake was on guard. But without further protest, she stepped into the cradle he made with his hands and pulled herself over the windowsill, hopping onto the porch below.

"After you go, I'll find a hiding place and wait for them outside. I'll get him in the open, before he can get into the house where he can hide. And I promise, nothing will happen to your daughter."

Rachel cast him a look of regret that he didn't see as he lowered his head through the window and turned away. She was already off the porch, standing in the rain, when he pulled himself through the window's narrow opening.

Jake looked up, and she began to run. Taken off guard, he jumped to the porch and stumbled, twisting an ankle. When he'd regained his balance, Rachel had disappeared into the thick covering of underbrush and trees bordering the back of the house.

Jake made a dash toward the door, ignoring the pain in his ankle, cursing beneath his breath. "Rachel! Dammit, this is no time to play a game of wills—come out!" He scanned the immediate area looking for a sign of the direction she'd taken and waited, hoping she'd see sense and come out without his having to search for her.

"This is ridiculous," he muttered furiously, when she didn't immediately step into view, "we're wasting precious time. Be reasonable! What if Gary returns while I'm gone?

"You're no match for him." Jake reminded her of the last time she'd crossed swords with the man, then paused to let that sink in, hoping it would elicit a response.

When it didn't, he tried again. "The sight of you could send him over the edge. What could you do to stop him, if he tried to harm your daughter? Have you considered that?"

Again his warning was met with utter silence.

"Rachel... *Damn you*," he muttered beneath his breath, "Be reasonable . . . please. . . ."

He waited a few minutes longer, but this time, when she didn't respond, he knew she wasn't going to. He had to go. Dryden might return at any moment, and it was ten miles to town.

He didn't want to leave her here, alone, but what else could he do? *Remember the last time.* The warning he'd offered Rachel echoed inside his own head. He did, and all too well.

Hurrying into the trees, he threw a glance toward the sky and noted that it had changed from a dull dirty-gray, when they'd first entered the house, to stormy black slate. It would be totally dark soon and fear for Rachel's safety gnawed at his insides.

"All right, Rachel, you win. I'll go make the call. But whatever you do, stay out of sight and away from the house. Do you hear me? Don't make your presence known or approach your ex-husband in any way, until I return."

Jake stood a moment longer staring at the trees, straining to catch a glimpse of her slight figure, before making a dash in the direction of the car. He returned to the vehicle in the same roundabout course that he'd taken to the house. He wanted to ensure that he left no tracks in the rain-softened earth for Dryden to find. The safety of Rachel and her daughter was in Jake's hands and he couldn't afford to make another mistake.

Jake damned himself heartily for not realizing before this that he'd need to contact the sheriff and preparing for it. He should have taken along a two-way radio, or driven an official car instead of using his own.

He hadn't been thinking! Slamming his fist against the steering wheel until he began to feel the pain, he forced himself to slow the car down and stay in the tracks. He couldn't afford mistakes—mistakes cost lives—*mistakes cost lives...cost lives...cost lives....* The words echoed through his brain.

Once out on the highway, he drove like a demon, passing no one on the road, making the trip to the town of Morris in record time. At the first gas station he spotted there was a bank of four phones. Jake slammed on his brakes, leaving a trail of smoke and rubber on the road.

He almost fell out of his car as he searched in his pockets for change. The first phone he tried was out of order. The second one took his quarter and gave him no dial tone, but on the third try he got the sheriff's department.

"Langly? Frost here." He didn't waste time with amenities. "We've found him."

"Where?"

"Town called Morris. A house just off Speedway Road about ten miles from the city limits—"

"I know the area. Is it the old Tenney place?"

"I don't know. It's a single-story house, set back down a lane, in a forest of pines."

"That's the Tenney place. I'll call Judge Wyman for the warrant and send backup. Do you think he might be armed?"

"I don't know—he wasn't there—but there's evidence to prove the child has been there. Look, I've got to go. Mrs. Dryden is back at the house—"

"You left her there alone?"

"Not my choice," Jake responded tersely.

"I see. Well, I'll deliver the warrant myself, within the hour. Be careful," Langly warned and rang off.

Jake dropped the phone to dangle on the wire cord and hurried back to the car. He checked the clock on his car's dash and realized he'd been gone twenty minutes. That was too long! A lot could happen in twenty minutes. Pushing from his mind the image of Lacy being held in her kidnapper's hands, Jake switched on the car's headlights and stepped down hard on the accelerator.

It was totally dark when Jake turned onto the lane to the old Tenney house where he'd left Rachel such a short time ago. All totaled it had taken little more than half an hour to accomplish his mission.

But it was still too long. As Jake wound his way on foot down the drive toward the house, forsaking the woods this time because he now moved under the cover of darkness, he

saw a black Ford parked in the drive in front of the house.
With a twist of fear, Jake knew Dryden had returned.

Where was Rachel?

Approaching the house with caution, he looked for her.
Stopping to within a few hundred yards of it, he called her
name softly. He edged closer, calling to her again, but
knowing instinctively that it was a waste of time. She was in
the house. That's probably where her child was, and that,
he was certain, is where he'd also find her.

Feeling the revolver Langly had given him earlier that day
rub against his spine, Jake reached around behind and
withdrew it from beneath the waistband of his jeans. For a
moment he wondered if he should have given the gun to
Rachel for protection before he left to make his call, but it
was only a fleeting thought. She probably didn't know how
to use one, and putting a loaded weapon in the hands of an
untrained individual was an irresponsible act.

Jake held the weapon with both hands and hunched low,
as he moved toward the house. Stopping to lean against the
side of the building, he eased toward a window and peered
warily into the living room. The lamp had been turned on
in the room, but no one was in sight.

It was the only window in this part of the house that
showed any illumination, so he decided to move toward the
back. Nearing what he knew must be the kitchen window,
he saw that a light had been turned on in that room, too, but
the curtains had been drawn, barring his vision.

With a shoulder against the house, he felt his way around
to the rear of the house. At the very back Jake shifted the
gun to his right hand and quietly tried the screen door. It
was still unlocked. Guessing it could be a trap, he moved
through it with great caution.

Once on the porch, he paused for a moment, squinting
through the dark and turned with the gun pointed in all directions. So far, everything had looked quiet, his way un-
impeded, but Jake was distrustful of the ease with which he
appeared able to gain entrance to the house a second time.

Looking for a trap, he moved toward the window he'd
used before to get into the house. He'd left it slightly open

when exiting it earlier. It was still open. If Rachel had used it to reenter the house, she'd been careful to leave it in the exact position she'd found it.

The window slid up the frame easily, making only a slight sound. Jake hadn't noticed it the first time, probably because he'd been vexed with Rachel. He stopped and listened carefully, while the thought of Rachel and the possible danger she could be facing at that very moment weaved its way along his nerves, stretching them tighter.

A moment later, he was in the house. Leaving the window open, he quickly but noiselessly made his way into the hall. He could hear voices coming from another part of the house, and it took him a moment to get his bearings and realize they were coming from the direction of the kitchen.

One of the indistinct voices was definitely feminine, and as he drew closer to the room, he recognized Rachel's throaty tones. Jake stood flattened against the wall, staring into the room.

The tableau inside induced a terrible memory. For a moment, Jake was propelled back in time, facing a coldly insane man who held a gun pointed at a child—while his cold, gray glance rested, unwaveringly, on Jake's frozen face.

An icy sweat broke out under Jake's arms and across his shoulders. Sweat popped out on his forehead and along his upper lip. An itch developed at the corner of one eye. He scratched at it ruthlessly. He swallowed with a dry mouth and tasted the thick, sour, taste of fear on the back of his tongue.

"If you hurt our child, I swear—crazy or not—I'll kill you myself."

Rachel's deadly calm voice penetrated Jake's fogged senses, slapping him abruptly into the present. He focused on the scene before him as it truly was.

Gary Dryden sat at the table with a small, dark-haired girl on his lap. At her throat, he held a long, thin-bladed knife that succeeded in keeping his ex-wife at bay.

Rachel stood motionless in the center of the room, fists clenched tightly at her sides, facing her ex-husband. Jake could see her in profile, and he'd never witnessed a look of such intense hatred on her face.

"You always were melodramatic, my dear," Dryden responded in deeply cultured tones. "And as I recall, you were always making promises you couldn't fulfill."

"You're referring to the money. Is that why you married me, instead of Marian Benning?" Rachel asked scathingly. "She had money, but you found out you couldn't control her. You thought I'd be easy—"

"You *were* easy—too easy. It was all over the campus. You were the wealthy princess all the jocks wanted to land, the darling only child of older parents, guaranteed to make some lucky man rich as Croesus."

"Only I didn't get the money," Rachel put in. "At my insistence, my parents left most of it to their favorite charities. And that's something you didn't foresee, isn't it—the fact that I wasn't as greedy as you?"

"You're a fool!"

"No, I simply loved my parents for who they were, not for what they could give me. But you don't understand that, do you? All you understand is *money*," she spat the word at him. She'd thought she'd be dealing with a crazy man. And maybe she was, but he didn't sound crazy at the moment, just vicious and cruel.

"Wrong!" he shouted. Tightening his hold on his daughter, he gazed up at Rachel with a mixture of triumph and outrage.

Amy whimpered, and Rachel made a quick move in her direction. "Don't," her ex-husband warned, pressing the knife closer against the child's throat.

Rachel froze.

"I know about love—I loved my aunt. I loved the stories she used to tell me about my grandmother."

"Is that why your aunt is dying all alone in a nursing home—kept by the state—because you loved her?" Rachel asked scornfully.

"So—you know about her. Then that means you must have met my dear mother as well. A wonderful woman, wouldn't you say?" he asked with unveiled sarcasm.

Rachel noted the feverish light becoming visible in her ex-husband's eyes and the way the hand holding the knife at their daughter's throat trembled. She was upsetting him, and that isn't what she wanted, not until Amy was free of him.

By going against Jake's command and making her presence known to Gary, she'd hoped she could reason with him and get him to release the child before anyone actually got hurt. It was still hard, despite her deep anger at him and all that he'd done, for her to stop seeing him as the quiet man she'd married.

Which was stupid of her, she knew, because he'd given her ample proof even before their divorce that his kindness and consideration had all been an act with which to deceive her, so he could get what he really wanted.

"Whatever your differences with your mother—whatever you feel toward me—isn't important. What's important now is Amy. Let her go—"

"Shut up!" Pulling the little girl tighter against him, eyes narrowing on Rachel's white face, Gary shouted, "Don't say another word to me! I despise you every bit as much as I loathe that bitch who spawned me and then abandoned me for her music."

A crafty light entered the narrowed blue eyes. "But I got even with her. I stole what she wanted most in the world— besides her *music*—I stole her inheritance, and I stole it right from under her very nose.

"And I've done the same to you, haven't I?" he asked with a smile. "I've taken the one thing in all the world you care about."

"Why Amy?" Rachel dared to ask. "You have what you want, you have your aunt's money and property. You don't want a child, an encumbrance—"

"Be still, you stupid bitch!" Spittle flecked the corners of his mouth. "You think you know it all, don't you? You think I married you just for your money?

"Well—you're wrong! You know nothing! I did it for her! Don't you understand that, you stupid cow? I did it all for her!"

Dropping his cheek against the struggling child's head, he looked up at Rachel and smiled. "She's mine," he crooned, "my child, my little Amelinda—the one thing no one can ever take away from me.

"My mother drove my father away with her coldness." The anger was back in his eyes. "But my aunt...she gave me something I could really love...she gave me Amelinda."

Jake knew it was time to make his move. He slid the gun into the waistband of his jeans, where he could reach it quickly if he needed to, and stepped into the room. "And you love her very much, don't you?"

"What's this?" Dryden's glance flew between Rachel and the intruder. "You brought a man along?" The expression of surprise on his face quickly changed to one of derision. "You always were disgustingly preoccupied with what took place in the marriage bed. Is this your new lover?"

Amy whimpered as the knife pressed tautly against the tender flesh covering her larynx. Jake's eyes darkened momentarily with anger, but he quickly controlled it. He wanted nothing so much as to get the man between his hands and beat the meanness out of him, but he had to remember the child—and the fact that he was dealing with an unstable mind.

Everyone in their anxiety had overlooked the child's reaction to what was taking place around her. Amy glanced from her mother's frightened face to the newcomer, looking for help. She didn't understand why her daddy had taken her from her mother and brought her here, where they had no friends. She didn't understand why he was angry with her, or why he was hurting her. And she didn't understand why her mother was crying. All she knew is that she had missed her mother and wanted to go to her right now.

"You do love your daughter, don't you?" Jake asked again.

"Who the hell are you?" Dryden demanded.

"Someone concerned about a child—your child. Look at her, you're hurting her. Is that what you want?" His eyes closely searched the other man's face. "Do you really want to hurt *her?*" Jake asked in soothing tones.

Gary was confused. Rachel's anger he understood. He even welcomed it, since it fed the anger churning inside him. Anger that had been building inside him for years, ever since he was old enough to understand that his mother didn't love him and didn't want him—yet she wouldn't let him live with the one person who did love him, his Aunt Beaulah.

He felt Amy squirming in his grasp and looked down at her small, heart-shaped face. This was his child, the spitting image of his grandmother—no, she *was* his grandmother—she was Amelinda, he had a picture to prove it.

His Aunt Beaulah had been too old to get him away from his mother, and he'd been unhappy for a long time. But, then, he'd dreamed of a way to find the one person in all the world who would love him—he'd dreamed of his grandmother, and she'd come to him and told him what he must do.

Aunt Beaulah had loved Amelinda more than anyone in the world, even more than she loved him, but that was okay. She was the one who had told him all about Amelinda, and how special she'd been. She'd said Amelinda was the most beautiful, gentle, gifted creature ever born. And Gary had listened in fascination to the one person who had taken the time to treat him with kindness, and believed all that she said.

He'd sat for hours, listening, while his aunt told stories about Amelinda's beauty and accomplishments. And when Beaulah had told him Amelinda would have been so very proud to have had a little boy like him, a little boy with beautiful manners who respected his elders, Gary had grown to love Amelinda even more than he loved his Aunt Beaulah.

He knew Amelinda would have understood what it was like to be lonely and sad, because he had no one to play with, because his mother couldn't abide the noise of children around the house while she was practicing her music.

But she was gone—the real Amelinda was gone. So, Gary had spent his whole life looking for someone just like her, someone to take her place in his life. But eventually, when he didn't find anyone, he'd given up and settled on the idea of producing a special child of his own.

During that time, he'd managed to get even with his mother for refusing to allow him to live with his Aunt Beaulah. He got his aunt to sign over everything she owned to him, and even though he knew at the time that it would be a while before he could actually use any of it, that didn't matter, as long as his mother didn't receive a penny.

With that out of the way, he'd gone looking for a suitable wife to produce his child. Marian Benning had been his first choice. She had breeding to produce the kind of child he wanted, and she had money, so that at a suitable time he and the child could disappear and live without ever being found.

But Marian hadn't wanted a marriage that included a child. And then he'd met Rachel. Rachel was perfect—she was young and strong, from a good family, and she was due to inherit a fortune.

It wasn't until after they were married that he learned there would be no money. And then his aunt got worse, and he realized it didn't matter because he would soon have his inheritance.

Gary made careful plans, and Rachel became pregnant. Nine months later, when he'd seen his daughter for the first time in the hospital nursery, it was like looking at one of the pictures his Aunt Beaulah had showed him of Amelinda. Amy could have been the same child.

That's when he realized that it must be her. Somehow, wherever she was, Amelinda had learned how much Gary needed her, and she'd found a way to come to him. He was elated.

Everything would have been all right—he'd have managed to sell off the property that he had inherited, and he and Amelinda could have disappeared someplace where no one would find them, if *the bitch* hadn't divorced him and tried to take his precious Amelinda away from him for the second time.

"Daddy," Amy protested in childish tones, "you're hurting—stop hurting—me."

Gary loosened his hold on the child, but the knife remained at her throat. He wouldn't really hurt her—unless he had to—and then, he'd do himself in, too. They'd be together for all time after that and no one would ever be able to separate them ever again.

"What do you want?" he asked belligerently, looking directly at Jake.

"I want to help you," Jake replied again in that moderate tone of voice, moving farther into the room, hiding the animosity he felt toward this man who dared to threaten his own daughter's life.

"Stop!" Dryden cried suddenly. "Don't come any closer or I'll—"

"It's all right." Jake raised his hands and stopped dead in his tracks. "I'll stay right here—don't get upset."

"I'm not upset!" the other man denied hotly. "I'm very calm." He took a deep breath and released it slowly to show them he was calm. "I don't get angry—I get even." He flashed a sudden smirk in Rachel's direction.

Jake decided to try a different tack. "I saw Amy's room. She has a lot of toys. Did you buy her all those things?"

"Yes . . . so what? And it's Amelinda. I never liked the short appellation *she* chose to use."

"Amelinda," Jake corrected himself. "She's a very lucky little girl to have a father who cares so much about her. I'll bet you didn't have things like that when you were a child."

"Ha!" Dryden laughed without humor. "My mother spent every penny she earned on herself and her music."

Jake shook his head in sympathy. "That's too bad, but it's her loss."

"Yes?" Gary's eyes sharpened. "And how is that?"

"She missed the enjoyment of watching you grow, sharing your youth and enthusiasm for life. No one has more enthusiasm for life than a child. Don't you agree? Just think of all the things you have already experienced through your daughter's eyes."

Gary looked reflective. "Yes, I know what you mean."

"You're a good father. It's evident you've taken very good care of her since she's been with you."

Gary's expression darkened. "I tried to tell the courts that, but they wouldn't listen—"

"What do they know?" Jake asked quickly, seeing rage gathering in the blue eyes. "I can see you not only love your daughter, but she loves you, too. Look at her."

Jake nodded to the child who was once again sitting quietly, listening in fascination to the strange man talk. Her daddy seemed to like listening to him, too, because he wasn't holding her so tight now.

"You know," Jake continued, "she looks very much like you."

"That's because she's really Amelinda Conroy-Wilkes, my grandmother. She's come back for me."

"Is that so?" Jake advanced a few steps toward the man, covering the move with feigned interest. "Then, you wouldn't want to see her hurt...now, would you?" he asked gently, standing less than a yard away.

Jake gauged his chances of leaping toward the man and successfully shoving the child out of harm's way before Dryden could use the knife. He estimated them to be somewhere in the neighborhood of slim and none at all.

Switching his attention to the little girl, he hunkered down so he was on a level with her. Meeting her wide blue eyes, he smiled. If there was only some way to convey what he wanted her to do.

"You have a very good daddy. I'll bet you love him a lot, don't you?"

"Y-yes." She tried to nod, felt the blade close against her throat again and put up a tiny hand to push her father's arm out of the way.

Gary allowed her the room, Jake noted with a surge of satisfaction, dropping one knee to the floor and leaning closer. There was a chance, now that the other man's guard was partially lowered, that he might be able to get the child safely away from him. But he knew he had very little time to do it. Before long, Sheriff Langly and his deputies would descend on them, and all hell would break loose.

In what might appear a reckless move, he drew the man's attention to the weapon at his daughter's throat. "Children are very curious little creatures. I'll bet she didn't realize how dangerous a knife can be when she picked it up."

Jake wanted to jerk the knife from the man and punch him in the face for what he'd put Rachel and this child through—but not yet... not yet.

Rachel, silent throughout the whole proceeding, drew a quick breath, wondering why, when he'd been doing so well, Jake had deliberately brought the knife into the conversation.

Gary looked at the knife in surprise, taking his attention off Jake for a split second. It was all Jake needed. Sweeping the child out of the way with one arm, he made a grab for the knife.

The other man recovered and made a move toward Amy, but too late. Rachel swept the child into her arms just as Jake struck a blow to the man's astonished face.

The blow knocked Gary back in the chair and the knife flew from his fingers. Jake made a leap toward it as Gary recovered and lunged out of the chair and onto Jake's back.

They fell to the floor, grappling for a hold on each other's gyrating bodies. Jake threw a punch to Dryden's solar plexus, rendering him incapacitated for long enough to reach the knife. But Dryden was on his back almost instantly, his arm around Jake's neck, throttling him.

Jake kept straining toward the knife with one hand, arm stretched, fingers extended, while he tried to break free of Gary's deathlike grip on his throat. All at once, he drew his arm up and brought his elbow back hard against Dryden's ribs.

Dryden grunted with pain but tightened his hold, locking his other arm with the first one and squeezing hard, slowly strangling the life from Jake's body. Jake had to give up on the knife, so he could use both elbows to deal Dryden a punishing blow to both sides of his rib cage at the same time.

Dryden gave a loud grunt of pain and let Jake go, grabbing his ribs with both hands and doubling over. It gave Jake the time he needed to get the knife. In seconds, he was sitting astride Dryden's chest with the knife at the man's throat.

"Knives are very dangerous weapons," Jake said coldly, ignoring the blood dripping from his own nose onto the man's shirt. "People can easily get hurt with them," Jake bit out through clenched teeth. "You wouldn't want that to happen, would you?" he asked, jamming the thin blade against the man's bobbing Adam's apple.

"N-no," Gary replied, looking up into a face twisted with hate. Who was this man?

Jake felt the muscles in his arms and back grow tense. It took every ounce of restraint he could muster to keep the knife steady, instead of letting it sweep across the man's throat to leave a thin red line in its wake. Dryden's face swam before his vision, and another face took its place.

Detached gray eyes locked on his and all Jake could see was cold deliberation in their depths. *Don't!* his mind cried, while his throat worked to produce the sound his lips couldn't manage.

"Jake?"

All at once, Jake became conscious of mother and daughter, holding each other tight, watching him with wide, frightened eyes.

"Take the child into the other room," he grated to Rachel.

"Why?"

"Do it!"

"N-no—what are you going to do?" Her eyes were on the thin edge of the blade pressed to Gary's throat.

Jake's nostrils flared with fury. "Do you care?" he asked with contempt.

"A-about him? No. But I do care about you. Don't do anything foolish, Jake—please. The sheriff will be here soon."

Jake stared at her thinly, knowing she was right, Langly would be here soon, but... He wanted to bash the man's head in. He wanted to rip him in two. He ached to—

"Mommy, why is that man sitting on Daddy's chest? Is Daddy sick?"

"No, honey, Daddy's fine and he's going to stay that way—isn't he, Jake?" She knew how Jake felt. A few minutes ago, she'd have liked nothing better than to get a few blows in herself for all the pain and worry he'd caused her in the last couple of years. But now that she had Amy in her arms, she was content to let the law handle Gary Dryden's punishment.

"He isn't worth it, you know," she whispered softly, turning away. It was Jake's choice, and he had to make it alone.

A long moment of taut silence, while anger fought with reason, followed. The images from Jake's past faded, leaving a clear picture of the pathetic man beneath him cowering from the knife and Jake's implacable anger. Jake climbed slowly to his feet and hauled Gary to his. Dragging him to the table, he shoved him down in the chair where he'd sat so calmly a few minutes ago, holding a knife at his own daughter's throat.

Rachel left the room slowly, taking Amy with her, but her thoughts stayed with Jake. It had been close, the ferocity of his anger had frightened her, but deep down inside she'd known all along that he'd make the right decision. Whether Jake realized it himself or not, he was a very humane man.

Chapter 14

"Well, here's the warrant." Sheriff Ben Langly flashed the document before Jake's eyes, but his own eyes were fastened on the man his deputies were leading away. "By the way, who's Amelinda? He keeps asking for her."

Jake shrugged. "His daughter, but I guess he thinks she's his reincarnated grandmother or something."

"The man's got some real problems," Langly commented with a shake of his head.

"Who doesn't?" Jake asked, thinking about his own.

Rachel walked up to the two men, holding her daughter in her arms. Was Jake about to disappear from her life now that she had her daughter back? She hoped not, because these last few minutes had made her realize how much she had come to love him. She had eyes for no one but Jake.

"Is it really all over?"

"It's over." Jake didn't know what else to say. He'd been dragged in on this case against his will, but once he'd become involved with it, he'd begun to hope that by its end, he'd feel different inside. All he felt was frozen. Like an engine that had been run without oil, he was locked up tight within himself and nothing moved—except anger. He was deeply angry with Rachel.

Sheriff Langly sensed the two had things to say to each other and decided to make himself scarce. "Would you like me to take the little girl?" he offered. It was starting to rain heavily. "I'll put her in the patrol car out of the weather."

"No—thank you," Rachel responded quickly, hugging her daughter close. It was going to be a long while before she'd willingly let the child out of her sight again.

"We have some papers for you to sign at the station," Langly continued uncomfortably, feeling like a fifth wheel, but business was business. "Can I give you a lift back to town?"

Rachel looked at Jake. Jake stared at the ground. She opened her mouth to reply, and Jake intervened abruptly, "I'll take them back to town."

There was no way out of it and he knew it, so he might as well give in gracefully. They were going to have to talk. Maybe it would be easier with the child between them.

The sheriff nodded and started to walk away. Jake stopped him with a quick motion of his head. The two stepped away from the lights and commotion.

"Here, you'll be wanting this back now." Jake pulled the gun from beneath his jacket and handed it to the other man.

"Thanks." Langly weighed the weapon in his hand and then looked up at Jake. "You been with the agency a long time?"

Jake shrugged. "A while."

"You ever get in the mood for something a bit slower paced, you give me a call."

"Thanks." They shook hands. "I'll keep that in mind."

"You do that." Langly turned away, touched a finger to his hat as he passed Rachel and climbed into the sheriff's car beside a young deputy. He waved as they drove off.

A few minutes later they were on their way, too. Jake traveled down the lane at a much slower speed than he'd driven down it the last time. Something bumped against his thigh and he looked down and saw that Amy had crawled onto the seat between him and Rachel and fallen asleep. Her head lay in her mother's lap, her feet in his. They looked like a family returning from a day's outing, but Jake knew better.

"I owe you an apology," Rachel spoke softly, mindful of the sleeping child.

"It isn't necessary." His voice sounded gruff.

"You're angry with me. I'm sorry, but I couldn't leave without—"

"Forget it," Jake cut across her words. "It's over now, so let's just forget it."

"I can't."

"Well, I'm going to."

"Can you?" She turned to look up at his profile in the light from the dash. "Can you forget . . . all of it?"

A note in her voice drew his eyes to her face. As their glances locked, she whispered, "I can't forget . . . any of it. I remember every moment together since our first meeting."

"Leave it alone." He returned his gaze to the road.

"Why?"

"It's better that way."

"Better for whom?"

"For all of us," he answered with a finality that made her ache inside. "It just wouldn't work."

"What wouldn't work?"

"Us—you and me . . . and your daughter."

"Her name is Amy. Say it—it won't bind you to us if you use her name."

Jake's jaw tightened. She was going to make this as hard as possible for the both of them. The silence between them, broken by the swish of the windshield wipers, thickened.

"Is it because she's his child?" Though it hurt, she had to ask the question.

"What are you talking about?" Jake asked with a frown.

"Is this wall between us built on the fact that I am the mother of another man's child?"

"Don't be ridiculous," Jake snapped.

"Then it's because I went back into the house—I disobeyed you—that's it, isn't it?"

"I told you to leave it alone."

"I won't!" Her voice had risen and she quickly glanced down at her daughter's sleeping face before demanding in quieter tones, "I want an explanation."

"And is that all that matters?" He ground the words out from between his teeth. "Does nothing matter to you but what you want?"

He slammed the heel of his hand against the steering wheel. The child between them moved restlessly in her sleep, and Jake lowered his voice to whisper hotly, "Well, what about what I want? I told you to stay put! I told you to stay away from the house—away from your ex-husband—but you didn't listen.

"You're stubborn and willful and—you could have been hurt! Don't you understand? If you'd have been hurt, I'd have been responsible—"

"Is that all that matters to you—" she asked, becoming angry herself, now, "—who would be responsible?"

"Your safety matters—"

"Does it?" she all but shouted and then quickly lowered her voice. "I'm an adult, so why don't you treat me like one? I take responsibility for my own actions. I don't need to blame someone else for them!"

"Then learn to act like an adult!" Jake responded passionately. "You aren't the only one who might have been hurt. Did you stop to think about that? You put your own daughter's life in danger, too, by your reckless actions. If she'd been injured, would you willingly have accepted the responsibility for that, too?"

The truth of the remark hit home, deflating her anger. "I'm sorry."

"Don't tell me, tell her—tell your daughter, it's her life you jeopardized just now."

"You're cruel," she whispered through stiff lips.

"Yes…I am," Jake agreed, hoping that would put an end to the conversation.

"You're going to leave us, aren't you?" Rachel asked after a long brittle silence, ice spreading through her at the thought.

"Why?" Eyes darkened with the pain of it darted in his direction. "Why?" she asked again when he didn't answer.

What did she want from him? *He knew . . . he knew . . .*

"Aren't you going to answer me? Jake—if what's standing between us has anything to do with what happened the last time, with that other little girl—"

"What's between us—or lacking between us—has nothing at all to do with that," Jake cut her off. He didn't want to have this conversation. He'd hoped to avoid it.

"Then what?" Rachel persisted. "What's taking you away?"

"It should be obvious—"

"Well, it isn't."

"It's me, dammit!" he said in a tortured whisper. "Don't you understand? It's me!"

"You? What do you mean?"

"I wanted to smash your ex-husband's head in a little while ago. I wanted to take that knife and . . ." He broke off, shaking his head.

"I know," Rachel took him up, "I wanted to bash his head in, too. Whether he's sick or not, I'd still like to do it. I hope they put him away for a very long time.

"But I still don't see your point. There's nothing wrong with having a healthy temper."

"There's nothing healthy about my temper. There's a violent streak in me . . . a legacy from my parents. It's a kind of sickness—like your ex-husband's. I won't inflict it on others—"

"That's nonsense!" Rachel protested quickly. "You're nothing like Gary. There's no sickness in you, just unhappiness and pain."

"No, you're wrong. I've seen a pattern, the same pattern my parents followed, and I won't—"

"What pattern?"

"The passion between us—"

"—is good—is wonderful!"

"It's destructive."

"My God . . ." She was startled by the thoughts flashing through her mind. "It isn't violence that's frightening you," she said in amazement, suddenly realizing the truth of it. "It's love—it's your capacity for caring about others that has you running scared.

"I thought it was me. I thought you were afraid of loving me. But that isn't it. It's the whole idea of love that turns you off. You've grown so accustomed to keeping yourself locked away from the world, you don't want to change things.

"I understand your being afraid of getting hurt, we're all afraid of that, but you have to take that chance, or...what's the use in living?"

"Don't be ridiculous! You don't know what you're talking about." Jake dismissed her indictment out of hand. He was doing this for her, why couldn't she understand that?

"Don't I?" Her tone had become chilly. "You accused me of being stubborn and willful, but you're a coward—an emotional cripple."

Jake seethed silently.

"What are you planning to do after you leave us?" she asked with an edge to her voice. "Are you going back to your safe house in the middle of nowhere, where you won't have to be a part of life?

"Where you won't have to face the possibility of encountering someone you might come to care for—someone who might come to care for you?" she continued mockingly. "Someplace where you won't risk getting hurt?"

Suddenly the mocking note left her voice to be replaced with one of heartfelt sincerity. "Jake, you can't run away from pain, any more than you can run away from life. You have to learn to endure it and pray that the next time it comes around, you'll be a little bit stronger and a little bit wiser for it."

"You should stand on the pulpit beside your Reverend Jasper on Sunday mornings," Jake commented sarcastically. "You're beginning to sound a lot like him."

"You think I'm preaching to you?" she asked, hiding the pain his sarcasm caused and becoming angry again because she couldn't make him see the point she was trying to make.

"Well, I'd rather be like him than like you. You worship at the feet of a shrine you've created out of your own pain. But if that's what you want, if you don't want me and Amy, then go back to your graveside vigil," she dismissed him passionately.

"Go back where you can hide from life, from emotion. Go back to the dead! That's the only place you'll ever truly be safe, because the dead are past feeling anything at all."

Rachel faced the front of the car, brushing angrily at the tears on her cheeks.

Amy stirred, looked up at her mother's face and whispered, "You crying?"

"No, honey, I'm fine. Go back to sleep."

Jake pulled into the motel drive and stopped before Rachel's door. "I'll let you out here," he said stiffly.

"You aren't coming inside?" she couldn't help asking.

"No."

"Will I see you tomorrow?"

"I don't know—I'll need to make my report directly to Washington in the next few days."

"Will you be leaving right away?"

Jake shrugged, giving nothing away.

"Then, I guess this is probably the last time I'll see you...unless...you come to visit us some time."

Jake didn't answer. "Are we saying goodbye, Jake?" Rachel asked in a thick, unsteady voice.

He understood her meaning perfectly. "I guess so."

She leaned slowly toward him, brushing a soft kiss on his rough cheek. "I love you, Jake. Doesn't that make any difference?"

"Would you like me to carry your daughter inside?" he murmured stiffly, his eyes fixed on the hood of the car.

Jake sat in his car and watched at a distance as Rachel and her daughter boarded the bus. He hadn't left Nacogdoches in the two days following Rachel's ex-husband's capture, as he'd told her he would. He'd intended to, but something kept him there. He did, however, move to another motel clear across town—so he wouldn't have to risk seeing her every time he left his room.

The bus closed its doors and the engine began to whine as the driver put it in gear. Jake tensed. His hand reached for the door handle beside him. *It wasn't too late....*

Yes, it was, too late for Jake and anyone, but especially a woman who already had a child. Rachel had asked if Amy stood between them and Jake had told her no. He'd lied.

His reasons for feeling that way were not caused as she'd suggested by the fact that the little girl was another man's child, but because of her very existence. The memory of his own suffering at the hands of his parents kept resurfacing in his mind—along with the fear that he might follow in their footsteps.

What if he gave in to this feeling he had for Rachel and sometime in the future the child was made to suffer for it? He couldn't do it! He couldn't put another child through what his parents had put him through.

Jake's eyes followed the bus to the edge of town. When its taillights had finally faded in the distance, he started the car's engine and drove back toward town.

He was stopped at a red light when he looked up and realized he was sitting on the corner of Birchwood and Elm streets. His head swiveled toward the tall building with the huge cross topping it. The Sacred Cross Church.

A horn honked behind and Jake jerked his attention from the building toward the green traffic light above him. "All right—all right," he muttered as the horn sounded again, becoming joined by a whole chorus in the next few seconds.

A week later, Jake pulled up to the curb on Birchwood and exited his car. Moving diagonally across the sidewalk, he approached the house with determined strides. On the porch, he pressed a finger on the doorbell and held it there.

Within moments the door was thrown back on its hinges and Jake stood face-to-face with the one person he'd never expected to see again in his life.

"You said to come by if I ever wanted to talk," he said aggressively, by way of a greeting. "Well, I've got a lot of questions I need answered."

The Reverend Lionus Jasper stared at him somberly for a long moment before stepping back and inviting him inside with a wide welcoming smile.

Rachel put another log on the fire and sat back on her heels watching the flames dance around it. Pushing a hand through her hair, she glanced up at the clock on the mantel and heaved a great sigh.

Amy had only been gone for two hours, but already she was missing her. They hadn't been parted for any length of time in the last six weeks since they'd returned to San Antonio. And if it hadn't been for the long talk, Jennifer, her best friend, had initiated last week, they'd probably be together right now.

Jennifer had even talked her into thinking about going back to teaching after the first of the year. Amy needed the companionship of other children, and Rachel needed the company of adults. Besides, she loved teaching, and though working in her glass shop had been enjoyable these past weeks, she needed the mental stimulation teaching would afford her.

Jennifer was even trying to talk her into meeting her second cousin, an eligible bachelor who was coming to town for the holidays. So far, Rachel had resisted the idea, but she was beginning to realize she was lonely.

Sighing, she stood and moved across the room and into the kitchen. She was making homemade eggnog with rum. The whole evening lay before her with nothing to do, except wrap Christmas presents and relax.

It was only three weeks now till Christmas and Amy was getting anxious, because there still weren't any presents beneath their tree. Everyone she knew, according to her, had loads of wrapped packages beneath theirs.

Rachel smiled at the memory of her daughter's twinkling blue eyes. She knew how much her mother had missed her and wasn't above using that fact to her advantage. But it was all right; Rachel approached every new situation concerning her daughter with enthusiasm. They were a family, and it felt good to be part of a family again.

Carrying her glass into the living room, her eyes fell on the stack of presents she had placed near the couch, waiting to be wrapped. A man's sweater lay on top of the heap.

Rachel set the eggnog on the glass-topped coffee table and reached for the sweater. Where was he? Where was Jake Frost spending Christmas?

She supposed it was foolish to buy a gift you had no intention of giving for a person you didn't expect to see, but she hadn't been able to resist. The sweater was knitted in shades of blue and dark gold on a creamy background. It had looked so right for him in the store....

Dropping the sweater on top of the heap, Rachel pushed the memory of his face and the remote expression in his hazel eyes the last time she'd seen him, from her mind. He'd made his choice.

The phone rang and she jumped, then hurried to answer it. It was Jennifer, checking to make certain she wasn't too lonely without Amy there for company.

"No, I'm fine," Rachel assured her.

"You wouldn't like me to sneak away and come over after a while...so you won't be alone?"

"I told you, I'm fine," Rachel answered quickly. She really was enjoying the time by herself. She'd forgotten how good it was to relax and let your mind go. She was so thrilled to have Amy back that she'd forgotten how trying an energetic four-year-old could be at the best of times, even one as well-loved as Amy.

"You're sure?" Jennifer asked, listening for hidden nuances in Rachel's voice.

"Go back to your television program. I can hear it in the background," Rachel said with a laugh.

"Amy said to give you her love—we love you, too."

"I know."

Replacing the receiver, Rachel picked up her cup and sipped the thick, creamy drink. Her eyes fell on a portrait of her parents taken the year before she started college. They'd have loved Amy, and she would have loved them, too, she thought sadly.

From the framed picture, she glanced at the Christmas card sitting beside it. Rachel had debated a long time before sending Alexandra Conroy a Christmas card. And the woman had sent them one in return along with a brief note. She wanted to see Amy.

Rachel hadn't yet decided what she was going to do about that. Turning away from the mantel, her eyes were drawn to the sweater.

Where was he? Would he be spending the holidays with friends?

She hadn't dared to let herself seriously consider the possibility of hearing from him, yet, every time the doorbell rang...

Sighing wistfully, telling herself not to be a fool, she picked up the control and switched on the television. Giving her attention over to the program in progress, she forgot her troubles for a little while.

It was eight o'clock when Rachel switched the set off and looked again at the sweater. Picking it up, she buried her face in its softness. Six weeks! It had been six weeks since she'd seen him. Why couldn't she forget him as easily as he'd apparently forgotten her?

Jake cruised slowly past the house, looking at the Christmas lights in the window. This was the fourth pass he'd made. Turning around, he drove back, passing a man stringing lights on a tree in his yard. If he didn't make a decision soon, someone in the neighborhood watch program would probably phone the police and turn him in as a possible burglary suspect.

This time as he neared the stucco house, he pulled in at the curb and parked, killing the engine. She was home. He had no excuse for leaving without letting her know he was there.

Easing out of the car, Jake approached the house slowly. The man two doors down had stopped working with his lights and stood watching him.

At the front door, Jake lifted a hand, hesitated and dropped it without touching the lighted button. What if he wasn't welcome?

What if she had gotten on with her life and forgotten him? What if there was another man with her?

It had been so long...six weeks...six long, agonizing weeks without her....

What if he wasn't welcome?

He'd left her, promising himself he'd forget her. And he'd done his damnedest to do it, for all of a week.

When Jake left Nacogdoches, he had every intention of finishing up in Washington, D.C., as quickly as possible and heading back to his house in the Texas hill country. But things hadn't worked out that way.

After talking to Gus for most of one whole day, Jake had turned himself over to an agency shrink. They'd talked for the next three days, it seemed now, almost nonstop. Jake had poured it all out to the man, telling him everything he'd kept bottled up inside for most of his life.

And in between his bouts of analysis, Rachel haunted had him. She tormented him awake and asleep, reminding him of her last words. She'd called him a coward, and he knew she was right. He was a coward. He'd been running away ever since the night Janet had taken him from his parents home in the midst of a blizzard.

Jake glanced nervously toward the man two houses down who had been joined by a woman—his wife, Jake presumed. They were both watching him now. He gave them a tight smile and lifted a hand to wave nonchalantly in their direction.

The hand moved of its own free will toward the doorbell and Jake closed his eyes as he heard the muted tone of it ringing somewhere inside the house. His nerve suddenly deserted him and he almost bolted, but his glance encountered that of the man moving in Jake's direction. Jake grinned at him sickly and turned back to the door.

Suddenly the door in front of him opened and Jake stood staring at the face that had haunted him religiously for the past six weeks...and he couldn't speak.

Rachel caught her breath. She wanted to speak, but her tongue stuck to the roof of her mouth. She wanted to smile, but her face was frozen stiff. She wanted to hurl herself into his arms, but her feet were encased in lead boots holding her to the ground. And then she got mad.

Chapter 15

"May I come in?"

Rachel stepped back without speaking. Jake moved inside and she closed the door after him. Again, without speaking, she led the way into the living room. There she turned toward him and asked politely, masking the anger seething inside, "Would you like to sit down?"

"Thanks, I'll stand." She could have been talking to an insurance salesman for all the warmth there had been in the invitation. Perhaps, the worse scenario he had imagined, that of finding her with another man, wouldn't have been as bad as this terrible reserve between them.

Jake looked around the room, remembering it from the last time he'd been there. Stepping up to the fireplace, he bent to warm his hands. "This is nice—cozy."

"Yes," Rachel agreed solemnly, hands folded together at her waist, watching him. "Amy and I both enjoy a fire in the evening while we read, or watch television."

"Is she in bed?"

"No...she's with friends."

"Oh. Is she all right? I mean, she wasn't traumatized by the kidnapping?"

"No, not really." There was a bit more animation in her voice when she talked about her daughter, even though the controlled aspect to her features hadn't changed. "It appears Gary treated her gently while she was in his care. And except for being concerned about me, and the fact that she'd had to leave her home and friends behind, she didn't really comprehend much of what was happening."

Jake watched her move across the room toward him. His eyes were drawn to her slender figure and the pale, rose-colored jumpsuit she wore, made of some kind of soft, flowing material that clung to every shapely curve of her body like a second skin.

The outfit looked all of one piece and didn't appear to possess anything resembling a button or zipper. He wondered how she got into the thing. The top overlapped securely across her bosom, but when she removed the screen from the fireplace and bent toward the fire to stir the flames, Jake caught a glimpse of soft round breasts and forgot everything except the flames stirring inside him.

Was she trying to arouse him deliberately, to remind him of what he'd voluntarily given up when he'd rejected her vow of love the last time they'd been together?

Rachel replaced the screen and crossed to stand behind the sofa with her hands resting on the cushioned back. Awkwardly she waited for him to say whatever it was he had come to say and then leave.

It had taken her a long time to get over him. Okay, so who was she kidding—she wasn't completely over him, yet. But she was getting there. After weeks of jumping every time the phone rang, and dashing to the door with her heart in her mouth, just when she'd decided to lock the memory of him away in a special place in her heart and forget him, he showed up tonight without any prior warning.

For one crazy moment, when she'd been confronted by him on her doorstep, she had thought he was there because he loved her. But now she'd already dismissed that idea as absurd. He didn't act like a man in love. He acted like the coldhearted man she'd left behind in Nacogdoches.

Maybe it was the practice of the FBI to make follow-up visits to the people they'd been involved with on a case.

"I'm glad."

Rachel glanced at him blankly, forgetting for a moment to keep her defenses in place, and Jake saw behind the aloofness to the misery in her gray eyes.

"I beg your pardon?" she whispered in confusion. She'd lost the train of their conversation in her own unhappy reflections.

Jake swallowed quickly and explained. "I'm glad Amy hasn't suffered any ill effects from her unfortunate experience."

"Oh—yes . . . thank you."

The room was warm and growing warmer by the minute. There was something so scxy about that vague expression on her face. Jake loosened his coat, wondering how to broach the subject he'd come to discuss with her.

"I understand your ex-husband's trial is set for the first of the year."

"Yes." Rachel's eyes withdrew from his. So, as she'd suspected, this was an official visit. He'd come to discuss the case with her. Her restless glance landed on her forgotten glass.

"Would you like some eggnog?" She needed an excuse to get away from him for a few minutes.

"No, thank you, I don't want to put you to any trouble—"

"It's no trouble. I was just having some myself." She indicated the glass sitting near the end of the sofa that she'd abandoned to answer the door.

"Oh. In that case, yes—thank you—I'd like something to drink."

Rachel turned toward the kitchen with a feeling of relief.

"Ah—excuse me . . ."

She turned back reluctantly.

"May I just lay this here?" Jake was shrugging out of his long overcoat.

"Yes, of course. I'm sorry, I've been so remiss, I should have asked for it right away. Give it to me." She held out a hand. "I'll put it in the hall closet—"

"No, that's all right, I'll just lay it over this chair. I won't be staying long."

Rachel stiffened, gave a short, sharp nod and turned away. Jake watched her go with a sense of relief. He couldn't think clearly when she was in the room, and he needed all his wits about him tonight.

Gazing around the room, his eyes landed on the Christmas tree sitting in front of the window. He moved closer, noting that it was a live tree, one that could be planted after the holiday season was past. It stood about six feet tall and was decorated with red and green Christmas bows.

The only light on it was the star at the top of the tree. His eyes moved downward, toward a lighted manger scene that had been placed at the base of the tree on a cotton skirt sprinkled with glitter. Man, woman, and child. It was a wonderful thought. Jake blinked and looked away.

Colored fairy lights edging the window twinkled on and off, capturing his attention. They were the lights he'd seen from his car outside. Turning suddenly away, he sniffed the air filled with pine and holiday spices and realized sadly that this house reminded him of the home he'd had with Janet.

Light bounced off a glass sphere sitting on the mantel. Jake moved toward it. Picking it up curiously, he looked at the winter scene encapsulated within the transparent ball, then, turning it over, discovered a key on the bottom. Jake turned the key, shook the whole thing upside down, then set it back on the mantel. The strains of "Silent Night" filtered through the room as the snow fluttered around the small village, filling him with nostalgia.

Moving down the mantel past a Santa dish holding hard candy and a candle shaped like a snowman, Jake picked up a Christmas card and read it. So, Alexandra Conroy was beginning to feel like a grandmother.

He returned the card, feeling suddenly out of place. This room told him better than any words that Rachel and Amy were getting along just fine without him. He should never have come—

"Here we are. I hope you like homemade eggnog. The recipe was my mother's and her mother's before her. It's my favorite holiday drink. I make it every year...." She let the words trail off.

"I'm sorry," she murmured, handing Jake a frosty glass without looking at him. "I'm chattering. It's just that I hadn't expected to see you again. I mean—"

"Relax."

Rachel's teeth suddenly snapped shut. "I am relaxed," she couldn't help muttering testily, before moving across the room to once more take up her stance behind the sofa.

"How are you?" Jake asked purposefully. This waltzing around what was really between the two of them was beginning to wear on his nerves. He had a lot to tell her, and he'd come a long way to say it. He just didn't know how to begin.

"I'm fine," Rachel answered lightly, reaching across the arm of the sofa for her glass. *He had no right to ask how she was in that tone of voice!*

"I've missed you."

The glass slipped suddenly from her fingers, shattering against the glass-topped table. "Oh, no!" Rachel reached for it in horror.

Jake put his own glass on the mantel and rushed to her side. "Are you all right? You didn't cut yourself?" Grabbing her hand, he carefully inspected each finger with a rare show of concern.

It only took an instant for the tension in the hand to transmit itself to him. Jake's eyes flew to meet hers in surprise.

Rachel jerked her hand away and demanded, "Why have you come, Jake? Why now—after all this time? What do you want from me?"

But Jake's eyes had suddenly become riveted on the sweater at the top of the stack of unwrapped gifts. Picking it up, he tested its softness between the fingers of one large hand. "Is there someone in your life?" he asked with his glance still on the sweater. He couldn't stand the thought of seeing the answer written on her face, before her lips formed the words that would damn him to a living hell on earth.

Rachel's eyes moved to the sweater. "No . . . yes . . . no."

Throwing the garment from him in a move that stunned her, Jake grabbed her by the shoulders and hauled her into his arms. "Which is it?" he demanded gruffly.

"I—I—"

"Answer me!" He shook her slightly.

All at once her eyes darkened with anger. "Take your hands off me! What gives you the right to question me about that—or anything else for that matter?"

"This . . ." Jerking her tightly against him, his mouth covered hers, devouring its softness.

Stunned, Rachel neither responded nor resisted. And then, suddenly, she was pushing against his chest, hitting his back with her hand. Wrenching her mouth from beneath his, she cried, "Stop this! Let me go! You can't do this to me again—I won't let you—I won't let you back into my life for a few days or a night."

Jake let her go and strode across the room, wiping a hand across his mouth. Keeping his back to her, so she wouldn't see how the touch of her lips—the feel of her in his arms— had affected him, he took a gulp from his glass, made a slight face, and placed it back on the mantel. He'd never liked eggnog.

When he had himself under control, he turned to face her. "Would you like to know what I've been up to these past weeks?"

"Is that why you came, to keep me abreast of your activities?"

Ignoring the sharpness of her answer, Jake said, "I've been to Washington to see Gus Davison . . . and I've been to Indiana."

"Indiana?" she asked with sudden attention.

"That's right. I helped tie up some loose ends on a case for Gus, and while I was there I dropped by to see my uncle."

"Your uncle?" she repeated stupidly, moving around the end of the sofa and dropping down onto it, forgetting the broken glass and spilled drink.

"That's right."

"H-how was he?"

"In good health, but confined to a wheelchair—a permanent result of the fall he took down the stairs that night."

He didn't need to explain which night he meant. Rachel understood. "Did he recognize you?"

"Oddly enough, he did. He said I was the spitting image of his father—my grandfather. We talked for a long time. He explained to me a little about my parents.

"Mother had ... problems, all her life. She was wild and uncontrollable even as a teenager—but I don't want to go into all that now."

There was still the fear, somewhere inside him, that someday ... But he was learning to deal with it.

"What else did he tell you?"

"He said he tried to talk to my parents about their ... treatment of me. He said they made it clear to him that if he interfered he'd be eliminated altogether from their lives.

"But it was because of his intervention that Janet was hired to care for me. He told my mother it would give her more free time to devote to her law practice if she had someone living with us to keep me out of her hair. And she immediately went for that idea. She was a totally selfish person."

"Have you forgiven him, then, for his part in what happened?" Rachel asked softly.

"It's going to take time." He shrugged. A faraway look dimmed the hazel eyes. "People can do some damned awful things to kids—in the name of love."

"Can you forgive him, Jake?" she asked carefully, watching his face. The answer was very important to her.

"I don't know. He's not the same man I remember—but then, the memory is that of a four-year-old child. Either he's changed, or I have...." He shrugged again. "We'll talk some more later."

Talking about his past made him feel restless. He lifted his glass, paused to look at it, wishing it contained something a whole lot stronger, then set it back down without taking a drink and began to wander around the room.

He stopped to look at the Christmas decorations adorning the room, picking things up and putting them down without really seeing them. Rachel followed his curious wanderings with a frown.

Pausing abruptly by the tree, with his back to her, he murmured, "He said they changed after I disappeared. He said things would have been different if I'd returned...before..."

"Do you believe him?"

Jake turned toward the fireplace, rocking back and forth on his heels for a long time without answering. Finally he shook his head and muttered, "I don't know."

"People do change, Jake," she reminded him softly. "And sometimes it's even for the better."

"I visited their graves," he said after a moment. "It was raining...a cold, winter rain, the kind that chills you to the bone. I stood there, staring at the graves of the two people responsible for my being here, and I felt...nothing."

Firelight glistened in his eyes as he turned fully to face Rachel. "I should have felt something...shouldn't I?"

She wanted to go to him—but she couldn't, she didn't have the right. He'd taken that right away from her that last night in Nacogdoches.

"After I came back to Texas, I visited Janet's grave, and all I felt was anger...." There was a faint tremor in his voice when he continued. "She gave up everything for me. I owed her so much...and I never got the chance to repay any of it."

Rachel couldn't remain silent. "Remember something, Jake. Whatever happens in the future, remember that she must have loved you very much to do what she did and that she's a part of you, too."

Capturing her eyes, he held them without answering and slowly crossed the room to her side. Stopping very close to her, he announced suddenly in a stronger voice, "I've just come from Ripley."

"R-Ripley?" Rachel blinked and looked away. She was under the impression he had just got in from Washington.

"Yes. I had some things to take care of there. Some were harder than others."

"I'm sorry," Rachel whispered awkwardly, knowing he was referring to Lacy and Mary Tolbridge. She wished he wouldn't stand so close. It made her uncomfortable.

"Don't be sorry. I'll never forget them, but I'm ready to admit that that part of my life is finished. I feel as though I can start my life all over again—and I owe that all to you. Thank you," he whispered deeply.

Rachel couldn't have spoken if her life had depended upon it. Now she knew the real reason behind this visit—he wanted to say thank you. Having him in her house was agony, but to know he'd only come to say...thank you...

Rising swiftly to her feet, she swept past his figure and went to look out the window. It was impossible to be so close to him and not...

She didn't want his thanks! He could take his thank you's and he could...he could...

"Rachel?"

Jake was standing behind her, so close she could feel the heat of his body along her back. The reflection of his taller figure loomed over her shoulder. She glanced into his mirrored face and quickly away.

She tried to speak in a normal voice. "I'm glad you've gotten things in perspective." His breath touched the back of her neck and she couldn't withhold a shiver—nor the question, "How long have you been back in Texas?"

"A couple of weeks."

"I...see." She moved away from him. "And I suppose you decided you couldn't start this new life you mentioned before tying up *all* the loose threads of your old one."

Jake frowned. That wasn't exactly how he would have put it, but...

"I've been assigned a new job. The agency is opening a branch office for locating missing children, here, in Texas. For the past two weeks I've been busy pulling it together."

"Good for you."

His eyes narrowed on her face. "Is that all you have to say?"

She whirled to face him. "What do you want me to say, Jake? You want my approval—you have it. You want my good wishes—you have them, too. What else do you want from me?"

"Your love?"

The room became so quiet Rachel could almost hear the blood surging through her veins, once her heart began to beat again. "What do you mean?" she managed to get past stiff lips.

"I mean, when I watched you get on that bus in Nacogdoches, I knew you were taking my heart with you." Emotion darkened the hazel eyes to a deep sea green.

"Y-you were there when we left?" The anger inside her began to waver as she tried to comprehend what she was hearing.

"I was there."

"Why?"

"Isn't it obvious?" he asked uncomfortably.

"No." She shook her head, her eyes staring hard at his face. "It isn't obvious to me—tell me."

"I . . ." Dammit, why couldn't he just say it?

Rachel's mouth turned as pale as her cheeks. "Why can't you say it? " she blurted, scarcely aware of her own voice. "I said it first in Nacogdoches—" she halted abruptly, cheeks flushing a hot red in embarrassment "—unless, that isn't what you meant . . ."

"Don't look at me like that!" Twisting away, Jake paced to the other side of the room. Now it was his turn to try to put some distance between them. Maybe if he explained. "I went to talk to the Reverend Jasper—"

"You went to see Lionus Jasper?" Rachel interrupted in amazement. "I thought you didn't like him."

"I never said that," Jake whirled about to deny quickly.

"You didn't say it," Rachel agreed, "but you made it obvious how you felt about him when you called him sanctimonious."

"I...may have been mistaken about that," Jake responded hesitantly.

"Mistaken? I would have liked to have seen his face when you showed up on his doorstep," she murmured, turning to pick up something off the table beside her.

"What are you doing?" Jake asked in amazement when she turned to face him with a cigarette in her mouth, holding a lighter to its tip.

Removing the cigarette, she looked at its glowing tip and then at him with a raised brow. "Smoking." Returning the cigarette to her lips she took a long drag.

"You don't smoke."

"I didn't." She shrugged. "But I do now."

Jake looked at her intently, then strode to within a couple of feet of her. "Well, you just quit," he replied curtly, removing the cigarette from her lips and throwing it into the fireplace.

"Hey! Who in the hell do you think you are—"

"What did you say?" he rounded on her furiously.

"I said—"

"I heard you! When did you start cussing? Shame on you, what if your daughter should hear you?"

"What are you, my conscience?" she asked scathingly.

"No!" he shouted. "I'm the man who loves you—"

"What—what did you say?" Rachel asked in a suffocated whisper.

"I said..." Jake put his hands on her shoulders "...I love you." It got easier with practice.

"Y-you do?" she asked on a thin whisper of a breath, staring up into his face with wide, wondering eyes.

"Yes, I do," he responded huskily. "None of this—none of the changes I've made in my life, the changes I've made in my thinking—means anything without you. You made me want to quit running and face life. That's what I'm doing right now...I love you."

Rachel was shaking her head. She wanted to believe. . . . "But I haven't heard a word from you for six weeks—*six weeks!*" Her hands found his waist and she gripped it with trembling fingers, needing something solid to keep her in touch with reality. "You let me walk away—and now you want to walk back into my life—just like that?"

Jake had no defense. "Yes," he answered solemnly, "just like that. You're all I've thought about since the day you stormed into my life and demanded that I help you.

"I was afraid of you then, because I thought you were the ghost of my dead mother coming to get me, and I'm afraid of you now."

"Me? You're afraid of me? Why?"

"I'm afraid you're going to tell me to get out—" the hands on her shoulders tightened "—that you no longer love me. And if that happens, you might just as well kill me—right here and now."

"Oh, Jake . . ." She wanted to believe, but . . .

"You created the man you see standing before you, Rachel, and now it's up to you as to what happens to him."

"No," she protested, faintly.

"Yes. I've had a good example in you. When you came to me desperate to find your daughter, even in your fear and anger, you were vibrantly alive. You had purpose, drive, and direction. You knew what you wanted—you wanted your daughter back—and you weren't going to let anything stand in your way.

"At first, I agreed to help you just to get you out of my hair. Once you were gone, I told myself, I'd be able to grieve in peace. What I really meant was that I could go back to burying myself from life.

"But, after a while . . . I didn't want you to leave me. But, now, I had a new worry. You brought out a side of me I'd kept hidden, buried under layers of anger and fear. You made me experience all the emotions I'd kept carefully locked up inside.

"And I rejoiced in it—in you—until my past reared its ugly head. Once I remembered my mother and father, I was scared again.

"Only this time, I was more scared than I'd ever been in my whole life, because I wanted you—and I knew I couldn't have you."

"Why couldn't you have me?" Rachel shook him a little in agitation. She wanted to hear it all, it all had to come out into the open, so she'd understand the truth behind his agonizing rejection of her.

"Because...what if I did something in a fit of anger to hurt you...or Amy?"

So that was it! "Oh, Jake! I thought it was because you didn't love me, or didn't want Amy."

Jake lifted a hand to smooth a strand of hair back from her face. His fingers lingered against her soft cheek.

"I wanted you." His voice deepened, his eyes smoldering with banked fires. "My God, how I wanted you. I couldn't look at you, accidentally brush against you—just the thought of you—" He broke off and shook his head, unable to go on. The hand at her cheek moved around to the back of her neck. He tilted her head and leaned his forehead against hers, fighting for control of his emotions so he could continue.

Rachel lifted a hand to his face and whispered, "You said I taught you all those things—how could I teach you anything? Until I met you, I didn't know the meaning of love myself."

Pulling her in against his chest, Jake pressed his lips against the hair above her temple and whispered hoarsely, "I can't go on without you. All my good intentions will fall by the wayside if you aren't there to keep me in line."

And then his arms were wrapped around her and he was kissing the side of her neck. "God—I've missed you, every minute of every day—and night," he added deeply, "I've missed you so much...."

Rachel moved her face so their lips met and answered his kisses with unabashed enthusiasm.

Jake took his lips from hers to ask, breathlessly, "Do you love me?"

"With all my heart!"

After a long, satisfying kiss, it was Rachel who evaded his lips long enough to whisper, "What about Amy?"

"What about her?"

"She needs a father."

"And I need a family."

"Are you sure?" she asked, eyeing him intently.

"Of you? Never. But that's what life is all about, the ups and downs and the surprises—right?"

"Right!"

"Then I guess I'd better start plighting my troth—"

"Your what?" she asked with a laugh.

"You know, planning my trousseau and all that stuff. Cause, I've discovered I'm an old-fashioned guy at heart. I plan for us to be together a lifetime, so I want to start things off right—with a wedding—a church wedding—"

"With Lionus Jasper to marry us," Rachel put in mischievously, and then, at the look on Jake's face she began to laugh merrily. "You didn't! You did—you asked Lionus Jasper to marry us?"

"Well..." Jake grinned sheepishly. "Unless you have another preference, I kind of agreed to have the wedding take place in Nacogdoches—"

"Oh, Jake." She hugged him tightly. "We're going to be so happy!"

* * * * *

AMERICAN HERO

You have spoken! You've asked for more of our irresistible American Heroes, and now we're happy to oblige. After all, we're as in love with these men as you are! In coming months, look for these must-have guys:

In COLD, COLD HEART (IM #487) by Ann Williams, we're looking at a hero with a heart of ice. But when faced with a desperate mother and a missing child, his heart begins to melt. You'll want to be there in April to see the results!

In May we celebrate the line's tenth anniversary with one of our most-requested heroes ever: Quinn Eisley. In QUINN EISLEY'S WAR (IM #493) by Patricia Gardner Evans, this lone-wolf agent finally meets the one woman who is his perfect match.

The weather starts to heat up in June, so come deep-sea diving with us in Heather Graham Pozzessere's BETWEEN ROC AND A HARD PLACE (IM #499). Your blood will boil right along with Roc Trellyn's when he pulls in his net to find—his not-quite-ex-wife!

AMERICAN HEROES. YOU WON'T WANT TO MISS A SINGLE ONE—ONLY FROM

INTIMATE MOMENTS®
Silhouette®

IMHER04

Take 4 bestselling love stories FREE
Plus get a FREE surprise gift!

Special Limited-time Offer

Mail to Silhouette Reader Service™

3010 Walden Avenue
P.O. Box 1867
Buffalo, N.Y. 14269-1867

YES! Please send me 4 free Silhouette Intimate Moments® novels and my free surprise gift. Then send me 6 brand-new novels every month, which I will receive months before they appear in bookstores. Bill me at the low price of $2.71* each plus 25¢ delivery and applicable sales tax, if any.* I understand that accepting the books and gift places me under no obligation ever to buy any books. I can always return a shipment and cancel at any time. Even if I never buy another book from Silhouette, the 4 free books and the surprise gift are mine to keep forever.

245 BPA AJCK

Name	(PLEASE PRINT)	
Address		Apt No.
City	State	Zip

This offer is limited to one order per household and not valid to present Silhouette Intimate Moments® subscribers. *Terms and prices are subject to change without notice. Sales tax applicable in N.Y.

UMOM-93   ©1990 Harlequin Enterprises Limited

A romantic collection that
will touch your heart....

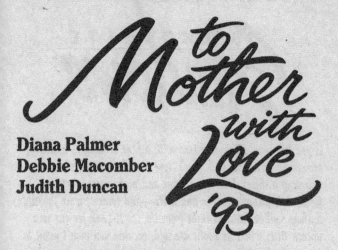

Diana Palmer
Debbie Macomber
Judith Duncan

As part of your annual tribute to
motherhood, join three of Silhouette's
best-loved authors as they celebrate the
joy of one of our most precious gifts—
mothers.

Available in May at your favorite retail outlet.

Only from  *Silhouette*®

—where passion lives.

For all those readers who've been looking for something a little bit different, a little bit spooky, let Silhouette Books take you on a journey to the dark side of love with

SILHOUETTE
Shadows™

If you like your romance mixed with a hint of danger, a taste of something eerie and wild, you'll love Shadows. This new line will send a shiver down your spine and make your heart beat faster. It's full of romance and more—and some of your favorite authors will be featured right from the start. Look for our four launch titles wherever books are sold, because you won't want to miss a single one.

THE LAST CAVALIER—Heather Graham Pozzessere
WHO IS DEBORAH?—Elise Title
STRANGER IN THE MIST—Lee Karr
SWAMP SECRETS—Carla Cassidy

After that, look for two books every month, and prepare to tremble with fear—and passion.

SILHOUETTE SHADOWS, coming your way in March.

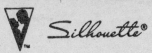 *Silhouette*®

SHAD1